Readers are not able to ~~put~~ down this
capturing, feel-good st~~ory~~

'Definitely has the **feel-good factor!** I coul~~dn't~~ put it down until turning the last page - I had to be sure of the ending I wanted! This is **a beautiful tale, set in glorious Cornwall.**'

Mags

'This book is a must for anyone wanting to really enjoy a new author who **transports them to a different place** with a want-to-read-more feeling.'

Caroline

'The predominant setting, in a cider farm in **picturesque Cornwall**, is the **perfect escapism.** A must-read for anyone who likes **romantic, family orientated stories.** It's beautiful.'

Holly

'Fab book! So many **twists and turns** along the way that you'd never guess the end from reading the first few chapters. Really enjoyed the cast of characters, as well as the **pure escapism** of most of the book being **set in Cornwall.**'

Leonie

'I could **feel the Cornish countryside** and felt like I knew the characters by the end of it.'

Jane

Lamorna would love to hear from you. Find her on:

 Facebook.com/LamornaIreland

 @AuthorIreland

 www.LamornaIreland.co.uk

Unexpected Beginnings

The Debut Novel

Lamorna Ireland

AUTHOR

Copyright © 2020 Lamorna Ireland

All rights reserved

No part of this book may be reproduced, or stored in a retrieval system, or transmitted in any form or by any means, electronic, mechanical, photocopying, recording, or otherwise, without express written permission of the publisher.

ISBN-13: 9798619903676

To my brave sister and all the other Cluster Heads around the world.

Chapter One

It had been eight hours. Eight long, cruel, excruciating hours since I'd surfaced from this particular attack. The Beast was doing his worst today. My limbs were tangled in stale bed sheets, an oxygen mask clinging to my face like something from the movie Alien, and there was a gaping hole in the plaster board next to my bed, where I put my head through at some point in the fourth hour. I think I'd hoped that it would stop the pain. After all, you don't feel the pain so bad if you're rendered unconscious - right?

I opened my eyes gingerly, only semi-aware that it was night-time already. The attack had started over my breakfast cereal earlier that morning. Another wasted day. Then again, the ever-so-slight comforting noise of a car alarm sounding through the street below gave me confirmation of my survival.

I'm still here. I'm pretty beat, though.

Coming up for fresh air, I peeled the oxygen mask from my swollen face and stared at the ceiling for a moment. There was that horrible metallic taste in my mouth again. And why did my teeth always ache, and my gums sting like a bad case of gingivitis afterwards? Not to mention, my tongue was all dried up from the oxygen.

I was in two minds at that moment. One was to dump everything and run. The second was to put a gun to my head and end it, right here in my minuscule Brooklyn flat. Both seemed rather extreme, but the prospect of both comforted me for now.

I carefully stretched out my stiff limbs and massaged out the pins-and-needles coursing through my legs whilst I was thinking. There were too many flaws to these plans. For one thing, I didn't have a gun, and how on earth could I out-run The Beast? The truth was, I couldn't. He was with me for the long haul it seemed.

"Trigeminal autonomic cephalalgia," the neurologist had

finally said, the day I had been formally diagnosed.

"And in English please?"

"Commonly known as cluster headaches," the neurologist had muttered, half distracted with writing up his notes. "It affects the trigeminal nerve. Carries sensations from your face to your brain - can be pretty painful apparently."

"Pretty painful?" I had thought out loud, indignant, willing the neurologist to tear himself away from his notes for just two seconds. "So, what now? Is it permanent?"

"Pretty much. No cure I'm afraid. The NIH has been working on CH research for the last 25 years, so I mean - hang in there. For now, oxygen therapy...could try steroid injections...verapamil if it gets really chronic. Other than that, avoid smoking and drinking and anything that might over stimulate..."

The rest of the neurologist's instructions had blurred from my memory after that and it was now a good four years of just 'hanging in there'.

I sighed, resigning to the fact that I had no way of escaping my life right now, and took the two steps from my bed to the kitchenette. A small, dingy corner of my poky little flat, the kitchenette had just one cupboard, a sink and an archaic fridge which often hummed noisily. It was quiet today. The limited counter space was piled high with dirty dishes and uneaten meals. I needed to have a clear up at some point.

Click.

The switch on the kettle sprang back up, refusing to connect.

Click.

It did it again.

I checked the socket was in the wall, then looked at the microwave. The digital clock wasn't showing either. I groaned, my shoulders slumping and my head bowing down. The electricity had been switched off. There had been multiple letters through the mail warning me of this, but of course I'd ignored them. I'd become an expert in the art of denial over the last six months.

My cell buzzed on the last bit of space on the kitchen worktop, balancing precariously on the edge. Well at least my cell phone plan hadn't been cancelled yet.

Glancing at the caller ID, I braced myself f
other end of the phone. "Hi Helen."

"Hi, Emily. I need an update."

No 'how are you?' this time, then. This wa
main desk at work, and her disapproval towar
absence at work was insufferable right now.

"Nothing new I'm afraid, Helen. I haven't been able to get myself to the doctors this week," - mostly because I couldn't afford the journey there, let alone the bill that follows - "I'm hoping to give you a better picture on Friday for a phased return."

"I'll let Donald know."

Helen rang off and I massaged my temple vigorously.

I placed my cell back on the worktop, deciding to tackle the small pile of ominous looking mail building up by the front door of the flat. Monica, one of the waitresses now working in the diner, often brought them up for me. Otherwise, I had to traipse down the stairs and into the diner to extract my own mail from the diner's, which I wanted to avoid if I could.

I'd lived above Gwynne's Diner for about ten years now. At first with Gwynne, when the flat had been twice the size it is now. Before it had been split in to two, forcing me to the very edge of the building. The colder side. The noisier side. The smellier side, above the extractor. Yeah, you get the picture. The diner had belonged to *him* after Gwynne's death. After that everything became pretty complicated.

Now, these notices had started coming through. From him, mainly. Like I said, things had gotten pretty complicated.

On top of all that, there was this stupid CH. At my worst, I could barely see, let alone function enough to leave the safety of my bed. I'd had symptoms since my early teens, undiagnosed and confused. It was the last six months where the symptoms had largely consumed my life. And this time, I had bills to pay.

I flicked through the mail, crimson words like 'NOTICE' or 'IMPORTANT' flashing menacingly at me. I slammed the letters back on the side and took in deep, shaky breaths, my hands trembling from the amount of blood pumping around my body. I knew it was inevitable; I was going to lose. He was going to get what he wanted, and I was going to be left with nothing. Again.

...ways been so good with managing what little money I... But there was only so much budgeting and organising of ...nces I could do before my outgoings were bigger than my income. My medication alone was costing more than my rent at the moment, which I wasn't entirely convinced was helping me anyway. The CH Beast was way too clever and unpredictable to be outsmarted by some tiny pink pills, sneering smugly as he brutally attacked the side of my skull.

My pay had been cut in half. That's what happened when finishing a whole shift without an attack became impossible. My colleagues had been so supportive at the beginning, but that support and patience soon dwindled.

"Going home again, Emily? You've only been back a few days - was there any point?"

"If you're going to be off for more than a week, can you give me some notice this time? We nearly lost the Hayes project to that new marketing company that's just set up on the other side of town because you bailed before presentations. Get your act together, Miller!"

Some of the colleagues I'd actually seen as friends had stopped texting me as well. In fact, nobody had checked to see how I was for days now. The only form of contact had been my friend Michelle and Helen's very charming 'check-up' just a moment ago.

"I could be dead," I thought out loud, feeling a pang of bitterness sweep over me as my voice rattled around in the near-empty flat.

No, I needed to stop thinking that way. After all, this thing that had taken over my life had inconvenienced everybody, not just me. I'd call the office and let them know I'd be back in work tomorrow, not Friday. Beast or no Beast.

There was an odd atmosphere as I stepped into the office the next morning. I'd done my best to groom myself to an acceptable standard. My brown hair lay flat and lifeless; my clothes clung to my bony frame; I lacked nutrition everywhere. Every part of my body had suffered recently, not just my head. I really did look like shit, but nonetheless I yanked my tights up for the fifth time that morning, heaved a deep breath and smiled my way through the sea of uneasy eyes. Why did everybody look so apprehensive? Helen's assistant, Meera smiled meekly while averting her eyes. She hadn't sounded her usual friendly self on the phone last night, when I rang to say I would be returning to work. Perhaps her son was playing up at school again. Yes, that had to be it. I would offer to make her a cup of coffee later.

I tried to ignore the nagging feeling that something wasn't right and opened the glass door into my office, taking a seat behind my trusty desk. Glass fronted and with a view, the office was bright and fresh. The disparities between the office and my flat often made returning back home dismal. I am fortunate though, to have been given an office after I was made Case Team Leader eight months ago. On sunny days, I liked to twist my chair around and watch the people of Manhattan enjoy their lunch breaks and soak up some vitamin D, reading their books, walking the dog or playing chess with the local geriatrics. It had always been a thriving community of busy, purposeful lives. I thought back to those working lunches with colleagues, the warmth of the sun mapping out a path of hope for my career before me.

Today the park was quiet. The sun was looming behind a thick mass of black clouds, unwilling to shed any hope on this occasion. *You're on your own Emily Miller,* it may as well have said.

Nothing new there then.

I glanced across the hall to Mark Trengrouse's office, an instant chorus of hyperactive butterflies exploding in my tummy. The lights were off and his desk clear; he wasn't in yet. I pinged up my emails on the computer screen. This was my only way to reconnect with the flow of the office again until my boss arrived.

No emails.

No reconnecting for a minute then.

I channelled my focus on my chair instead, which hadn't been feeling right since I sat down. I bent forward, re-adjusting whatever had been tampered with. Then, I picked up a strange, bright-pink stapler with caution, as if it was about to attack me at any moment.

Whose stapler was this, and why was it on my desk? Come to think of it, a lot of things were out of place in this office, and there appeared to be a few new additions. A feeling of displacement suddenly washed over me, causing me to look up to my office door. Through the glass I could just make out an unfamiliar name etched in bold, white font.

Sophie Paulsen, Case Team Leader.

Just then, Mark Trengrouse sauntered past my office, eyes fixed on his phone, a curt wave in my direction before disappearing into his office. I was so flustered with the door fiasco, I hadn't had time to react in the appropriate school-girl-crush manner I usually adopted around Mark.

He took a seat behind his desk. Only two layers of glass between us, and he was oblivious. Oh God. Perhaps he was angry with me. He wanted me to do some research on the policies in place for United Ltd. I'd never got round to sending him my findings and the presentation deadline had been and gone by now.

I fidgeted in my seat, smoothing down my skirt and straightening my keyboard. I smoothed down my skirt a second time and straightened the mouse this time, simply for something to do. I was about to get up and offer Mark a 'peace-offering' coffee when my eyes locked with his through the glass walls. He was looking pleasantly surprised, much to my relief.

"Miller. Bloody hell, you're back," Mark boomed as he burst into my office. His smooth British accent had always made me a little giddy.   "You're better then?"

"Well, kind of...for now," I stuttered. "As I've said before, it's a condition. It comes back."

"Yeah, pain in the arse, that. Good to see you."

I pressed my hands together and levelled my eyes to Mark's. *Keep it casual. Don't show him you're upset.* "Hey, Mark? What's with the name on the office door? Who's Sophie Paulsen?"

"You haven't been told? Was wondering why you were in here. Yeah, you've been moved," Mark answered, matter-of-factly. "Perhaps you should speak to Donald."

Donald - as in Donald Blake of Blake & Company Ltd - was perhaps one of the most unreasonable, intolerable old timers I'd ever met. A big lump of a man, with wandering eyes and an archaic view on women in the workplace. As the founder of our company, we didn't really see him that often - thank goodness. But I'd always seemed to be 'blessed' with his presence in all the wrong moments - this moment of vulnerability being one of them.

So, of course, a conversation with Donald only made me feel smaller. A one-sided argument which only resulted in me being escorted to my new - much less private - cubicle office, complete with three free-standing walls and just enough room for my desk and computer. I logged in with forced calmness, my cheeks burning from humiliation as I desperately focused on the firm's logo flickering at me from the computer screen. I winced as I thought back to the day I'd received my own office. The way I'd strode through the sea of desks in this very room. How gleeful these people must be to see me now.

My ears were pounding from my racing heart. I was in shock. A demotion. From Case Team Leader to Associate Consultant. Just like that. The last two years of hard work, undone with the snap of Donald's sausage fingers.

The worst part of this new position: I was practically scraping the barrel in hierarchy now and was expected to report to Mark, attending to his every need. Did I mention Donald's low opinions on women in the workplace? I may as well be that silly, naive intern again, who'd spent her first week getting well-acquainted with the coffee machine and photocopier.

Since Mark had hired me two years ago, my infatuation over his British accent, and rather pathetic weakness for his charismatic arrogance and good looks, had often got in the way. In his presence I would often feel flustered and inadequate. Luckily for me - depends on how you look at it - I would never be the type of girl Mark would pursue. I could not be further from his usual type - which is long-legged, blond and big-boobed - I myself having mousy-brown hair, average-length legs, and a skinny frame with barely any shape. So it was safe to say, I would never stand a chance with Mark Trengrouse. It never hurt, however, to sneak cheeky glances across the corridor to where he sat behind his desk, often engrossed in a file or something important on his computer. At least in a senior role I had started to feel like his equal, but as an assistant now - I could not feel more inadequate.

These things set aside, I was a professional. Minutes later I was sat in front of Mark, a steaming pot of coffee between us, with pen and pad to hand, ready for a brief on my new duties.

"You look tired, Miller," Mark began the conversation. Good start.

"Thank you Mark, so kind of you to notice," I quipped, clicking my pen vigorously.

"Just saying. Are you sleeping?"

"Haven't very much, recently, no," I tried not to sound too condescending. You didn't tend to get much sleep during cluster bouts. Then again, it seemed that no one, not even my former neurologist, understood the condition. I wasn't entirely sure I understood it, so how could I expect Mark to? All he knew was that it quickly racked up my sick leave.

"Anyway," Mark continued, as if dismissing the previous conversation. "Before I go into the boring details of your new job role, I want to tell you something exciting. The company have put me in charge of a new expansion. I'm going to be opening the first UK branch of Blake & Co."

Trying not to let my recent demotion get in the way of being pleased for Mark, I slapped on a smile. "That makes sense - because you're British!"

Mark frowned. "Well I'm hoping they're giving me this opportunity for more reason other than my nationality."

"Of course they are, sorry. That's brilliant news! I thought only Partners were in charge of office openings? Wait, are you being made a Senior Partner?"

"If the UK opening is successful, then yes," Mark confirmed, his chest puffing proudly.

I knew how much this meant to Mark. He had been acting Principal for the Manhattan branch for over two years now and had every potential to become a partner. His ruthless leadership skills and cut-throat approaches to turning around failing businesses made him one of the most effective Business Consultants in the area. Who else better for the job?

"I'm really pleased for you," I smiled, more sincerely, though my gut was twisting.

"Thanks," Mark grinned. "It's in London. Best city in the UK.

Being my new, personal associate, you're coming with me, of course."

With that, the grip I had on my mug was suddenly compromised and I gave a little squeal as hot coffee spilt all over my lap and notebook.

"Ow, shit," I cursed, getting up and rubbing myself down. Mark chuckled and handed me a napkin. "Thanks. What do you mean, I'm coming with you? To London? I can't go to London."

"Why not?" Mark shrugged, almost bored at my reaction. My mouth opened, then shut, then opened again, like a demented goldfish.

Why couldn't I go to London? Good question, and a question I didn't really have an answer to. There was no legitimate reason as to why I couldn't go to London. But the real question at hand bounced around in my head like a wild pinball: why me? The one who had been on and off sick for the last six months? Not to mention the most mundane-looking woman at the office? Wouldn't Bachelor Mark Trengrouse want to take one of the more charismatic female associates, so he could mix business with pleasure, so to speak. Something he was very well-known for.

"I take it you don't actually have a reason," Mark continued, sitting up and straightening his tie. "Look, I spoke to Donald. He's fine with it all. Think of it as a way to redeem yourself, get yourself back up that ladder. Maybe even by-pass your previous position before...you know..."

"I loved that job!" I scoffed, indignant. "Besides, I can't go any further in the company without finishing my business degree. You know that."

"I do. Which is why I'm thinking that very incentive sounds pretty good right now."

"What, finishing my degree? You have got to be kidding me?" I scoffed again, but louder. "Yeah, alright. Donald's going to pay for my final semester after he's just demoted me for poor attendance."

"Who says it'll be Donald? Once I'm senior partner, I can sort it out myself. I'll even give you some time in London to study."

I looked up at Mark, determining his expression.

"Why would you do that for me?" That wasn't supposed to be

an accusation. But there was a defensive tone in my voice that I couldn't quite shake.

"You were a great team leader and could one day make a good manager. You've progressed quickly over the last two years, despite your lack of qualifications. You help me. I'll help you."

"I need to think this through," I heard myself saying.

"Fine, if you must. But don't take too long. I have plenty of other people who would jump at the opportunity. Now go get me another coffee, assistant," he winked and flashed me a grin, "and we'll talk about your duties."

And just like that the conversation was halted, with it my sinking heart as reality pulled me back down to Floor 12. Before any of these prosperities could come true, I first had to endure being Mark's assistant: one coffee at a time.

Chapter Two

Mark left the office late that night, feeling irritated. At least Emily had agreed to think about his proposal, though he couldn't understand why somebody in her position wouldn't snap up such an opportunity. He couldn't help but feel disappointed over her hesitation. Though recently a little less reliable, she did have a knack for keeping things organised, and it meant that she could take care of the tedious paperwork that he hated.

Mark grimaced a little as he realised what he had just promised Emily. He wasn't sure why he had been so ambitious in his promise to send her back to business school. But he needed her on board with this trip to London. The only other person who was willing to travel with Mark was Bob, another Manager within the company. But given that Bob was neither female or remotely interesting, it was never going to work. Besides, Mark had always liked Emily. He was the first one to recommend hiring Emily two years ago and the first to defend her when Donald was considering the termination of her employment. He would never let on to Emily just how close she was to actually losing her job. That this move to London was the only way her employment could be saved.

Mark remembered well the day Emily came into the office, looking for a job. It still amused him thinking back to that moment when he first met Emily. She had been caught in a heavy rainfall, squelching her way down the corridor as she came across Mark's office.

"Excuse me?" Emily had gasped, her hair dishevelled and her face burning red. "I'm here for the job interview. Which way to conference room B, please?"

"Which job are you here for? We're enrolling in several areas," Mark had replied, looking her up and down in amusement,

noting the puddle she was forming in the threshold of his office.

"Um, it's the internship for Associate Consultancy."

"Well, you're a little late for that. Interviews started at midday."

A look of panic had crossed Emily's face as she'd rummaged in her sodden bag. "I checked my letter over and over, and I'm certain it said two o'clock."

Hands in his pockets, and leaning on his desk patiently, he'd watched this water-drenched girl dig frantically to the bottom of her bag. Mark had felt a spark of interest, as well as pity, towards Emily that he couldn't quite figure out.

"Ah-ha!" Emily exclaimed, drawing out a soggy piece of paper and waving it in Mark's face. "Here we are! See! Start time..." Emily had paused, staring at the letter defeated, before folding it up and putting it back in her bag. "Thank you. Sorry for wasting your time."

In that moment, Mark's gut had told him to help this haphazard girl. He'd observed her with altered concern as she'd tried to steady herself, closing her eyes and drawing a long breath through her nose. Mark recalled her face looking drawn and hollow.

"I'm heading out for a late lunch. Care to join me?" Mark had asked.

"Sorry?"

"Come on, you can tell me all about your attributes over a sandwich."

"Oh, I don't have my..."

"Lunch is on me. Stop faffing. Come on, get your interview face on!"

"Umm, thank you! Mr?"

"Mark Trengrouse," Mark shook Emily's hand.

"Emily Miller," Emily had smiled, shaking Mark's hand.

Two years on, Mark found himself still occasionally looking out for her and patching up her poor decisions in life. That usual mixture of endearment and pure frustration towards Emily continued to confuse him.

Mark pulled his thoughts away from Emily for a second to make room for another concern on his mind. The thought of returning to the UK after all these years. He had left his home-country for good reasons and he wasn't sure he was ready to return. But this promotion to Senior Partner meant more to him than anything. He would make it work.

One thing was for sure, he wouldn't be setting foot in Cornwall, not when he knew exactly what was waiting for him. No way - he would make a quick visit to London and that was as far as he would go until his job there was done.

For the next few weeks Mark and Emily worked closely together, making sure any loose ends were tied, and all paperwork was up to date. Having Emily as his assistant was already having its advantages. She had cleared some forms he'd been putting off for days and kept him fuelled with endless amounts of caffeine.

"I got you double-espresso; a sandwich for later," Emily routed through the paper deli bag, her brown hair glistening from the drizzle outside. Did that girl ever wear a coat? "Ooh, and some blueberry muffins. I forgot about those."

"Any change from that twenty I gave you?"

"Yes, sorry. You didn't need to buy me lunch as well. I'll pay you -"

"Oh shut up, Em. It's on me," Mark took his espresso. "Thanks. You know, you should really wear a coat when you're out in the rain."

"Okay Pa!" Emily snorted, shaking a few droplets out of her fringe.

"Just saying. You look like a drowned rat," Mark teased.

"And there's me thinking it's because you care about my health," Emily threw a napkin in Mark's direction, grinning ear-to-ear. That smile. What was it about that smile?

"By the way, your friend Michelle called," Mark continued, taking a big mouthful of his blueberry muffin.

"What? At the office?"

"No, your mobile. You left it here, on my desk," Mark held up the phone as evidence. "I told her you were too busy at the moment to get to the phone and you would call her when we're finished."

"Finished with what? What are you talking about?" Emily

asked, nervously. Mark grinned and his eyebrows danced in a suggestive manner. "Oh, my God! Great, she's going to keep pestering me now until I give her the dirt on something that didn't even happen."

"Sorry. I'm sorry - it was too easy," Mark hooted with laughter.

"Do you even know how insufferable she is?"

"Why are you friends with her then?" Mark snorted.

"It's not that simple. We go way back."

"Seems simple enough to me. Just cut her loose."

"Is that what you do? Just cut people out of your life, just like that?"

There was a pause as Mark let the salt settle into a very old, very deep cut. He quickly recovered.

"Look, would it be easier if something did happen?" Mark shrugged, casually changing the attention back over to Emily.

Emily chucked another napkin at him and continued typing up some meeting minutes, blushing ferociously and trying not to smile. Mark knew he had an effect on her, and shamelessly enjoyed it. The only thing that was different with Emily was she never acted upon it. Mark had an effect on a lot of women, but the effect on Emily was often incomplete and unsatisfying. After Catherine left him two and a half years ago, it was a guilty pleasure: making women feel beautiful but discarding them when it suited him. Most women he wooed returned the affection and pounced on him before he'd had a chance to tell them his name. But no matter how much he pushed Emily, all he got in return was a nervous giggle, the occasional 'fuck-off' and a variety of things chucked in his direction. She was in no way sexy - pretty, but not sexy. She was also funny, quirky and completely adorable. The fact she didn't have a single bit of sexual confidence was what made it even more fun and sometimes desirable for Mark.

"What's this?" Emily pierced Mark's train of thought, picking up a brown, white laced envelope. "An invite?"

Mark leaned across and snatched the envelope from Emily's grasp before she had a chance to read it. "A wedding invite. Clashes with the weekend in London, so no good."

"Oh, that's a shame. Whose wedding?"

"Just a mate's."

Mark tried to concentrate on his work, feeling Emily's eyes on him. She was always very good at knowing when Mark was lying, but this was a road he really did not want to go down. "Any more thoughts on London by the way?"

"I'm still thinking."

"Well don't take too long?" Mark's mood took a turn and he was suddenly irritated. "Anyway, enough chit-chat. Let's get on with this next business proposal."

That evening, Mark twiddled the wedding invite in his hand, turning it over and over as he trailed into deep thought. He thought about his family, whom he hadn't spoken to in over three years. He thought about the people who were hurt along the way. The loss he had felt. He couldn't go back, not even for his sister's big day. What would he say to them, after all this time?

Then, reluctantly, his thoughts trickled over to Catherine. It had been two and a half years since she broke his heart, but the feeling was still raw. He had loved her, moved to America for her: he was entirely devoted to her. Then one day, without any explanation, she packed her bags and left with Jack, a Senior Partner from the California branch of Blake & Co.

"Jack can give me stability," she had said. He'd heard those words uttered from her before.

Mark should have known that Catherine would go for the upgrade. After all, it was exactly what she had done when she'd left for America with him. Well, supposedly.

Mark shook his head, bringing himself back to reality and trying to squish the familiar sting of guilt back down to the basement of his feelings. Instead he occupied his mind by looking at the flights from JFK to Heathrow, London. Hypothetical until he got a proper answer from Emily. He then occupied himself further by carefully selecting the right hotel. After all, when the firm was paying, he needed to get all the perks he could.

After only twenty minutes of searching, Mark decisively chose one. It was modern, only a mile from the new office, and had a very swanky indoor pool and spa. Mark expected it was a far-cry from what Emily was accustomed to, mildly confused at how much he looked forward to exposing her to such luxuries. He didn't know everything about her, but enough to know that any form of opulence was a rarity for the poor girl. Perhaps he would show her the website tomorrow to seal the deal.

Eyes beginning to ache, Mark tore himself away from his smart phone, and poured himself a large glass of whiskey. He walked through his spacious apartment and stood before his panoramic window, drinking in the views of the Upper East Side Manhattan in all its glory. It was even more beautiful at night, thought Mark fondly, with its dazzling lights and constant buzz of life below. He couldn't think of a better place to live. He thought of his damp little bedroom where he grew up in Cornwall. The paint and plaster crumbling over his bedsheets from a harsh winter. Dad being too tight to put the central heating on. The central heating that took them until Mark was at least thirteen to finally get round to installing, in their 250-year-old farmhouse. The walls, that were so horrifically wonky and lumpy, meant hanging pictures or posters was near impossible, his furniture never quite sitting flush with the wall.

Now, at the prime age of thirty-one, here he was. In New York City, soon-to-be Senior Partner of a successful Business Consultancy. Bachelor of his own luxurious, deliciously straight and rectangular, modern apartment - overlooking some of the best views in the city. Yeah, he had done pretty well. He'd proved them all wrong. He was in exactly the place he needed, and wanted, to be.

Screw them.

Downing the whiskey, allowing the warming liquid to trickle down his throat, he received a text.

Trengrouse.
Lots of lovely ladies out tonight.
Get yourself down here before all the good ones are taken! CJ

Mark grinned, checking his appearance in a nearby mirror. *Well*, thought Mark. *When in Manhattan.*

Chapter Three

"A bit more to the left. Left...Bloody hell Gary, I said left!"

"No offence, Sarah," Gary puffed, gripping on to the bar with white knuckles. "But this thing weighs a bloody tonne. Where's your brother? We'd get this done in no time."

"That's a good question," Sarah muttered through gritted teeth. "Okay, just leave it there for a minute. I'll try Tom's mobile again."

Sarah Trengrouse, on a good day, was a force to be reckoned with. But in a couple of weeks Sarah was going to be a bride, and at this moment in time nothing was more important to her than the smooth running of her carefully planned wedding. Things were beginning to feel more real now. The marquee had been delivered and would be erected end of the week. Now Gary and a couple of the young lads from the distillery were trying to heave the massive wooden bar, which Tom had hand-crafted himself, into the barn for one last coat of paint.

Tom, her dear eldest brother, had made a huge contribution to this wedding. Working into the early hours of the morning to build her a bar, a wishing well, a sweet trolley...she named it, he made it. He had always been good to her, and she loved him for it. But he was also so frustratingly dedicated to the family business that it was hard to pin him down sometimes.

She tried his mobile again.

Straight to voicemail.

That would mean he had no signal, which could only mean he was down in the bottom orchard, pruning back the apple trees. Last winter had been harsh and some of the trees had taken it hard; the farm had lost a lot of crop and the business had felt it financially. The hours Tom had spent, cooped up in his tiny little nook of an office, hunched over the accounts and desperately trying to find a way to make ends meet.

Sarah sighed, putting her phone back in her back pocket. She wouldn't pester him now. Besides - Steve, her soon-to-be husband, would be back any moment from his delivery rounds.

Steve had worked for Sarah's family for nearly nine years now, starting off as a weekend boy who helped collect the apples during harvest. Steve had fancied Sarah since the beginning, but Sarah had been too blind to notice - too loved up with her school sweetheart, Jason. That infatuation soon came to a messy end when they got to college, Jason pursuing every girl in the college. Sarah was left humiliated and heart broken.

Steve had nervously asked her out on a date just a week later, and she had gladly accepted. Eight years later and here they were, finally tying the knot.

Sarah sent Gary and the distillery boys back to work, took herself back into the farmhouse and stuck the kettle on the AGA to boil. With a heavy sigh, she sat down at the head of the large table, its chips and stains engraved into the wood from years of family meals and checked her seating plan for the tenth time that day. She rested her head heavily on her hand as she analysed the carefully drawn seating plan before her. She had made sure guests were sat with people they knew but had also mixed them up enough so the two families could mingle. And she had been completely traditional with the top table. Her mum Karen was to be sat next to Steve's dad and Tom was to be sat, in honour of their father, next to Steve's mum.

Sarah steadied herself as she thought of her dear father, who had died almost four years ago from pancreatic cancer. He had suffered from it for only four months, but that short period of time had been excruciating. They had all chipped in to nurse him from home, but it was Sarah and Karen who had been in the room when Roy Trengrouse had finally taken his last breath. Tom had been out in the fields, vigorously harvesting the apples, trying to keep the family business afloat in its most vulnerable time and her other brother Mark had been working up in London, trying to establish himself as a business consultant in the big city.

Mark. She focused her attention to his name, carefully written onto table 3 with plus 1 next to him. She knew he wouldn't be bringing Catherine. Thank god. But she also knew her brother well enough to know that if he was to come to the wedding, he wouldn't come alone.

"There she is," a familiar voice cooed behind her. Steve wrapped his arms around her shoulders, glancing at the seating plan from behind. "Sweetheart, why is Mark still on the plan? He hasn't even bothered sending us an RSVP."

"Neither have half of our evening guests. It doesn't mean they're not coming," Sarah scoffed. "He's my brother. I'm not removing him from the plan. There will be a place for him if he decides to show."

"I know he's your brother - and don't get me wrong, it would be wonderful to see him make the effort to support you on our big day - but Mark is an ass-hole."

"My brother might be an ass-hole. But he's family, and no amount of bullshit that he pulls will ever stop me loving him."

"I know," Steve said gently, kissing the side of Sarah's head. "That's why you're amazing. You forgive too easily. Tom, however -"

"Yes, well," Sarah jumped up at the sound of the kettle whistling. "Let's not go there, shall we?"

"Why aren't you at the tearooms by the way?" Steve asked.

"I was attempting to direct Gary and those other muppets into the barn with the bar, but they couldn't get it through without nearly knocking the whole thing down."

"That thing weighs a tonne mind," Steve said in Gary's defence. "I'll get Tom to help us later. He's got the strength of two men anyway."

"Besides," Sarah continued, as if she hadn't been listening, "the tearooms have been dead all morning. I've left Poppy in charge."

"Wasn't dead when I walked up the yard just a minute ago. Looks like the care home has brought a minibus of their residents over for afternoon tea again."

Sarah's eyes widened in horror, "Shit! Why didn't you say something, you pleb!"

Before Steve could reply, Sarah had darted out of the farmhouse, down the yard, jumped the fence and skidded into the tearooms, finding every seat taken by an elderly person. Bustling in between the tables, frantically taking orders, was a flustered Poppy.

"Poppy, I'm so sorry! I didn't know it had got so busy!"

"Shit, Sarah! Like, bloody hell!" Poppy hissed, as she steamed the milk for the coffee with ferocity.

"You're burning that milk," Sarah added. "Why didn't you call me or something?"

"I couldn't even get to the phone! They just flooded in, demanding their tea and cake!" Poppy squealed.

"Alright, alright. Pipe down, will you!?" Sarah begged. "You'll break their hearing aids at that pitch."

"They can't hear bugger all. Took me ten minutes to get the right order for bloody Mrs. Patmore over there. Oh shit, she's looking over. Smile, just smile. Daft cow."

"Okay, you're officially hysterical. Go into the kitchen and make the cream teas. I'll make the hot drinks."

Sarah pushed her frantic employee into the kitchen, and made a start on the coffees and teas. It wasn't long until all the customers were slurping away at their chosen hot beverage - a fresh, warm scone with oodles of jam and cream being placed in front of them minutes after. Sarah then made Poppy a cup of tea to calm her nerves.

By the time the elderly folk had finished their afternoon treats, paid up, and clambered one-by-one back onto the minibus, it was time to shut. Poppy gladly turned the sign to 'Closed', flipped the chairs up onto the tables and swept the floor. Sarah made a start cashing up the till, knowing it was going to be another dismal day in earnings, despite the last-minute invasion.

When Sarah had first conjured up the idea of renovating one of the outbuildings into a tearoom two years ago, she had had a very different vision of the business. She imagined her tearooms being a roaring success, people travelling all over the South West for her famous cream teas. She envisioned it having a positive impact on Tom, helping with the cider farm's footfall. The only positive impact it was having on Tom so far was easy access to a hot lunch every day, not to mention unlimited coffees. As for her own benefits... well, she wasn't sat in front of a computer screen punching numbers into a spreadsheet anymore. That was something.

They were now into their second year of running the

tearooms, Sarah needed to keep reminding herself. They were still relatively new, in business terms. But the summer season was over, the tourists had gone home, and September was proving to be the coldest and wettest it had been in years. This made their idyllic spot in the Cornish Countryside, down several muddy and bumpy lanes, not so appealing to customers. Sarah was grateful of her loyal regulars. The elderly residents of Oaktree Care Home always guaranteed her a fair income. If only they could come daily.

She thought fondly of Mr and Mrs Jenkins, an elderly couple who lived in the nearby village and came three times a week for their usual - two sparkling waters, a round of marmalade toast and two lattes to finish up. It wasn't much, but their frequent visits always made Sarah smile.

Then there was Mr. Potter, who reminded Sarah so much of Captain Mainwaring in Dad's Army - a charming, delicate sort of a man who had recently lost his wife of fifty-six years. Every day he came in, sat in the same armchair by the wood burner, ordered a Pot of Tea for One and a Jacket Potato with cheese and beans, and read his newspaper. Then, without fail, he would plump up the cushions, take his finished plate and crockery to the counter, dip his hat to Sarah and be on his way.

Yes, Sarah was lucky to have such loyal customers, but she did wish some new, and perhaps younger customers would give her a try, perhaps make the place a bit more lively. Of course, she'd have to invest in more staff. It didn't bode well that between her and Poppy they got flustered from a few geriatrics turning up at their door.

Sarah checked the tip jar. The elderly certainly knew how to tip. And low and behold: about £4 in coins and a £5 note sat in the bottom. She emptied the money into a brown envelope and stuck Poppy's wages in with it for the day.

"Here you are, chick," Sarah dangled the wage packet for Poppy. "You go home, I'll finish cleaning up."

Poppy had a little peek in her wages, then looked up frowning. "You've put too much in here."

"Those old birds are good tippers. You earned it this afternoon," Sarah winked.

"Thanks, Sarah. Are you sure you don't mind me going? I can

stay longer."

"No way! It's a Friday night. Go and have fun!"

"If you're sure," Poppy said this as she hopped from foot to foot, forcing them into her wellington boots.

"Close the bottom gate when you get to the lane, will you? Tom will be after you if you leave it open again!"

"Tom? After me? I wish!" Poppy sighed dreamily, before facing the late afternoon chill.

Sarah tutted in amusement as she locked the door behind her. Sticking some music on, she got to work on cleaning up, humming away contently as she went.

Chapter Four

"They can't just boot you out of your office like that! What they're doing isn't legal, surely!" My colourful friend, Michelle, was expressing a small percentage of her equally colourful vocabulary, as she cussed her way through my dreary recount of the last couple of weeks.

We were sat in our favourite coffee shop, exactly a mile between my place and Michelle's, back in Brooklyn. Michelle's frizzy red hair was blazing scarlet in the late-afternoon sun, matching the fury she felt for my mistreatment back in the office. I really should give her more credit where it's due. She's certainly loyal in that respect. Although Michelle's empathy was often over the top and theatrical, I couldn't help but feel better for it, like she justified my feelings. I wasn't really a melodramatic person, so having Michelle do it for me was somewhat satisfying.

"No, I'm pretty sure everything is perfectly legal so far," I stabbed a fork into Michelle's slice of cake. "I'm digging into that frosting by the way."

"Help yourself. I don't get it - you're an F-ing lawyer, sort them out!"

My fork paused at my mouth; I stared at Michelle in wonder.

"I work for a business consultancy company. I'm not a - why did you think I was an F-ing lawyer?"

Michelle shrugged, nonchalant, "Dunno. Sounded cool. They can't fire you though, can they?" Michelle was now tucking in to her chocolate cake, batting my fork away.

"Not yet, no. Urgh, I don't know - I don't know the first thing about employment law. There are so many loopholes. If they want to get rid of me, they'll find a way."

Just then, it felt like my heart literally plummeted to my feet as realisation hit me. I sat back in my chair, twiddling my fork in my hands, holding back tears.

"Being an F-ing lawyer would come in pretty handy right now. Hey," Michelle hushed as my sniffs caught her attention, "you'll be okay."

"Well there's always this job proposal in London," I screwed my face up, unsure what to make of the whole thing.

"Well, obviously you have to go!"

"*Obviously* I have to go? What is obvious about any of this?" I groaned, holding a hand to my forehead in defeat.

"Oh come on Emily! I practically fall asleep just at the thought of your life at the moment. It's so dull! This little British adventure is exactly what you need."

"I resent your comment!" I tried, and failed, to look offended, knowing full well that in comparison to Michelle's life, I really was as dull as it came.

"Resent all you like sweetie, you know I'm right. Besides, how can you resist this opportunity to have Mr Mark Trengrouse all to yourself?"

It made me shudder the way Michelle practically drooled out his name. Honestly, she was sleazier than most men and, like a lot of men, her mind was constantly on the topic of sex. She was also infuriatingly beautiful, her fiery red curls catching the eyes of every man in New York. Of course, once she opened her fiery loud mouth, most ran a mile.

"There's another thing," I began, the fork in my hand now working overtime as I spun it round and round from nerves. "I've been receiving notices for eviction."

"Oh, Em. Is it from... him? You told me you had your finances under control."

"Well, clearly I lied didn't I?" I snapped. "Sorry! Sorry, I don't mean to... It's just... scary. Michelle, I could be made homeless - any moment now. I'll have let Gwynne down and he'll have got his way..."

"You won't be made homeless, sweetie. It's not going to get to that point. He won't be able to just evict you like that."

Just one week later, Michelle was proven horribly wrong.

"Evening, Emily. What, no welcome party for your friendly landlord?"

I clutched hold of the door in an effort to support my legs, which had buckled underneath me. Fear seeped into my pores and rendered me speechless. A wicked smile spread over his face as he noted my reaction.

"You gonna let me in or what? I only own the joint and all, y'know?"

I shuffled to the side, my mind racing through the abridged list of options I had.

I cleared my throat and tried to find my voice, "I returned to work the other week, so money will start coming in again soon."

"Good. That's good," Sal nodded, taking the flat in. Thank God I had tidied up some of the mess. Sal hated mess. "Gonna have to be a fair pay check though, to cover your debts."

Sal paused in the middle of the room, his hands in his pockets, and set his eyes on me. Hungry and sinister. I wanted to bolt, straight out of the front door. But no good came from that.

"Come on Em. Enough is enough, y'know. You took advantage of Ma's kindness enough. Don't take advantage of mine."

"I never took advantage of Gwynne," my response was barely a whisper as Sal took a large step forward. He wasn't much taller than me, but somehow managed to tower above me all the same.

"Tell you what," Sal's voice was dangerously low. "I'll make this simple. You get every single cent owed to me before October. Down to the last quarter. You get that and we're good. You don't? I'll be doing what Ma should have done a long time ago and I'll be chucking you out on that street faster than you can say diner."

His last words tickled my ear as he leaned in, his words coated with such venom. I willed the tears to stay in place; I didn't want him having that satisfaction.

"Unless of course, you want to explore that other option I offered you last time?" Sal's hand traced my upper arm and the sensation ran through me like a cold trickle of water, bile rising in my throat as that familiar feel of entrapment washed over me. I batted his hand away before it reached my cheek.

"I'll have the money by October," I snarled.

A cruel smile stretched across his face. He dropped his arm, nodded and opened the door.

"Good to hear. I'll be downstairs checking the diner. Think I'll stay for a couple of nights. Get the bed sheets prepped in the other flat, will ya?"

"You've rented it out to that Chinese couple - Mr and Mrs Chung."

"Fine, then you go stay at a friend's and I'll have your bed."

"You can't be serious?"

"Unless you wanna get all cosy tonight?" I couldn't suppress my shudder. "Then get packing. Will be good practise for if the money don't come through."

In an instance he was gone, his heavy footsteps pounding down the stairs into the diner, leaving me to crumble in a sobbing mess as I closed the door behind me in futility. He had a key. He could return whenever he wanted, so I packed my little duffel bag as fast as I could and headed straight to Michelle's.

"Hey Em!" Michelle stepped to one side to let me through, bringing the bags onto the right side of the threshold. Her hair was clipped up untidily, her sleeves rolled up, and there were smears of dried clay across her face. She must be in the middle of a piece.

Michelle's apartment was a splash of different colours, all ricocheting off one another in a hectic clash. Just like Michelle herself, the apartment was loud and obnoxious, the vibrant mint green kitchen already causing a strain on my sensitive eyes. Every piece of furniture wore a throw, that of the crocheted kind, and in every corner, on every work surface possibly available were piles and piles of books. Books on art, books on culture, books on photography. And where every corner and every work surface wasn't covered with piles of books, it was scattered with art supplies of every kind. Brushes, acrylics, dirty paint water, rags. The list went on.

Suddenly, I craved the solitude of my beige walls. All four of them. A feeling of sadness swept over me as I realised the huge possibility of losing them forever if I did not deliver on the first week of October. Through all its faults, it was the closest thing I'd had to home in a very long time.

"How are you doing?" Michelle asked brightly, pulling her sweater over her head and chucking it haphazardly across the room.

"Okay!" I forced myself to say, practically feeling my skin crack. I glanced over to the TV unit to have my weary green eyes lock in with two amber glass ones. "Still got that creepy bird thing then?"

"As long as Nicky is here, Peter stays."

Nicky was Michelle's slightly eccentric, outlandish roommate. He too was an artist, but unlike Michelle who focused more on sculptures, Nicky preferred to practise the more intrusive, illegal art of street graffiti. Peter was his stuffed pheasant that he had had imported from Europe whilst touring for a project that resulted in his being arrested. Something that happened on a regular occasion.

"So, make yourself comfortable. The futon just pulls out from there, and there are spare sheets at the bottom of those drawers. We're getting take-out later, do you want Nicky to get you anything?"

"Oh...no it's fine. I'll just-"

"Em, it's on me. Don't sweat it. Oh please don't start crying!"

"He's just there...in my flat. In my bed!" I wailed, my voice thick from the tears.

"This has got to be illegal, Em. You've got to get a solicitor involved."

"I can't afford one," I sniffed, curling myself into the nearest chair and covering my legs with a nearby blanket. What was the point of a crochet blanket when the heat just escaped from all the holes?

"Emily. In all seriousness now," I heaved a shaky sigh as Michelle steadied my juddering shoulders with both hands, asking, "have you spoken to Mark about London yet?"

"No, but I will."

"I think that's a good idea. Now get some alcohol down that skinny neck of yours. Bottle's in the top cupboard. And pour me one too, before I lob this crappy pile of clay down the trash chute."

With a looming payment deadline and Sal lingering in my flat, it was all I could do not to snatch up Mark's offer. Mark was over the moon and just three weeks after that, with my new passport clasped firmly in my hand, we were heading to John F.Kennedy Airport.

It had seemed like the right thing to do, without a trace of doubt. Soon, my life would be bagged up in duffel bags at the foot of Michelle's futon bed. I mean really, what did I have to lose? The few hours spent in the delights of the First Class Lounge Bar had distracted me enough, but it wasn't until Mark and I were boarding the plane, the noise of the engine deafening until inside the aircraft, that the extent of what I had committed to began to hit home.

"O-o-o-k," I breathed to myself, shuffling down the aisle to find my allocated seat. "O-o-o-k." I could feel Mark's eyes appraising me from behind, probably with amusement.

"You're okay, Miller. Keep going."

I wished I could be as cool and collective as Mark, but something about the idea of being ascended 32,000 feet in a tiny seat crammed onto the side of an aircraft was suddenly causing my body to twitch in involuntary ways. I was about to start hyperventilating when the breath got knocked out of me entirely at the sight of my allocated seat - or should I say suite.

"Suite 6B," I muttered, checking my boarding pass. "Holy shit, is this all mine?"

"Yep, and this is mine," Mark declared, settling in to the opposite suite across the aisle. "I've got the window seat. Do you want to swap?"

"No, no. Being away from the window this is just fine," I stepped in to my little pod, pressing buttons like an excited toddler, a small hint of hysteria giving away my nerves.

"Good grief, Em. You'd think you've never flown before," Mark exclaimed, as he tucked his laptop bag into the storage under his TV screen. The look of alarm on my face must have said it all as Mark released a heavy breath of exasperation. "You've never flown before, have you?"

"I've never needed to," I squeaked. "How long is the flight again?"

"Seven hours."

"Oh shit! Is there another way?"

"Across the Atlantic? No, Em. Sit down and relax, will you?

You're in First Class and complimentary drinks are on their way. I suggest you have an alcoholic one."

"Good evening," a friendly flight attendant said, her bright white teeth illuminating behind ruby red lipstick. "Can I interest you in a complimentary beverage?"

Her tinkering British accent and warming manner immediately calmed me and I smiled warmly back, accepting a flute of prosecco.

"Thank you," Mark muttered, also taking a flute of the crisp bubbly drink, oblivious to the fluttering of the flight attendant's eyelashes. He really did look like some sort of celebrity in his blue linen shirt and perfectly styled hair. My presence on the upper-class deck definitely looked like some sort of admin error.

"This is insane. I had visions of us being elbow to elbow, surrounded by screaming babies."

"That's economy. I wouldn't subject you to that sort of torture," Mark winked, adjusting his seat.

"You're so privileged," I laughed, shaking my head in mock disgust.

"Hey, Little Miss Judgey! I've flown economy plenty of times in my time, thank you very much."

I chuckled and started exploring my little suite, in awe of the way space-saving hadn't compromised luxury. Honestly, there was more in the way of facilities in this little pod than there was in my entire flat - although, actually, that didn't take much.

An eighteen-inch TV screen popped out by a click of a button and it took a lot of restrain not to squeal out in glee. I hadn't had access to this many film options in years, having my cable cancelled and my TV taken away by the first round of bailiffs last summer. Shaking those toxic thoughts away, not wanting them to spoil this moment, I busied myself with rooting through my Virgin Atlantic Goodie Bag.

"Are you going to fidget the entire way over there?" Mark huffed, looking across the way to me.

"Sorry," I mumbled, scarlet lines forming on my cheeks. "Am I embarrassing you?"

"No," Mark smiled, gentle with me. "It's cute that you're so excited. But seriously, stop fidgeting and drink your prosecco."

An hour into the flight, I was taking delicate, disgusting sips from the whiskey Mark had insisted on buying me to calm my nerves, trying my best not to pull a face. The taste practically burnt my taste buds and a shudder ran down my spine each time I swallowed the malty liquid.

"If you don't like it, don't drink it," Mark stated.

"It's fine. It's just got a bit of a kick, that's all," I reasoned, looking around the plane at all the passengers fixated on their laptops, tapping away on their keyboards with agitated importance. "I feel like we should probably be doing some work."

"Pfft! Screw that," Mark scoffed. "This is as close as we're getting to a holiday in a while. May as well enjoy it! Another?"

I shook my head, pushing my glass away. I was beginning to feel a little queasy, and the constant popping of my ears was beginning to take its toll on my already tender head. I'd looked into the cost of a portable oxygen tank a week ago, but it had been an extortionate amount of money so I'd had no choice but to hide my trusty oxygen cylinder at Michelle's, with hope that I would be able to purchase another one in the UK. For this long-haul flight, I was on my own.

Out of idleness, I found a Country Living magazine tucked in the corner of the foot-well and flicked through the pages, gazing at the pictures of idyllic green and blue scenery.

"They make the countryside seem so magical and inviting in the UK, don't they?"

"They paint a pretty picture," Mark gruffed, not taking his eyes off his screen, his redundant half-screen across offering him semi-privacy. "What they fail to mention is the constant damp weather, the midges and the endless smell of dung. Not to mention the tractors continuously blocking the roads."

"Got first-hand experience, have you?"

There was no response, and when I glanced over in Mark's direction, I found him watching his screen with intense concentration. Something told me that he had no intention of replying.

Another couple of hours passed and Mark had fallen asleep, his headphones slightly off-centre from his head. He looked peaceful, younger even. It had never occurred to me, the strain that Mark must be putting himself through to climb up this corporate ladder. He was naturally one of the best in his industry and I had admired this about him for the last two years of knowing him. But I felt a little ashamed at realising that this was perhaps the first time that I was looking at him as just any regular guy, somebody who stripped himself to the very core of exhaustion to meet his goals. I'd taught myself to endure his arrogance, accepting it as a result of his success - but how much of that was survival tactics to get through the brutal politics of the corporate life? Well I certainly knew what it was like to need survival tactics, just in a different way.

It was now dark, and the effects of my drinks were beginning to leave me sleepy. A prickling sensation was forming around my temples and my left eye was beginning to feel droopy. The Beast was waking up.

"Excuse me," I stopped a passing flight attendant, trying to ignore the tone of panic rising in my voice.

"Is everything alright, Ma'am?"

"Would I be able to get some ice please? Wrapped in a towel?"

The flight attendant frowned in confusion then smiled politely before heading towards the bar to meet my request.

I tried repositioning myself, worried that if I moved too much, I may provoke The Beast. Then I remembered that my seat could recline in to a flat bed and if it wasn't for the fact that the shadows of pain forming were beginning to compromise the muscles in my face, I would have giggled with glee as I was lowered into a more comfortable, horizontal position.

The flight attendant returned promptly and handed me a small hand-towel filled with cubes of ice, along with a bowl to put it in afterwards. Thanking the steward gratefully, I pressed the ice-cold bundle to the back of my neck and felt an immediate, albeit temporary, relief. The prickling sensation melted away and the biting of the ice-cubes spread across my skull. Settling myself down into a comfortable sleeping position and closing my eyes, I slipped into a cold, yet relatively painless, sleep.

"Ladies and Gentlemen, this is your captain speaking. We will shortly be arriving at London Gatwick. The local time here is 07:00 hours. On behalf of myself and the cabin crew, we would like to thank you for choosing to fly with us and hope you enjoy your stay here in London."

The pilot's voice penetrated my sleep as the cabin crew paced up and down the aisle, ensuring that passengers' seat belts were fastened, and chairs were reclined back up in the upright position. A member of the cabin crew stopped next to Mark and addressed him gently.

"Sir, we're preparing to land. Would you mind bringing your tray up? Thank you kindly," the pretty flight attendant twisted around towards me. "Excuse me Madam, we're preparing to land. Would you mind returning your seat to its upright position?"

"Mmm, yeah sure…sorry," I mumbled and then squealed as I adjusted my head. The back of my neck was soaking wet, as was the top half of my shirt.

"Jesus, what happened to you?" Mark exclaimed, accepting a hot towel from the flight attendant. Pulling my much colder towel out from behind me, I then remembered the ice.

"I asked for some ice for my neck and must have fallen asleep. It's all melted - what a mess!"

"Honestly Em. Can't take you anywhere!" Mark tsked, sipping at his coffee. "You missed the coffee run. You were out for the count."

It was clear that Mark wasn't the kind of man to rush with anything. Once we had retrieved our luggage in arrivals, Mark led the way to the Clubhouse arrivals lounge where I was able to indulge in the best shower I had had in years and gorge on a fully cooked breakfast.

"I could get used to this," I groaned, rubbing my stomach in satisfaction.

"There was me thinking you didn't like your food," Mark chuckled at me, impressed by my efforts. "You're as skinny as a rake."

"Thank you," I replied, deadpan, scrunching my nose up at this comment. "It's not by choice. Not everybody has food on demand like this."

"Alright, touchy! Most girls would be delighted with that compliment," Mark teased, then checked his watch. "Right, grab yourself a coffee. I've booked the Uber for thirty minutes time."

The Uber driver yanked the vehicle vigorously into a parallel space outside the new office an hour later.

I tried not to let it show on my face, as my heart stumbled slightly in disappointment. Lacking the elegance and glamour of its sister branch in Manhattan, the building I would potentially create new beginnings in, stood before us. Then again, it was an attractive, historical terraced building, sandwiched between others, all in a uniform chain. The upper half of the building was dark from the exposed London stock brick and the bottom half gleamed white, the black iron railings contrasting against it. The wide, black front door with its brass knocker reminded me of the iconic image of 10 Downing Street. It had charm, and I admired the window boxes overflowing with an explosion of summer flowers. But I just couldn't help but note the size.

"What do you think?" Mark asked, enthused.

"It's...small."

"Yes, well the rent in London is colossal," Mark said, pressing the buzzer. "I think we struck lucky with this really. Wait until you get upstairs; it's got a wicked view of the park behind."

"Blake & Co?" A female voice sang through the speaker.

"Morning Janet, it's Mark. We've spoken on the phone."

"Mark! How lovely! Come on in."

The speaker buzzed and the front door unlocked. Inside was a work in progress, with desks, filing cabinets and randomly placed office chairs littering the foyer. Instead of polished marble effect walls and matching floors, this place had outdated panelled wood, busy patterned carpets, and an unidentifiable damp smell. The sash windows did not allow for much light either - a far cry from a glass-fronted skyscraper.

"There's going to be a desk here, and I'm currently having a large sign made to go up there. Though, going by the pictures I was emailed I thought this space would have been bigger. May have to adjust the order and have a smaller sign."

Mark talked me through his plans as he led the way up the varnished wooden staircase to the second floor. He spoke with a passion and excitement that I hadn't seen from him in a long time. I smiled and listened intently as he talked through the advertisement and marketing plans, all the while trying to convince myself that this was all going to be a good idea.

Poking his head into empty rooms, Mark finally located the employee break room. A handful of people sat amongst boxes, enjoying a tea break.

"Hi everyone. Just coming to introduce ourselves. I'm Mark."

Mark shook hands with each person, carrying with him an air of confidence and authority. He really was very good at this.

"This is Emily. Your new recruit. Let's see if I can remember all your names from recruitment for Emily's sake. This is Keith from Legal Support. This is Janet, she's one of the secretaries, along with Polly here. This is Harry. Outstanding C.V mate. Great consultant. Em, you'll learn a lot from this guy."

I shook hands with each person as Mark introduced me. They all seemed warm and friendly. Janet offered me a cup of coffee and a biscuit and it was from that factor alone that I decided I liked Janet very much. Harry then invited me to shadow him in a day's work, claiming that the best way to learn was to watch a professional. His offer was clearly an ego-boost for himself, but I thanked him all the same. Maybe it wasn't going to be all that bad. If I had a good set of colleagues to work with, who cared about the fancy office, right?

The rest of the day flew by, time trickling away unnoticed. I had been given the task of chasing potential marketing leads and ensuring our advertisement would be live as of next week.

I spent most of my lunch break taking a good look in every room. This didn't take long seeing as the entire building was the same size as just one floor of the branch in Manhattan. The rest of my lunch was spent chatting with Polly and Janet, as if we had been friends for years. Polly was in her early twenties but acted like she was well into her forties. She dressed far beyond her years and her hair was a rusty red, stiffly styled into a 50s beehive, while a string of large pearls clung tightly around her neck. Her smile was contagious and warming behind her glistening ruby lipstick.

Janet was possibly in her mid-fifties, her dress-code much more beige than that of her colleague. She dressed for comfort but still carried off the professional look expected in an office environment. I'd noticed very quickly that Janet's main priority in life was to make sure everybody around her always had a cup of tea and a biscuit. How very British of her.

I barely saw Mark that day, but when five o'clock ticked by Mark had found me nestled deep inside a cupboard where I was housing the new filing cabinets, labelling the drawers and beginning to create some sort of an admin system.

"Alright Miller? You seem in your element there," Mark smiled, leaning on the door frame.

"You know me. I love organisation," I winced as I stood up. I had been cross-legged on that floor for at least an hour and a half.

"You've done great. Everybody loves you," Mark complimented. This seemed genuine, to my surprise. "Time to head back now. We'll grab some dinner at the hotel. On me."

"Don't you mean, on the firm?" I corrected.

"Yeah. But this way, I'm the generous one."

Chapter Five

It had been a successful first day at the office, and Mark was satisfied with his choice of team - though it was still yet to expand. Mark knew that Emily didn't like the office. It was clear from the way she over-compensated her enthusiasm one minute and scrunched her nose up the next when she didn't think Mark was watching. It was small, a little run down, and didn't boast that clean-cut, modern design like the office back in Manhattan. The building itself was old, creaky and damp, while the interior hadn't been updated in a few decades. The firm would not be spending money to bring it up to date until the office started making money. If Mark was honest, he was glad it was Emily who would be working here and not him.

He was now sat in the hotel restaurant, with Emily scrutinising the menu opposite, with a pained expression on her face.

"What's the matter with you?"

"It's really expensive," Emily whispered.

"So? You're not paying, so don't worry about it."

"Well that's good really," Emily scoffed. "The appetisers alone cost more than my water bill."

Mark chortled. "Just order what you want. We won't be able to make a habit of it, but first day and all... we've earned it."

Emily ordered a sirloin steak with the waiter moments later and Mark ordered the sea bass. He then proceeded to order a bottle of red for the table.

"Have you missed England?" Emily asked when everything had been ordered and the wine was flowing.

Mark was taken back by the question and paused for a moment. Had he missed England? London, maybe. The mannerisms of the British, the etiquette? Yeah, he'd missed it. But he also loved New York. The cleanliness of the city, the architecture of the modern skyscrapers, the people. He had felt more at home in New York than he had anywhere else.

"Not really," Mark replied, simply.

"Really? Not even a little?" Emily sipped her wine, an air of self-consciousness about her as she did. "Isn't it Cornwall that you're from? At least you can visit your family for a bit while we're here."

Clutching his wine glass, praying that it didn't snap under his tightening fingers, Mark paused for a moment to think of an appropriate answer.

"Yes, Cornwall. But it's very far from here. We won't have time."

"But when do you ever get to come back to England?" Emily continued, unaware of Mark's tensing posture. "Surely it's worth covering those extra miles."

"We would have to fly down which is extra cost. And like I said, we really wouldn't have time," Mark smiled falsely, his lips tightening over his teeth.

"Couldn't we-"

"Can we just drop it? We're here on business, nothing more."

Sensing that he had been a bit harsh, Mark tried to soften his features, offering Emily some more wine. She didn't say anymore on the matter.

"Can I get you anything else?" the waiter asked routinely.

"No," Mark replied, waving him off.

"No, *thank you*," Emily chimed.

There was a pause as Mark tucked into his sea bass. It was good, and he hadn't realised how hungry he was.

"Why do you do that?"

Mark looked up at Emily, confused at her question.

"Do what?"

"Speak to people like that? People who serve you?"

Mark washed his food down with a swig of wine, all the while his eyes fixed on Emily's. She looked irritated all of a sudden.

"Speak to them like what? They're used to it, they're-"

"Oh! Oh no, don't do that! Don't be that guy!"

Mark chuckled now, incredulous at where the conversation was going.

"What? Jesus, Emily! Let me eat my food, will you?"

"You were going to say 'just a waiter', weren't you? You know, I was 'just' a waitress once. And I hated it when people spoke to me how you just spoke to that poor man."

"Alright! Alright, you're right! You're right, I'm sorry. I'll leave a tip, how's that?"

"A big tip!" Emily was grinning now. "Just because you've never done manual labour before -"

"Hey, whoah whoah! Big assumption there, Miller! I've done my fair share of manual labour thank you very much. But you're right. I was very rude. You have taught me a valid lesson. I will strive to be more polite."

"Good. I'll hold you to that."

The smile on Mark's face felt like it was growing the more he fought against it and he suddenly felt goofy. He cleared his throat, a way to smoothly compose himself.

"So, where did you used to waitress?"

"Is this your way of taking an interest in us little people now?"

"Oh shut up Miller and answer the damn question!"

"Umm, well I-"

Mark sat up as he realised how distressed Emily looked in answering this question.

"You don't have to tell me if-"

"No, no it's fine. I just haven't talked about it for a long time, y'know? So, the diner I worked at was my foster Mom's...Gwynne she was called."

"Was?"

"She passed away when I was seventeen."

"I'm sorry. What was the diner called?"

"Gwynne's Diner. Ha, no I'm serious," Emily chuckled as Mark let out an involuntary snort. "I know, really original. But it's great. It's outdated and falling apart, and on the roughest street in Brooklyn - but it's busy and popular and... the closest thing I have to home."

"So, you're still there?" Mark tried and failed to keep an edge of criticism from his voice.

"Yep, still there," Emily raised her eyebrows in what seemed like bitterness as she pushed her food around her plate.

Silence fell between them, and for once Mark didn't feel

compelled to fill it. He regarded Emily as her eyes glazed over at the memory, a look of pain flashing across her small face.

Mark was useless when conversations turned sinister like this, so he cleared his throat for the second time and nudged Emily's plate towards her.

"Eat up. This food was expensive you know?"

Emily smiled, seemingly relieved that they had moved on from the conversation.

An hour later, their dessert plates empty and their stomachs full, Mark ordered them each a brandy to finish the meal. He was surprised to find he had enjoyed Emily's company this evening. He wasn't sure why he was so surprised; he supposed that Emily had always seemed so plain against the other girls he usually wined and dined. The big difference was, however, that Emily had real class and was attractively intelligent. It became clear, as the evening went on, that she was wasted as his assistant. Suddenly that empty bribe of promising to get her into business school was something he wished, and hoped, he could guarantee.

"So," Emily began, running her finger along the top of her brandy glass with ponder. "Hypothetically speaking... if I decided to take this job here in London... "

"Yes?" Mark encouraged her.

"I'm just trying to get my head around it all, really. Will the firm pay the costs of my move? Everything?"

"Visa. Working visa. They'll also pay your first month's rent," Mark added. "Just to make sure you're all settled before you begin."

"Wow," Emily sat back, twirling her brandy in circles at the bottom of her glass, with no intention of drinking it, it seemed. "With everything that has happened recently, I felt sure I was going to lose my job. I never would have guessed they'd consider me for this?"

A small twist of guilt rose in Mark's chest, which he tried to fight off. Oh, if only she knew the real reason she was here. Mark tried to convince himself that all of this had Emily's best interest in mind. It didn't - but it would be good for her... eventually. She'd get the promotion she deserved even if it was in a different country and in a much smaller office. She'd get a fresh start. Yeah, that was it.

Mark always thought Emily to be a quiet sort of girl - not much of a social life. She had that ridiculously annoying friend - what was her name? Michelle? But he had never heard her talk of nights out with her girls, or anything that involved a group of friends at all. If he was honest, she always came across as a bit of a loner. He imagined her, every evening after work, ordering a Chinese for one and devouring several chick-flicks before going to bed at exactly 10pm. Maybe earlier. So really, what difference would it make if she was here? She'd find a new favourite Chinese takeaway, maybe even get a cat, and live happily ever after.

Perhaps the idea of Emily leading a remarkably dull life was why she was taking Mark by surprise tonight. Here she was, in London, dining with him and looking remarkably pretty in her black dress; nothing like the usual Plain Jane he was used to seeing at the office.

This made Mark think back to an office Christmas party two years ago, when Emily was still fairly new to the firm. The evening was uneventful, as always. Full of pretentious conversations and debates between colleagues, people sat at desks working, cleverly disguised in party hats to give the impression of having fun, while sneaking in some extra work at their desks in between sips of eggnog. Mark rarely enjoyed the Christmas parties for those reasons alone and given recent events with Catherine and his supposed friend Jack, Mark had taken it upon himself to join the trend of working through the party. He had just opened his emails when the door was wrenched open, Emily stumbling in whilst leaving a trail of wine in her wake.

"Sorry, sorry. Wrong room!" Emily staggered. "Thought this was where the drinks were being kept."

"You're enjoying yourself," Mark had stated, keeping his eyes on the screen in hope that she would depart quickly.

"So are you. Doing your favourite thing. Do you ever stop working, by any chance?"

"Of course," Mark had replied, loading an email from Donald in regard to a new client's account. He sensed Emily hovering by the door. "Can I help you with anything? No booze in here I'm afraid. Though, I wonder if you've had enough."

"Had to do something to numb the boredom. Worst Christmas party I've ever attended."

"You're right there."

Mark recalled Emily wandering away from the door and propping herself on his desk.

"I haven't officially thanked you for landing me this job," Emily spoke softly now.

"I didn't. You interviewed well. You landed it yourself."

"You have no idea how much I needed this job. Any job. You saved my ass, Mark. Seriously."

Concerned at her words and her sudden change in tone, Mark had looked up from his computer screen to see Emily fragile, the drink and her emotions getting the better of her.

"Crikey Miller, don't start blubbering," he had never dealt with emotional females well and wasn't one for successfully consoling another human being either. "Tell you what, I'll-"

Before he could finish his sentence, Mark had found his lips locked in by Emily's as she'd thrusted herself upon him. Despite the slightly unfortunate lingering taste of wine, Emily was a good kisser. Fierce and determined. Mark had liked it. Too much. It was just as he recovered from the initial shock of being pounced on that she'd ripped herself away, a look of horror spread across her face.

"I'm so sorry! That was so inappropriate! So unprofessional of me! I'm so sorry!"

And with that, Emily had scampered out of his office, quicker than lightning, and disappeared for the rest of the night. They never spoke of the incident directly but occasionally Mark indulged in making her uncomfortable. Flirting with her just enough to make her squirm. Besides, there was something about her innocence and the way he easily made her blush that Mark liked. Emily was not one-night-stand material. An odd sense of protectiveness came over him at the thought of doing that to her. But he liked making her nervous, and as the weeks went by he realised that he enjoyed the challenge.

"Right," Mark snapped himself out of his train of thought, catching Emily yawning. "Bedtime. Lots to do tomorrow."

"Good idea," Emily sheepishly placed her untouched brandy on the table. "I can't believe how tired I am. I thought I'd be wide awake considering the time difference from the states."

"You got pretty stuck in today. Like I said, everyone was really impressed with you. Come on, I'll walk you to your room."

Mark led a slightly tipsy Emily to the lift, up to the top floor of the hotel and along the corridor to her room.

"I've enjoyed this evening," Emily said as she fumbled with the key card to her room. "I don't get opportunities to eat in nice restaurants, so thanks."

"No problem," Mark replied, smiling at how accurate his assumptions were of her.

Then she surprised him for the second time that evening by closing the gap between them and pecking him affectionately on the cheek. Such a sweet, non-sexual gesture, and yet it sent a current of electricity across his face.

"Thank you for your kindness. Night Mark."

"Goodnight, Em."

Once she was safely inside, Mark meandered back to his own room, which was located just down the end of the same corridor. He'd upgraded his room with a balcony overlooking the River Thames, the London Eye glittering majestically on the other side of it. He wasn't a regular smoker, but on perfect evenings like this he couldn't help but enjoy a well-cut cigar on the balcony, soaking up his privileged view. Yep, this was the life. He wouldn't have it any other way.

Unlike Emily, Mark was wide awake and in no way ready to call it a night. An hour was spent enjoying his brandy and cigar on the balcony, another half an hour was spent enjoying a long soak in the bath. He was just about to settle down in bed to watch a movie when his phone pinged. Glancing at the screen, he could see a Facebook notification.

'Emily Miller says she was with you at The Savoy in Covent Gardens, London.'

If anybody could witness the blood drain from Mark's face at that very moment, they'd say he had seen a ghost, with a pickaxe, ready to murder him. Mark suddenly felt sick, faint and panicked all at the same time.

Since when did Emily tag him in anything on Facebook? He wasn't a fond user of Facebook and had quite forgotten he was even friends with her on the damned thing. He wasn't the type to regularly update the world on his geographical whereabouts and he didn't take Emily to be one of those people either. Just how drunk was she? Perhaps he should have confiscated her phone.

His palms suddenly clammy, Mark jabbed his pass code into the screen and brought up the post. There it was, in clear black and white and with an excruciating amount of emoticons to follow (aeroplane, smiley face, cocktail glass, smiley face with tongue stuck out, another aeroplane and a kitten face - not sure what the kitten was for). Proof that Mark Trengrouse was back in England, for the first time in three years. He thought of his sister, back in Cornwall, with growing anxiety. The only family member he was friends with on Facebook, mainly out of obligation. She was bound to read this and question why he hadn't been down, and why he hadn't RSVP'd her wedding invitation. Without the 3,500 miles safely between them as a reputable excuse not to attend the wedding, Mark didn't really have a leg to stand on. Not going now would be petty and unforgivable in Sarah's eyes.

Mark looked frantically at the time that it was posted. Two minutes ago. Could he untag himself? Yes! 'Remove tag'. But what if Sarah had already seen it? If it was then made clear that he had attempted to remove himself from the post, it would surely look even more suspicious. Deciding that was a smaller risk worth taking, he thumped the 'Remove Tag' button with his index finger, quickly proceeding to message Emily a curt text, ordering her to remove the post all together. What was she thinking? Mark had always seen Emily as being much more private than that.

Mark poured himself another brandy and decided to reach for his emergency pack of cigarettes, reserved only for moments of unbearable stress. He hadn't expected the source of his stress to come from a post on social media.

He checked his phone again, trying to hold onto the possibility that he had got away with this one. Except he hadn't.

There it was, the post giving him away like a beacon on a

mountain top. A single 'Like', a bullseye on his once unreachable target, and this 'Like' belonged to Sarah Trengrouse.

He'd been located.

Chapter Six

It was early December 2006. Gwynne's Diner had shut its doors for the night, and I began the onerous task of sweeping the chequered tile floor, flipping chairs up onto the tables as I went. Christmas shopping was now in full swing, so Gwynne was adamant we stay open later to lure in those weary shoppers with a hot chocolate and slice of pie. Of course, she'd been right and was now counting her dollars with glee.

"Emily sweetie! Be a doll and bring in the chairs, will ya?" Gwynne said over her cash flow.

It was bitter cold outside on the street, the hairs on my skinny arms demonstrating just that. I was feeling fed up, sulking like the teenager I was for having missed another night out with my friends, who by now would be at the movies watching The Holiday, huddled up over one box of popcorn. Not me though. As always, I was cooped up here, waiting tables and refilling endless cups of coffee.

I knew I sounded ungrateful. Gwynne had fostered me now for two years and had honestly saved me from either getting arrested or worse, killing myself from all the stupid things I had done before. I had not been in a good place, and it was Gwynne's tough but nurturing approach that had slowly pulled me from my dark place. Of course, it didn't stop me from doing the typical teenage thing and resenting her when she pulled the plug on my plans to touch base with my rebellious side every once in a while.

She'd say, "Doll, d'ya know what happens to girls who play in the street after dark? They end up in the gutter. You wanna end up in the gutter sweetheart, or d'ya wanna make something of yourself?"

Almost at a pinnacle moment, I spotted a homeless man settle himself down for the night in the threshold of Pins and Needles Tattoo. He busied himself, burying his legs into his bivvy bag and blowing hot breath into his tattered gloves, attempting to cover his hands. I paused from wiping a plastic bistro table and found myself simply staring at this man, a look of utter defeat on his face as he bristled his unkempt beard and buried half of his face into his scarf in an attempt to keep warm. Even when his greying eyes looked up to meet mine, I didn't look away. His gaze shot through me like a warning signal, as if he was telling me 'don't end up like me. Keep sweeping those floors. Things will get good in the end'.

"Why don't you take that poor fella over some coffee?" Gwynne's voice spoke soothingly from behind me. She placed the warm coffee into my hands and gave me a gentle nudge in the right direction, like she always did. Checking the streets were clear, I closed the gap between myself and the man, who was watching me warily all the way from the diner. He smelled musky and of stale tobacco. I stretched out my arm and offered the steaming cup of coffee, which the man took with his blackened fingers. I watched with an odd sense of fulfilment as the man's eyes closed from pleasure over the warming liquid now warming him through.

"Thank you. You got something to eat?"

"Oh, um yeah. Probably. Just a second."

A slight spring in my step and with a new purpose to my evening, I jogged back across the road to Gwynne who smiled proudly as she passed me the last few slices of the pumpkin pie we had planned to eat that night. When I placed the takeaway box, full to the brim with the pie, into the man's hands just seconds later, it was like I had undergone a transition.

"God bless you," the man nodded his thanks and tucked into the pie.

Once back in the warmth of the diner, I turned the key and shut the blinds. I then found Gwynne in the kitchen, who was struggling to mop the floor. Instinctively, I wrapped my arms around her neck from behind and planted a kiss on her soft, powdery cheek.

"Have I ever said thank you?"

"For what?"

"You know what." I said, feeling self-conscious.

Gwynne's shoulders bounced as she chuckled. "You have. You do every day, in your Emily way. You're a good girl."

I took the mop from Gwynne's tired hands and led her in the direction of the nearest chair, "I'll finish the cleaning up Gwynne. Why don't you put your feet up?"

"As I said, you're a good girl."

"Am I? I very nearly wasn't." My voice trailed to barely a whisper as tears compromised my vocal cords.

"You've always been a good girl, sweetie. You just lost your way, that's all. Your actions don't define you."

As always, Gwynne's astute words sank in and cleansed me of the bad thoughts that often kept me awake at night.

"Now pull yourself together. You're slow at your work when you're brooding."

It was now 6am, early September 2019, and I was waking up to the sound of hotel doors slamming shut and other guests making their way down for breakfast. I had an acute hangover that was leaving me foggy and a little worse for wear. A stark contrast to last night, where I'd felt composed, chic in my black dress. Mark had actually enjoyed my company, I think - I know - I'd seen a different side to him last night. A side that opened up to me and spoke to me like I was his equal. Not his assistant. Not the one he pitied. Despite the hangover, I'd woken up with a smile on my face this morning, looking forward to Mark's company once again. A moment of sadness trickled through me as I remembered my dream from last night, taking me back to my days with Gwynne and threatening to start me off on the wrong foot for the day, with nostalgia sitting heavy on my heart. I gave myself a shake and started getting ready for another day at my new office. After all, Gwynne always hated when I moped.

I knocked on Mark's hotel door about forty minutes later. No answer. I knocked again, a little louder in case a similar hangover to mine was compromising Mark's get-up time. Still no answer. Deciding that he must have made his way down to the breakfast room early, I headed for the elevator.

Downstairs, I had no more luck in finding Mark in the breakfast room. I was hungry though, so hoped he would find me while I indulged in my favourite pastries. A phone call came through on my ancient brick cell just as I stuffed my mouth full of croissant.

"Hello?"

"Hello love, it's Janet. From the office. You alright, pet?"

"Oh, hi Janet. Yes, fine thanks - just having breakfast and waiting for Mark."

"Yes, that's why I've called actually," Janet replied, suddenly sounding uneasy. "Mark is already here and has asked me to let you know that a taxi will be picking you up outside the hotel at 8:30."

"Oh," I glanced at my watch. It was 8:10. "Okay, thank you Janet. See you in a minute then."

Once at the office, I wanted to find Mark straight away. He was obviously concerned about getting things done and perhaps needed my help. I shouldn't have slept in so long. A fresh smile crept into the corners of my mouth as I thought of last night and I suddenly felt a strange urge to find him faster, to continue where we left off.

I found Mark soon enough, hunched over a desk in the room he had commandeered as his office for the time being. His hands raked through his thick black hair and he was tapping his pen with agitation on his notebook to the right of him. His phone was coming alive on the desk in front of him as message after message, and phone call after phone call seemed to be coming through.

"Is everything alright, Mark?"

"Yes, thank you," Mark replied curtly, without looking up from his phone screen, which appeared to be permanently illuminated.

Things between us had changed dramatically since last night, it seemed. But why? I scanned nervously through my hazy memories as I stood in the threshold in thick silence. Had I said something to offend him? Had my little goodnight kiss made him uncomfortable? No, this was Mark we were talking about. No form of female contact made this bachelor uncomfortable.

"You got here early," I pressed on. "Did you not sleep very well?"

"I slept fine."

I bit my lip nervously. I had definitely done something wrong, and he was making this very clear. But what on earth had I done?

"Umm, okay. I'll go and make us both some coffee, shall I?"

"Emily, for future reference, can I ask that you not include me in your childish social media updates. I do not need the whole world knowing what I am doing in my spare time. Thank you."

His instructions were so direct, so cold and so pompously articulated that I didn't reply straight away. I gaped for a few seconds, my mouth opening and closing as my brain processed his demands and tried to construct an appropriate response.

"That's why you came to the office without me? Because I tagged you in a Facebook status?" I asked, incredulous.

If I was entirely honest, I had forgotten all about the Facebook status, and come to think of it he had messaged me that evening to ask me to remove it. I did it straight away, of course - but I didn't think it had left things sour between us. As far as I was aware, it had been out of sight, out of mind. I'd gone to sleep and that was that. Was Mark seriously holding a grudge over it now?

"Fine. Sorry I tagged you on Facebook," I finally retorted when Mark didn't say anything. Saying my apology out loud made it sound even more ridiculous. I went to leave but leaned in with one last quip. "Just want to add: I hardly ever go on Facebook, and I rarely have something interesting to say on the stupid thing. I suppose I enjoyed my evening and felt like I wanted to share it. But I won't be doing that again!"

I remembered the unexpected desire to share to my rather limited Facebook world. I remembered thinking about how anti-social I had become in the last year, how isolated I had become since The Beast took over my life. How Michelle constantly made me feel like a cooped-up loser with as much ability to have fun as a Priest at a strip club. Last night was the first time in forever that I had felt remotely sexy or glamorous. So yes, dammit, I had wanted to share it on social media. I'd wanted to prove to everybody that Emily Miller was still interesting, and that I could live the high life too.

I went to leave a second time, but Mark had other ideas.
"Miller!"

Turning on my heel, I glared at him. His face softened and it looked, for a moment, like he was going to change his tune.

"You need to check that Harry doesn't need anything before

you wander off to do your own thing."

It took all my strength not to throw a particular gesture in my boss' direction as I turned my back and rounded the corner down to Harry's office.

I worked through my lunch, later in the day. Not only because I was fully immersed in a job I wanted to finish, but also because it kept me busy and my temper calm. Mark had many ways of infuriating me and there had been times when I really wanted to thump him. But this time he had really got under my skin. Perhaps this was all down to last night. Perhaps I had seen a rare side to him that I actually liked; then the real Mark reared his ugly head, leaving me unarmed and disappointed.

"Everything alright, love?" Janet bustled into the room cautiously, holding a mug of hot coffee. "I've brought you up a coffee. You need something to eat? Can I go out and get you anything?"

Sitting back on my heels, I smiled warmly up at Janet. I'd been categorising potential and existing clients, spreading them out on the floor for better room. But now that I had stopped, I'd realised how stiff I was feeling.

"Thanks Janet. I'm okay, honestly. I'm still full from breakfast."

"You sure you're alright? In yourself, I mean? I don't know you all that well but I can see something is bothering you."

Something warm and inviting about Janet made me want to spill all of my hopes and worries to her, offload every ounce of shoulder weight that I bore.

"Just Mark. We had a bit of a disagreement this morning," I replied, diplomatically. I hastily added, "but it's fine."

"Must have been some disagreement, pet. You've both been miserable as sin all morning. I asked Mark what the matter was when he asked me to call you and he just shrugged and said, "lots to do". At least you were less cryptic."

"Mm, well - I'd best not say any more if he is being so reserved. Don't want to give him any more reason to be annoyed. Thank you for checking on me, Janet. I do appreciate it."

"Ah, you youngsters. Never mind, will be water under the bridge tomorrow, I'm sure. Let me know if you get hungry, pet.

There's a sandwich shop just across the street. Wouldn't take me long. I'm getting cabin fever behind my little desk."

I smiled my thanks and Janet shuffled off to attend to her desk once more.

The rest of the day continued the same as it started. By six p.m everybody had gone home, and I was forced to seek Mark out to see if he was ready to return to the hotel. A small part of me hoped he had gone back without me. I'd rather venture back by myself if it meant avoiding another argument with Mark. I was sadly disappointed when he beckoned me in impatiently. He was on the phone, his back facing me. His shoulders were tense and his shirt sleeves rolled up.

"Yep. Yep. Sure. Sounds good."

His short responses suggested that whoever was on the receiving end was dominating the conversation entirely. Mark appeared to be merely agreeing for the sake of it.

"Well, I'll try but... okay, tomorrow. It's not for another ten days, you know that right?" Mark rubbed a hand through his thick hair, exasperated over the conversation. "Okay, okay, keep your hair on. Yep, looking forward to it. See you tomorrow."

Mark ended the conversation and put his phone down. From behind, he seemed defeated - exhausted even. I even felt sorry for him for a moment, though I wasn't sure why after his behaviour earlier.

After a thoughtful pause, Mark finally turned around and faced me. His expression morphed from angry to anxious, and he no longer seemed to be glaring at me. He suddenly looked terribly tired, and his voice came out quiet and steady.

"Looks like we're going to Cornwall after all."

"Really? What for?"

"A wedding. My sister's wedding actually. Come on, we'd better get back to the hotel. I have some phone calls to make and we both need to pack. We're leaving first thing tomorrow morning."

I felt momentarily disorientated. What had just happened?

"But we've only done two days here. Is everybody going to be okay with us just... disappearing to Cornwall?"

Mark didn't answer. Instead he started tapping a message into his phone.

"Obviously, it's super important. It's your sister's wedding. But I'm not sure they'll understand me going with you. Perhaps I should stay behind and get things done here in London."

"No, you need to come with me," Mark finally replied. "You got me into this mess, after all."

He wasn't angry, but his stillness was more unnerving.

"What mess? How did I... what have I done this time?"

Mark rounded on me and a familiar sense of fear temporarily paralysed me.

"My family didn't know I was in England. Not until you tagged me last night. My sister has been ringing me all day, demanding I come to the wedding after all."

Suddenly, I recalled the invitation that Mark had snatched from me a couple of weeks ago. "Why wouldn't you tell your family that you were in England? This is the first time in, what, three years?"

"It is. But - and this is without me getting too honest with my personal affairs - I didn't necessarily want them knowing I was in England."

"Why?"

"As I said... I don't have to explain myself to you. I just didn't. But I have no choice now - I have to attend this bloody wedding. I'm not facing it alone. So, you're coming with me. End of story."

Mark's final words were fierce. I decided not to argue, but a new bubble of anguish began to form in the pit of my stomach. I sat down and watched helplessly as Mark called Janet up, spinning a quick tale of lies that we were heading down to Cornwall for a potential project lead and wouldn't be back until the deal was signed. How quick and effortless it was for him to lie to people to cover his tracks. How had I become a part of this?

Later, as I was packing what little clothes I had, I forced myself to get excited about the next ten days. I tried googling images of Cornwall to psych me up. Beaches, rolling hills, tiny little villages peppered across the countryside. A little excitement bubbled away, and a small dose of apprehension bled into the mix, spoiling the thought of it. Mark wasn't happy about these new plans and he blamed me for it entirely - so it was also clear he wasn't going to give me an easy ride. Another small measure of curiosity added to my jumble of emotions: what was waiting for Mark in Cornwall that made him so afraid? One thing that was for certain, I was going to pay for this minor mishap one way or another. For now, I suppose, I would just have to try and enjoy the journey before the storm.

Chapter Seven

Sarah came off the phone to her brother, fit to burst with mixed emotions. She was buzzing from the idea that in less than 24 hours she would get to see him again, after so many years. Deep down she knew that Mark had had no intention of letting his family know he was back. At the risk of feeling hurt, she pushed that thought to the back of her mind and pretended he had come to England especially for her: just for his little sister's wedding.

Sarah immediately felt a twinge of guilt for her other brother, Tom. How was he going to handle this? How would he react when Mark finally arrived? Oh god - would he start a fight with him? No, don't be silly Sarah. Tom may be a naturally built rugby lad, but he certainly wasn't the violent sort. In fact, he was an extremely reserved man, made even more silent since that awful day his and Mark's relationship plummeted to hell.

What if he refused to come to the wedding? Sarah would have been thoroughly saddened if Mark hadn't made it, but without Tom, her absolute rock and guide in life, she would be devastated. It wasn't a 'favourite' thing, but Tom had always been the reliable one. Mark was Mark.

Cashing the float for the day and locking up behind her, Sarah followed the scent of her mother's cooking back to the main house. Beef stew with Karen's famous dumplings - one of Sarah's favourites. Karen was just dishing it out as Sarah took a seat at the table.

"Molly!" Sarah trilled as Molly, the eldest whippet, jumped up and dug her claws into Sarah with demanding affection. "Hey girl. Where's your sister? Oh, there she is. Hey Lula!"

"How were your takings today, sweetheart?" was her mum's automated response, sliding a large plate of stew in front of Sarah.

"Mum, easy on the portions. I've got to fit in my dress next Saturday, remember," Sarah protested, though she still helped herself to a wedge of bread.

"Oh, get on with you," Karen waved her off. "You eat like a horse and never put an ounce of weight on. You're hardly going to start now. I'm sure you'll burn it off playing rugby, anyhow."

Her mum was right of course. Sarah was extremely lucky with her metabolism. She had a naturally athletic physique, measuring to a tall 5ft 11inches and sported an appetite bigger than most men. Her mum however, though by no means overweight, had not been the bearer of the athletic gene. She was much shorter than Sarah and stood around 5ft5. She comfortably carried around a little extra weight but was impressively active, especially given her age. Sarah guessed that her years of physical labour and endless gardening had kept her body supple.

"You still haven't told me how your takings were today," Karen pointed out.

Sarah shrugged through a mouthful of bread and stew. "Same old. Not great, but not zero."

"Don't be too disheartened, my love. Summer holidays have just ended; you're bound to have a lull -- will you stop stuffing your face and at least wait for your brother and husband-to-be?"

Reluctantly, Sarah put her fork down. Tom and Steve were always late for dinner, which really irritated Karen, though she never admitted it.

Karen tapped rhythmically on the table as the front door opened and slammed shut.

"Ah, good. Right, now you can tuck in."

"Sorry we're late, Mum," came the deep, gentle voice of Sarah's eldest brother, Tom. He towered to the ceiling in their mum's old country kitchen and seemed to fill it just by standing in the doorway. Steve, though tall, was dwarfed beside his best friend. "Delivery came in late for the bottles."

"That's not a problem, my darlings," Karen sang warmly, bustling around the kitchen for an oven glove and removing their plates of stew from the heat of the AGA. Sarah rolled her eyes as she chewed her food. Tom's presence always put their mother in good spirits. "Sit down, sit down both of you. There's more bread where that came from. Though, Sarah has scoffed most of it, I'm afraid."

"I had two pieces!" Sarah protested through a giant mouthful of dumpling.

"By the way, sis. I've sorted that bar out," Tom grabbed a piece of bread before Sarah could grab another, spreading a thick layer of butter onto it as he talked. "It's now in the barn. Though those blokes must have loosened something in the joint work when they were shimmying it down the lawn. Bloody fairies, the lot of them."

"Thanks - I thought it seemed looser. Sorry, I just wanted it in place before the chairs and tables arrived. Mum!" Sarah suddenly shouted, catching Karen feeding the dogs scraps of her food from under the table. "Stop feeding them from the table! No wonder they constantly have their noses in people's food."

"Well just ask me next time," Tom continued the previous conversation. "Don't ask them lot from the distillery. They can barely lift a keg of cider!" Tom and Steve chortled in unison, elbowing each other in agreement.

"That's all very well," Sarah quipped. "But you're never available when I need you. You're always too busy."

Tom rolled his eyes but didn't answer. Sarah knew he never had a come-back for that, but she knew he couldn't help being so busy. He had a lot of responsibility and, most days, found himself tackling the job of up to four men by himself. She didn't like to make him feel guilty over the matter so dropped it and changed the subject to the big topic of the evening. Although, this wasn't going to be much easier.

"So, I have a little surprise," Sarah began nervously. "Guess who is coming to the wedding."

She glanced at Steve; it was clear by his equally nervous expression that he had already worked it out.

"A bit late for RSVPs," Karen huffed. Sarah knew she was thinking from a catering perspective.

"This won't affect numbers for the food, Mum. He was counted in from the beginning."

That alone had been a big enough clue when Tom's fork dropped with a clatter. Sarah chanced a peek at Tom's expression which was cold and stony. His jaw clenched as he gritted his teeth.

Karen worked it out purely on Tom's reaction. Her voice was small and hopeful.

"Mark's coming?"

Sarah nodded in reply. She didn't want to say too much at this point, what with her brother steaming in the seat opposite her.

Tears began to fill her mother's eyes as she patted her daughter's arm for more information. "When is he coming? Saturday morning?"

"No. He's on his way now... from London. He should be here late evening... tonight. I'm sorry, I know it's short notice, but... everything happened so fast."

"Well now," Karen sniffed. "This is unexpected. How wonderful! Tom, darling. This is good news, isn't it? For your sister's wedding?"

Karen's tone was stern and challenging, almost urging Tom to be okay with this, but Sarah sensed he was far from okay. He was handling it may be better than she had expected; he hadn't stormed out, after all. Though his chosen reaction was perhaps a little more unnerving as he sat in silence, finishing his meal with intense concentration. He wiped the plate clean with the last wedge of bread, stuck his plate in the sink and grabbed his coat.

"Thank you for dinner, Mum. Delicious, as always. I'm going to lock up the barns and call it a night."

"Tom... " Sarah began.

"Not now, Sarah," Tom replied before stomping out of the house in his steel-capped boots, brandishing a torch light ready for the dark September evening.

Silence fell over the dinner table, Tom's heavy footfalls crunching into the distance as he crossed the yard.

"I feel awful," Sarah groaned, cradling her face in her hands. "But it's my wedding day - I need Mark there."

"Think nothing of it, my darling," Karen soothed. "Tom will come around. It's going to be difficult at first - but it's been three years. It's about time we put the whole ordeal behind us and forgot about the wretched thing. And I need to see my son! Can you two do the dishes please? I'm going to put some fresh sheets down on Mark's bed."

As were all of their rooms, Mark's room was exactly how he'd left it before he had moved out to study Business Economics at university, all those years ago. Karen had never been one for minimalistic living and rather took comfort in what Sarah and Tom always mocked as her three little shrines for her three not so little children. The attic was brimming with baby clothes, toys, old schoolbooks, anything and everything Karen could possibly hoard away. She just couldn't seem to bring herself to chuck anything of any sentimental value.

"Mark is bringing a plus one as well," Sarah added.

"Oh? A girl?"

"He is 30. It is allowed," Sarah scoffed.

"They can't both sleep in a single bed though," Karen worried, wringing her hands like she did when she was pondering over the smallest of problems.

"Stick her in Tom's old room then. Not mine, obviously. I might sleep in there night before the wedding."

"Right you are. I'll change both beds then," Karen began to fuss, dragging out a dust cloth and some polish from under the sink. "Best give both rooms a bit of a dust and vacuum as well. Ooh, wish you'd told me sooner - I feel ill-prepared now."

Steve and Sarah both rolled their eyes in unison and chuckled under their breaths.

"Do you think I'm an awful person?" Sarah pouted at Steve.

"For what? For wanting your whole family present at our wedding? No, definitely not."

"Tom though... this is going to be so difficult for him."

"Perhaps not. It's been three years. Mark, by the sounds of it, has a new girl on the scene. Maybe if Tom sees him with her it'll take the whole thing out of context, and they can learn to move on. I'll speak to him tomorrow. Don't worry yourself over it."

It was moments like this that Sarah was reminded why she loved Steve Bray so much. He had a way of saying the exact thing that Sarah needed to hear, at the exact time that she needed it the most.

It was an agonising wait for the rest of the evening. Karen busied herself frantically around the house, making her home presentable for her guests (though it already was). Steve lit the fire in Karen's front room, and they stuck a movie on to pass the time. It was nearly 11:30pm when the yard was filled by headlights as a car crunched into a parking space in the yard. Her heart racing, Sarah jumped up and rushed around, trying to find her shoes.

"They're here! They're here! They're here!" Sarah squealed childishly through the house. She heard Karen drop whatever it was she was doing, rushing downstairs to join Sarah and Steve out on the yard. She ushered the dogs out of the way frantically as they clawed at the front door, sensing the excitement.

It was a crisp evening, probably the coldest one so far to begin their transition into autumn, and their hot breaths lingered in the air as they waited for Mark and a pretty young girl to climb out of the car. Both looked tired from the journey, but Mark had a big smile plastered across his face, his arms held out as he approached their mother. He looked expensive, Sarah noted. His carefully structured hair, his black suit coat and his polished black shoes all represented Mark's success. Suddenly Sarah felt an unusual wave of shyness and inferiority towards this brother of hers that she hardly recognised.

"Hey Mum," Mark cooed, softly. Karen was already crying and he tutted at her for being so emotional. "What are you like, Mother?" He wrapped her up in a big hug and she sobbed freely into his shoulder. He then moved on to Sarah and gave a more sheepish grin. "Hey Sis."

"Hey Bro," Sarah smiled fondly. Her worries melted away at that moment. This was good. This was going to be okay. She allowed herself to be folded in one of Mark's best hugs and breathed in his expensive cologne. It was unfamiliar. Mark was unfamiliar. "I really appreciate this," she added with a tender note.

"Don't sweat it," Mark waved her off, a touch of Americanism in his manner. "Ah, Steve!"

Mark acknowledged Steve politely and gripped his hand. Steve returned his handshake with grace, though both men seemed to be competing in hand strength.

"Good to see you, Mark," Steve forced himself to say, gruffly.

Sarah looked over Mark's shoulder and noticed the girl he had come with standing rigid on the spot. Sarah had never seen anyone look so uncomfortable and out of place as this girl. She had to be mid-twenties; a petite frame, which was made to seem even smaller in clothes that hung from her slightness. She was exceedingly pretty, but plain - not a single ounce of makeup or fake nail in sight. An unusual companionship for Mark who, Sarah knew, preferred the more extravagant looking women.

"Are you going to introduce us to your girlfriend, Mark? Poor girl looks terrified!" Karen chuckled happily, beating Sarah to the mark.

"Oh... umm... yeah, sorry," Mark stuttered, oddly. "This is Emily Miller... my girlfriend." Mark steered Emily around, so she was standing level with him. If it was possible, she looked even more uncomfortable but smiled gently and held out a delicate hand.

"Pleased to meet you," Emily shook all their hands in turn. For such delicate hands, she had a firm grip and a steady voice.

"Oh, you're American!" Karen cried, delighted.

"Well, he has just been living in America for three years, Mum!" Sarah rolled her eyes and looked apologetically towards Emily. Honestly!

"Well come on in. Let's not stand out in the cold," Karen ordered. "Steve will help you with all your bags, Mark. Sarah, why don't you show Emily her room for the week. She looks exhausted, poor pet. Don't mind the dogs, Emily. They're vocal but friendly."

As Sarah led the way into the house, she couldn't help but notice a small twitch of Tom's curtains in the downstairs window of his cottage across the yard. Riddled with guilt she took Emily into the warmth of the farmhouse, silently vowing to make it up to Tom, somehow.

Chapter Eight

Pacing tracks into the royal blue carpet of my new room for the week, it was all I could do to keep myself calm.

Girlfriend? Girlfriend??! What was he thinking? I was furious with him. There was no way I could keep this up for the entire week, especially around his family. I just couldn't understand; what good did it do him?

Here I was, seething and panicking behind closed doors, trying not to allow my state of emotions provoke The Beast in any way. He had been on his best behaviour so far. I couldn't afford to fall apart now, I'd look like a complete idiot - more than usual.

I should have been comforted by the fact that Mark's family were, by all accounts, simply lovely. And there was a part of me that was slightly drawn to the rosy family shenanigans of hot cocoa by the fire and late-night chats. But who was I kidding? This wasn't me. I never did well in these scenarios and they never served me well neither. They had really tried to put me at ease, but by the time I was finally allowed to scuttle up to bed, I'd felt harassed, pulled at every angle, interrogated to within an inch of my life. Why did complete strangers want to know so much about a nobody they had just met? Oh yes, that's right - because they were under the impression that I was next in line for a spot in the perfect family portrait. Stupid Mark and his stupid web of lies!

Bags in the correct rooms, the Trengrouse family and I had spent an hour before bedtime literally drinking hot cocoa around a giant solid-wood dining table, centred in the middle of Karen's beautifully traditional country kitchen. It was heaven, except I spent the entire time with my eyes burning a hole in the door, my flight mode on stand-by as I took awkward sips of my hot beverage, social paralysis almost getting the better of me. I also hadn't realised how cold I had been until I'd sat near the AGA, which radiated the kind of warmth you didn't get from an electric heater. Okay, so that had been a positive and perhaps settled any urges to flee a mile, at least just for that moment while I'd thawed out.

The main instigator of my interrogation was Mark's terrifyingly charming sister, Sarah. She was naturally beautiful, with strong facial features, and towered above me in height. Her naturally wavy chestnut hair fell graciously past her shoulders and her cheekbones stood out prominently, without the help of makeup.

Eventually, I was deeply relieved when Karen had insisted everybody head to bed. They'd catch up properly over breakfast the next morning, Karen had said, and my interrogation was sure to continue.

I now propped myself on the edge of the single bed. How could I be so exhausted and yet so far from ready to go to sleep? I took in my new surroundings while layering up on my bedclothes (it was going to be a cold first night until - or if - I adjusted to the temperature), my attention first falling on the handful of trophies lined up on the shelf above the fireplace. To my disappointment, the fireplace was boarded up and hidden behind plaster, the mantelpiece left for display purposes only. Some of the trophies represented unusual categories such as 'Fastest Young Sheep Shearer of the Year' and 'Young Farmer of the Year'. The rest of them were rugby related. I'd heard of this sport. Similar to American Football, but no padding or cheerleaders!

This had been the other brother's bedroom growing up, perhaps in his teens, so I couldn't help but note how sophisticated, albeit dated, the bedroom was for a young teen. The carpet, a rich royal blue colour, was the first part of the decor to set it back a decade or two and the walls were half cream, half blue, with a silver strip of wallpaper separating the colours along the middle. There was a single yellow-pine desk and a blue office chair, a chest of drawers to match and, of course, the single bed which was tucked away in the corner, fitting perfectly sideways in an alcove where a fitted wardrobe had perhaps once sat. Tom (I was sure that was his name, from what Sarah had said) obviously liked keeping things simple, even as a teen.

I twitched the curtains to peer out of my bedroom window. Complete darkness. I recalled, on our arrival earlier, the streetlights being no more on the last twenty minutes of our journey and Mark's car plunging into darkness down a narrow, bumpy lane with grass growing in the middle. It was safe to say that we were 'in the sticks' as they say.

My curiosity soon diminished to sleepiness as I tucked myself under the crispy clean covers and shut my eyes in hope of a quick slip into slumber. It wasn't until I was perfectly comfy that I realised there was no bedside lamp and that I'd need to cross to the other end of the room to switch the main light off. This room was going to take some adjusting to.

The twittering of birds outside, with the room still plunged in darkness, told me that I had awoke in the small hours of the morning. I was wide awake and, for a moment, disorientated from my surroundings. The bed had been surprisingly comfortable, and I hadn't been as cold as I thought I would. But as I stretched my arms out of the covers and sat up to check my phone, I soon realised it had only been the effectiveness of the winter duvet cocooning me in my own body heat. The cold air of the room leeched onto me, sucking the reserved heat from my body. In desperation I dug into the contents of my suitcase. Nothing warm. Nothing practical. All suitable for a day at the office.

That was, after all, the original reason I crossed the Atlantic ocean.

I proceeded in rooting through this Tom person's old chest of drawers and quickly found a collection of old sweaters. I yanked on the first one my ice-cold hands could grasp and found that I was drowning in material. Tom must be a big guy, I thought. But I was already beginning to thaw and found myself indulging in the warmth.

5am. It wasn't time for the sun to rise just yet, but the birds' happy morning song gave a hint that it wasn't too far away.

Not wanting to sit in bed for the next two to three hours, and feeling increasingly thirsty, I wondered whether it would be intrusive to make my way down to the kitchen to fetch a drink. It wouldn't hurt to pop down quickly and grab a glass of water at least. I could then take my medication in private.

The rest of the house was peaceful and deathly still. I wasn't used to such quiet surroundings, and without the rumbling of traffic and beeping horns outside, the silence seemed almost maddening. But then, I couldn't remember ever waking up to a chorus of birds outside my window; that was enough to put anybody in a good mood.

Tiptoeing through the house, the coldness of the flagstone tiles leading to the kitchen penetrating my socks through to my already numb feet, I was startled to see the kitchen light on. Had somebody accidentally left it on last night? I suddenly felt like an intruder and started retreating away to head back upstairs when I walked straight into a large wall of a figure. Grabbing my mouth to stifle a pathetic cry of shock and almost stumbling backwards from the impact, the large figure grabbed my shoulders to steady me. I couldn't make out features, only the silhouette; he had to be at least a foot taller than me.

"Sorry, dint mean to startle you," came a voice from above me. The voice was deep, yet silky smooth, his West Country accent soothing to the ears. "Are you alright?"

"Ye-yes, I think so. Sorry. I shouldn't be- " I stumbled on my words, feeling increasingly stupid. A worrying thought flashed through my mind for a moment at the idea of him being the intruder.

"Come and sit down. I've just put the kettle on."

Okay, well an intruder wouldn't be arrogant enough to make himself a cup of tea. I felt a little more assured and allowed myself to be led by the mysterious man into the well-lit kitchen, the heat of the AGA already showing its benefits.

Once I was sat down, I sneaked a glance at the mystery man. He really was very tall, with broad shoulders and a powerful physique. He seemed to intimidate everything in the room. His body structure was very pleasing to the eye, especially in his black polo-shirt, his waist and behind even more pleasing in the tan-coloured work pants that were currently bulging with an array of tools, gloves and his phone. My head tilted in interest. I was suddenly feeling very exposed in my tiny gym shorts. At least my borrowed sweater was long enough to cover my own behind.

"Coffee? Or tea?" The man asked over his shoulder, as he spooned his own coffee granules into a travel mug.

"Actually, just a glass of water would be great."

The man turned around and faced me, his deep brown eyes fixing onto mine just for a moment. My stomach jolted uncomfortably.

"You're American."

It wasn't a question, more a statement - almost an accusation. I frowned a little at his tone. Now that I could see his face clearly, it became apparent to me that this must be Sarah and Mark's other brother, Tom. He was unbelievably attractive, his jawline set tensely, square and sturdy - his short but unruly beard only making him more masculine. He shared elements of Mark's features, though they were much more rusty and weather-worn.

"I am American. Well observed," I tried to reply with a cool, steady voice.

"Sorry, didn't mean to sound rude. I just didn't realise my sister had an American friend."

"Actually, I'm here with Mark. I met Sarah for the first time last night. And your mom, Karen."

Suddenly, I wondered if I had said something wrong as in that instant Tom's demeanour changed as he went rigid with tension.

"I see. Well nice t' meet you," Tom cleared his throat awkwardly, filled a glass with some tap water for me and grabbed his mug. "Help yerself to a hot drink if you wan' one."

Tom marched towards the door noisily, proceeding to exit. Strangely, I felt the need to extend the conversation.

"Thank you for allowing me to borrow your old room for the week," I blurted out, lamely. What was I doing? "It's very comfortable."

Tom looked confused for a moment.

"That will explain why you're wearing my hoody."

"Oh shi- I'm sorry! I'm such a - it's cold, and I didn't pack the right things..."

A small smile twinged in the corner of his mouth. "S'alright. I haven't worn it in years. Help yerself."

This was followed by a very long, tense silence. I suddenly wished I'd never come down for water.

"Right, I better get a move on."

Departing from the house, Tom left me to my solitude in the

silent kitchen. I could hear the faint crunching of Tom's tread across the yard, with the rumbling of the AGA next to me. It had been an odd exchange of words between us and I noted how sinister the conversation felt once I'd even mentioned Mark's name. Weren't they brothers?

I suddenly felt very foolish and childish for getting so giddy at the sight of Tom. I decided to blame it on my disrupted sleep patterns, coming to the conclusion that sleep deprivation did strange things to one's hormones. I thought of Michelle and how she acted like a predator with her wandering eyes and decided I didn't want to be like that.

Taking my glass of water back upstairs to my room, I took refuge under the covers and waited for movement from the rest of the house. At 6am I heard Karen make her way down to start breakfast, the scratching of excited dog claws sliding around on the downstairs tiles and the smell of bacon wafting through the house soon after. The front door opened and closed, followed by the murmuring of conversation between Karen and Sarah. This was clearly a household of morning bloomers.

Summoning some bravery, I got changed and made my way downstairs. The dogs greeted me as soon as my foot reached the bottom step, sticking their cold wet noses where-ever they could for a good, informative sniff. I petted them nervously and gently shooed them. I wasn't quite used to the overbearing affections of the canine sort.

"Good morning, Emily!" Karen sang, cheerfully. "Did you sleep well? I hope you're hungry."

"Good morning, Mrs. Trengrouse. Yes, thank you, I slept really well. And smelling that bacon - I am super hungry!"

"Good. I like a girl with an appetite. Though you wouldn't think so, looking at you. Seen more meat on a butcher's pencil."

"Mum!" Sarah scolded her mother as she poured boiling water into numerous mugs of coffee. "Honestly. Sorry, Emily. Coffee?"

"Yes please," I chuckled, winking at Karen to show that I wasn't offended. At the table Mark was fixed to his phone, tapping away manically on the keyboard as usual. "Morning, Mark."

"Morning," Mark replied distractedly, not taking his eyes off the screen.

"Put that bloody thing away, will you?" Karen waved towards Mark's phone, as she dished scrambled egg onto plates. "You haven't taken your eyes off of it since you came down."

"Sorry, Mum. It's the office. I'm just replying to an email, and then it'll be put away."

"Can I help with anything, Mrs. Trengrouse?"

"Oh, Emily my dear. Call me Karen. No need to be so formal. And no, we're fine. Just sit down and relax. I'm just serving it all up now."

Within minutes, we were sat around the table with the largest fried breakfast I had ever seen. Everything was cooked to perfection. I usually hated breakfast, often not bothering to eat until lunchtime. A few days in a hotel had already started to break that habit, but here I couldn't wait to dig in.

The front door opened as we were tucking in, and Steve stormed into the kitchen, looking a little weather-beaten.

"Bleddy 'ell, it's freezing out there! Wouldn't think it was summer a couple of weeks ago!"

"Ah, about time! Your breakfasts are in the AGA."

"Sorry, Karen. Can't stop. I'm just grabbing mine and Tom's. We'll eat it at work."

"Oh fine, just treat me like a bloody takeaway kitchen, won't you!"

"Sorry! We're just so behind on delivery and Jimmy's called in sick again," Steve gave Karen a kiss on the cheek on his way out with the plates of food. "Thanks Karen. Looks delicious!"

"So, what are you and Emily going to do today?" Karen asked Mark. "Perhaps you could take her for a nice walk down the lanes; take the dogs with you."

"Um... yeah? Could do," Mark hesitated, sticking his nose up at the idea of walking down some muddy lanes. "Not sure if Emily has the right gear for a country walk. It's going to be muddy."

"You can borrow some clothes from me, Emily," Sarah offered, enthusiastically. "And I've got loads of wellies. What size are you?"

"I'm around an 8."

"What's that in UK size?"

"Size 5," Mark pointed out, looking it up on his phone.

"Great, well I definitely have some wellies in that size. I'll fish them out for you."

"Well, let's just see first," Mark interjected, leaving me completely out of the decision process - as people usually did. "It might be that I'll have to do some work to send back to the office. Emily, you don't want to go traipsing through the lanes in this weather, do you?"

"Well I might, if you gave me a chance to speak," I fired back, flinching seconds later as I knew I would pay for that comment later. Though I couldn't help but enjoy the gleeful reaction from both Karen and Sarah.

"Ha! You tell him! The girl has a backbone, love it!" Sarah laughed. "Tell you what, Em. I have to open the tearooms later this morning. I'll give you a little tour and you can sample some cake."

"Sounds great," I smiled, glad to have *somebody* here who wanted my company. My frustration towards Mark grew as he finished up the last mouthful of his breakfast before immediately returning to his emails. What was so important that work already had his eager attention?

Once the table had been cleared, dishes had been washed and put away, and coffee had been guzzled, everybody departed in different directions to begin their days. Karen mentioned something about plans to hit the supermarkets and stock up on the last of the ingredients for the wedding food and Mark muttered about needing to reply to those emails upstairs on his laptop, even though he had spent most of breakfast typing away furiously into his phone. This left me and Sarah alone in the kitchen, along with the whippets who were now curled up together in front of the AGA. They were rather cute, I had to admit.

"Do you fancy coming with me to the tearooms then? I've got to make up the salads and put a quiche in the oven. Sorry, it's not very exciting... but you can eat as much cake as you like."

"Don't know if I can squeeze in cake quite so soon after your mom's delicious breakfast. But I'm happy to help, if you like. I used to work in a diner back in Brooklyn, before I worked at Blake & Co."

"Ha! A diner! So cool!"

The tearoom was a hidden gem inside the old dairy, one of many old stone-walled buildings dotted around Trengrouse Cider Farm. Unlike some of the more tired looking out-buildings, this one had been re-pointed and given a new slate roof. A wood-burner flue stuck through the roof, already billowing out smoke, the little dwelling practically inviting us to step inside.

It was a tiny space, with no more than five tables able to occupy three to four diners at a time. The wood-burner sat enticingly in the corner, and a basket full of blankets and cushions could be seen on the far side of a comfy-looking 2-seater sofa. The counter was simple and cladded with driftwood, and the coffee machine gleamed on the back counter.

"Tom must have been in to light the wood burner," Sarah sighed, mainly to herself. "You stick the coffee machine on - switch is on its right. It'll take about five minutes to warm up, then you can make us a coffee."

I did as I was told, then started familiarising myself with some of the necessary tools to make a decent coffee. My hands fell into the familiar movements as I poured fresh coffee beans into the grinder and measured the milk carefully into one of the jugs. After five minutes, I was happily steaming the milk to temperature and pouring it into the coffee shot to create intricate patterns. I'd forgotten how much I enjoyed making lattes and proudly presented Sarah with one topped with hearts and a leaf.

"No way! You're a pro!" Sarah exclaimed. "It's taken me months to perfect a simple heart. Most of the time I end up accidentally creating a cock and balls. You have to teach us how to do this."

"I'll try," I replied, through giggles over the 'cock and balls' image. "I'm not very good at explaining it. I kind of just...do it. I can do animals as well."

"Oh, that I have to see later. Poppy is going to love you. She'll be here in an hour. Or an hour and a bit - she's always late. Go and take a seat in front of the fire, if you like. I'm nearly done with these salads."

I wandered over to the sofa with my own coffee whilst taking in my surroundings. It really was a unique little tearoom - full of character and charm. But we were literally in the middle of nowhere.

"How long have you been running this tearoom? Looks quite new."

"Over a year now," Sarah called from the kitchen. "It has its busy periods occasionally, but we're on a bit of a lull at the moment. Post-summer and all that."

I wondered how such a small business gained any footfall at all, so far from civilisation. Then I could see the many reasons why people would return and return again. My self-restraint lasted half an hour before I just couldn't help but get involved, opening the doors for Sarah and donning an apron. Business was slow, but the occasional influx of customers dwindled in here and there throughout the morning.

I met Poppy once she eventually arrived; Sarah insisted that I teach Poppy the basics on latte art, stating that the accidental 'willy' shapes and hap-hazardous blobs that Poppy was currently creating on top of her lattes were not exactly creating the right effect.

I soon forgot about everything, all the reasons I was here, and got lost in the familiar routine of coffee-making, customer-pleasing and order-taking.

It felt so good.

Chapter Nine

Tom was a man of a calming disposition. At least, he usually was. That was until the return of his brother Mark. Tom wasn't usually the kind of person to hold a grudge. But this grudge was highly justified.

It was Tom's intention to avoid Mark as much as he possibly could for the next week, and get this wedding done and dusted. Mark could bugger off home back to where-ever he was living, and things could go blissfully back to normal. He knew this was a childish approach but that was the effect his younger brother had on him, and he resented him even more for that. Then there was the American girl. Mark had kept her suspiciously quiet. Tom was surprised that this was the first they had heard of this new relationship, given that an excuse to boast how happy he was never usually went amiss.

Since Sarah's announcement over the arrival of Mark, Tom had found his mood taking a dramatic descent. Even Steve was tiptoeing around him.

"Mate, where do you want these crates?" Steve asked. They had finished wolfing down Karen's warming fry-up an hour ago and had got straight back into working the large delivery that had arrived early that morning.

"Crates of what? I've got a fair few here!" Tom barked.

"Bloody hell, mate! Stop biting my head off, will you?" Steve retorted back, looking hurt. "The crates of empty bottles. The new ones."

"Put them in the back room behind the distillery," Tom sighed, scrutinising the invoice. He felt sure he had been over-charged again. Ashamed of his shortness towards Steve, he called after him. "Steve. Sorry, mate. I'm being a dick."

Steve nodded, loaded the trolley with one of the many crates that were currently blocking the entrance into the main barn and wheeled off into the distillery.

Tom dropped his clipboard with a clatter onto the stack of boxes and rubbed his face with a large sigh. What the hell was the matter with him? Mark pissed him off to no-end, yes. But he hadn't even seen him yet.

They were on the border of harvest season and his sister had chosen, of all the times in the year, September as her wedding month. And yes, his employees were dropping like flies, and the ones who were left were as much use as a chocolate tea pot. Apart from Steve. Steve was the most solid employee he had. He was like a brother to him, and literally would be in a week's time. This increased his guilt even more. He would need to make up for his foul mood to Steve when this delivery was done. The numbers becoming a blur on the page, Tom decided to take a step back and grab a coffee from Sarah. He'd have a chance to warm up a bit whilst putting a couple of logs into the wood burner. He'd been standing in that yard now since 5.30am and, though he rarely succumbed to feeling the cold, today's wind had a bit of a chill to it.

A couple of tables were occupied when Tom walked in. It was a relief to see. Tom knew Sarah's trade had been slow recently.

"Morning Tom," Poppy sang sweetly, fluttering her fake eyelashes at him.

Tom smiled politely but didn't make eye contact. Sarah had recently warned Tom of Poppy's infatuation with him, and that she had once found one of Poppy's college notebooks plastered with his name and love-hearts. Since then, Tom had kept pleasantries with the young Poppy to a bare minimum.

Leaning into the kitchen to announce his arrival to Sarah, he was surprised when he saw the American girl spooning some clotted cream into small pots.

"Hello again."

The girl looked up and flashed Tom a dazzling smile. He hadn't noticed before, but she really was pretty, and Tom felt a little guilty that he couldn't remember her name. She had introduced herself only a few hours ago.

"Hey! Tom, is it?" Crap! She remembered his. "Sarah's just getting some more milk. Can I get you anything? You want some coffees brought out to you guys?"

"Urr, yes. That'll be lovely. I mean, you don't have to do it. I can whip up my own." Although Sarah always scolded him if he went behind the counter in his dirty work gear.

"It's no problem. Won't take me long. How many do you want?"

Tom stood back so the girl could walk behind the coffee counter, a flowery scent wafting his nose as she squeezed past him.

"Just two please. Black Americano and a cappuccino."

The girl got busy grinding the coffee and steaming the milk. She was right, she was a lot faster than him. Realising that he was staring at the back of her, Tom decided to busy himself with putting the logs into the wood burner. By the time he had replaced the hatch and heaved himself to a standing position, the girl had walked over and placed two hot coffees into his hands.

"There you are," the girl said happily. "Just let me know if you want anymore. We don't seem to be very busy. Do you want some cake?"

"No... we're fine. Ur, can you let Sarah know we'll have our lunch at two today. The delivery is never-ending."

"Sure, no problem."

Once in the yard with Steve, the cappuccino a peace offering for his rudeness before, Tom's thoughts wandered over to the girl, and how she was different from who he expected Mark to be with. From first impressions she seemed neither high maintenance nor self-involved. Two of Mark's favourite assets in women. In fact, Tom's head was suddenly foggy from the natural beauty of the girl.

"What's that girl's name? The one who arrived last night?" Tom asked Steve, as they sat in the yard, their hot breaths in front of them.

"Emily. Sarah loves her. Wouldn't stop going on about her last night," Steve chuckled. "They make an odd couple though, don't you think? Her and Mark, that is."

"I was just thinking that, actually."

"Damn, this is a good coffee. I take it you didn't make this?"

"Cheeky shit," Tom chortled, relieved that the banter had returned between them.

The coffees drained, the two men heaved more of the delivery into its rightful place. They worked solidly until 2pm, their growling stomachs reminding them that it was time to eat again.

Back in the tearooms, the atmosphere seemed different to normal. The place had a real buzz to it. Though not completely full, it appeared busy and full of movement.

Behind the counter stood Sarah, Poppy and Emily, huddled around Sarah's iPad. Sarah looked up, her face beaming with excitement.

"Emily and I have just posted a special American Pie event on my new Facebook page for tomorrow!" Sarah squealed.

"What, the film? Bit inappropriate!" Steve sniffed.

"No, you plonker! Pumpkin pies, key lime pie... you name it, this girl has the recipe! The post has been shared four times in the last ten minutes, and ten people are interested!"

The men smiled politely, and something shifted in Tom as his eyes met Emily's.

"Sandwich or panini today, boys?" Sarah sighed, realising her excitement was lost on them.

"Have you got pulled pork?" Steve asked, taking a seat with Tom on their preferred table, which was tucked away in the corner, past the counter. It was their usual spot, ensuring they were out of public eye, and could eat peacefully without being pestered.

"Yeah, I think so. I'll check. Tom?"

"Same, please."

Steve began talking to Tom about strategies to get the apples picked in time for harvest. Only half listening, Tom's eyes trailed over to Emily who was now guiding Poppy through her attempt at latte art. Both girls were smiling with satisfaction as Emily formed a cat coming out of the mug. To be fair, it was impressive stuff, but Tom wasn't sure he'd be that fussed with it on his own coffee. He took in her mousy brown hair, which fell in natural little waves, and her small facial features. Her nose was particularly petite and rather complimented her small frame. Her looks seemed almost extraordinary and yet perfectly natural. He was just beginning to scrutinise her long eyelashes when suddenly they flicked up, and her green eyes landed directly on his.

"Sorry. I should be sorting you guys out with a coffee, not

playing with milk foam," Emily blushed. "Steve, what can I get you?"

"Another cappuccino please, Emily. The last one was proper job."

Emily chuckled, a tinkering sort of laugh that was pleasant to the ears and awoke something inside of Tom. "And Tom?"

"Can of Coke will be fine," Tom grumbled, suddenly feeling a little agitated. In danger of sounding rude he added, "thanks."

Ten minutes later, the two were sinking their teeth into their hot crispy paninis, all conversation of work coming to a temporary halt. Tom was beginning to relax for the first time that day when a familiar figure walked into the tearooms, immediately setting his teeth on edge. His appetite was suddenly gone, replaced with a bitterness that couldn't be justified with words. His back tensed and his hands formed fists on the table. It was Mark. Tom was thankful of his discreet table in the corner and hoped Mark wouldn't see them. Steve had obviously sensed his anguish, keeping unusually quiet whilst finishing his lunch.

"What the hell are you doing?" Tom heard Mark demand when he had reached the counter.

"What does it look like? I'm making coffee," Emily replied.

"This isn't a community centre where you can volunteer to do coffee-duty," Mark hassled. "It's a functional business. Does Sarah know you're making coffees?"

"No, I just sneaked in when she wasn't looking and started pressing buttons. Don't be so patronising, I used to work in a diner, remember?"

"Well, how much longer are you planning on playing 'Happy shoppers'?"

How much longer are you planning on interrogating the poor girl? thought Tom, his skin radiating in anger.

"Mark, give me a break. You're the one who left me with total strangers to answer some emails. Sarah was showing me around the place, found out I *can* make coffee, and I've been showing Poppy how to do latte art. No big deal."

"Fine. Well I need you now, to do some work for your *real* job. So, tell Sarah you're going back to the house. And take that apron off, it's filthy."

Tom stole a chance to look up from his hideout spot, seeing the previously cheerful girl looking down-trodden and humiliated. She peeled off her apron, scuttled into the kitchen to tell Sarah she was going and nudged past Mark with force. As Mark spun on his heel to follow her, it was then that he noticed Tom and Steve. Steve kept his eyes focused on his lunch but Tom, fuelled with both old and new anger, was up for the challenge, and burned murderous eyes into his brother. How dare he speak to her like that? Who did he think he was? Tom already felt there were a lot of things that Mark did not deserve. This girl was suddenly at the top of the list. He suddenly felt a bizarre sense of protectiveness over Emily.

Nobody moved a muscle as the two brothers continued to lock glares. Every muscle in Tom's body was tensed. A tiny glimmer of a smirk played in the corner of his mouth as he saw Mark's eyes waiver from his. The coward couldn't even hold his composure. Defeated, Mark backed down, sniffing indignantly before storming out of the tearooms and slamming the door behind him.

Somewhat satisfied but infused with built-up rage Tom left the remainder of his lunch on the plate. He set back to work, hopeful that the routine would keep him from doing something impetuous.

"Where've you lot been? You're late!" Tom barked at the two young lads making their way up the yard, as he ducked his head through the tearooms door. This time, he didn't feel bad for being rude. These two drove him nuts.

"We couldn't remember if you said one o'clock or two," Stuart, the youngest of the two said.

"We was squeezing in a bit of revision. Got mock exams next week," Tim, the other one piped up.

Both were in their last year of secondary school, and yes they probably did have mock exams next week. But knowing these boys, Tom called bullshit on them revising anything.

"There's a crate of Hockings Green in the press house. Go and start on those, will you?"

The boys exchanged affronted looks and scurried away to the press house. At least that batch of apples was being sorted now. It would free up another crate for more picking tomorrow.

"Mate, you've got to chill out," Steve said, giving Tom an encouraging slap on the back. "I know having Mark here is difficult..."

"Did you see the way he spoke to the poor girl?"

"Yes, mate. But that's none of our business."

Tom's jaw clenched and his mouth became dry. He wanted to find them and remove her from the situation.

"Mate, what is the matter with you? Get a grip!"

"Do you think he..."

"We're not going there! We're not thinking about that! Come on, let's take our anger out on some apple picking."

Chapter Ten

Humiliated, belittled, and unbelievably furious. I spent the rest of my day sending pointless emails and completing meaningless admin tasks for Mark, confined to my room like a punished teenager. I couldn't see what the significant rush was to get them done anyway. Some of the analysis reports weren't due for another fortnight yet and it was Mark who seemed to think it was perfectly fine to be away from the office right now, lying to my new colleagues about a non-existent lead. What if they found out? I was already on thin ice with my job.

I had always known Mark to be arrogant, perhaps difficult at times as a manager. Sometimes I even liked and admired him for it. Since this damn trip, however, I had witnessed an irrational side to him - a nasty side, which I didn't like at all. I shuddered as I thought about who he reminded me of when he was being like this. No, don't think about him - for God's Sake, don't think of him.

Fidgety and now anxious, I checked Sarah's tearoom page on Facebook, which I had added about an hour ago, and was pleased to see that her page likes had gone up since announcing the American Pie event. I just hoped that Mark would let me see it through. I also prayed that Sarah hadn't witnessed my humiliation, equally hoping that Poppy hadn't said anything about what she had witnessed, given that Mark had belittled me right in front of her.

I crept across the creaky hall to the bathroom, splashing my face with water and fixing my hair. I scrutinised myself in the tiny mirror above the sink, considering myself a pushover. In fact, even more of a pushover than I was already guilty of being. Next time he was rude to me like that, I would have to put my foot down and tell him, outright, that I wouldn't put up with it. Yeah, that would go down like a lead balloon.

Just outside of the bathroom, a narrow little landing before the descend of the main staircase, I admired the scattering of family portraits on the wall. Photos of the Trengrouse's altogether. Photos of Baby Tom, Baby Sarah and - oh my goodness - Baby Mark. My gaze hovered over a photo that instantly made me sad from the core: a photo of Tom and Mark. Both perhaps in their early twenties, they had their arms around each other in a brotherly embrace, each with the biggest smile plastered across his face. What had happened for their relationship to break down to such an extent?

I practically jumped out of my skin as Karen hollered up the stairs that dinner was ready. My previous anger now mixing horribly with sadness for the family, I closed my bedroom door and made my way downstairs. My mood improved considerably however when I lay eyes upon the spread Karen had put together, the plates of home-cooked goodness taking up every inch of the large farmhouse table. A mountain of crispy roast potatoes, oodles of carrots and swede, every green vegetable I could think of, masses of creamy cauliflower and cheese and a tumbling pile of puffy pastry things that Sarah informed me to be Yorkshire puddings the size of side plates made my mouth water. My stomach practically danced with joy as I realised I hadn't eaten this well since living with Gwynne all those years ago.

Sarah smiled widely at me, slipping a large glass of red into my hand and leading me to a seat around the feast.

"This girl is a saint," Sarah announced to the room. "Not only has she awoken my business page from its Facebook slumber, but she can make a bloody good coffee as well. Not to mention, so many customers went home with extra takeaway cake - Emily was so persuasive."

"Well done Emily," Karen smiled, as she stirred the gravy. "It's very kind of you to get so hands on. Sarah showed me the page on that Facebook thing. Very impressive!"

"Yeah, thanks Em. Really appreciated," Steve said as he washed his tired hands in the sink from a long day on the farm.

I wasn't used to this praise and, though a bit of me liked the change, it made me a little uncomfortable and relieved that my prickly boss wasn't in the room to witness it.

"The pleasure was mine," I waved them off, taking a seat.

"Sarah has done a great job already."

Sarah smiled gratefully at me and added to my untouched wine. I'd have to take it easy. I was wise enough to know that The Beast played cruel games after the influence of too much alcohol.

Taking a seat next to me, Sarah slid her iPad in front of me. Can you show me how to boost my post?"

"It costs to boost your post on Facebook, and honestly I wouldn't bother," I advised, slipping into my work voice. "Why don't you set up a competition and share it on some local sites? Much cheaper."

"See! Saint!" Sarah praised, striking a silly choir note in my direction and making me giggle. My giggle practically died in my throat as Mark walked through the door and this didn't go unnoticed by his sister being seated right next to me.

"Mark, my love. You look stressed. Would you like a drink?" Karen fussed over her son as he took a seat on the other side of me, looking thoroughly irritated. Without waiting for an answer, Karen placed a bottle of beer in front of Mark and squeezed his shoulder with affection.

"Thanks Mum. Emily, did you get those reports typed up and sent?"

Almost pulling a muscle in my neck, I felt myself stiffen. "Yes, all done."

"Must be so weird. Having your boyfriend as your boss, I mean," Sarah considered, eyeing us both suspiciously. She turned to Steve, "I think I'd have killed you by now."

"It comes with its challenges," I retorted just as Mark shot me a warning glance. A smirk played in the corner of my mouth and my eyes dared him to do something about it. Oh no! I was morphing into rebellious Emily - now he'd done it!

"Sarah, plate up some food for your brother. I don't think he's coming."

I couldn't help but notice Karen glance nervously at Mark who was shuffling in his seat and sipping his beer in silence. Curiosity pulsed through me like a current. What was the deal here?

"Right, tuck in everyone. Tuck in!" Karen refused to sit down until everyone was catered for, dishing out large servings of every item onto each person's plate. I gladly accepted a portion of food that would usually have sufficed for a week, a little terrified at the food challenge I had just taken on. With all of this wine and extra food I would need an extra seat on the plane home.

Sarah passed Karen a full plate of roast dinner, who then disappeared to take it to her eldest son. It was then that the front door opened and closed, some hustle and bustle in the hallway before Karen returned with Tom in tow. The busy scraping of knives and forks on plates stopped for a moment as everyone looked up, surprised to see Tom joining them.

"You know how it is, Mum," Tom continued. "With being short staffed at the moment, it's just taking a little longer to lock up in the evenings."

"I wish you would take it easy. You're going to make *yourself* ill."

"Not until harvest season is done, oh and this party-thing that these two are having."

"Bugger off!" Sarah grinned, chucking a piece of broccoli at her eldest brother.

"Hello Emily," Tom smiled warmly across the table, as he took a seat next to Steve.

I was taken by surprise and stuttered a timid 'hello' back. I instantly felt Mark, already rigid, practically radiate with tension beside me.

"Oh, lovely! So, you two have met?" Karen gushed, as she finally sat down.

"Only briefly, Mum. Emily here makes a good cup of coffee."

Okay, my cheeks were about to set on fire and I was pretty sure the redness was working its way down my neck.

"Understatement!" Sarah chimed in. "Mark, can I borrow her again tomorrow for the American Pie event? Oh, and tonight too, to - you know - make the pies!"

"Well, actually... " began Mark.

"Oh please! Emily, you don't mind, do you?"

"Not at all. Mark? Can you manage without me for a few hours?"

Mark grumbled and shrugged in annoyance. "Fine. But I would like to spend some time with my girlfriend this week, Sarah. If that's not too much trouble."

Before I could stop myself, a dignifying snort escaped the back of my throat - far louder than I had meant to - which brought more unwanted attention my way. Where was Michelle when I needed her? She was usually enough unruliness to reel me back in or at least distract people enough to make me blissfully invisible. I looked down at my plate of food, my cheeks officially on fire. Why was it that at times like these, when your boss/pretend boyfriend is already hacked off, that a nervous little giggle threatens to escape. I just couldn't help but find Mark's commitment to the charade of me being his girlfriend a little pathetic.

Luckily for me, it fell to a contented silence around the table as everybody feasted on Karen's delicious roast. To avoid any further embarrassment, I focused hard on the celebratory fanfare going on in my stomach as the beautiful rich food, with all its flavoursome glory, brought my palate to life. This food, by far, was winning against the overpriced steak I had had back in London.

When it was time for dessert, I happily offered to negotiate a dollop of clotted cream onto everybody's apple cobbler, considering myself an expert after my practise with the thick, silky substance today. Despite my best efforts not to antagonise Mark, my face and side was aching from laughter as everybody teased and scrutinised my handling of their native favourite. Quips like 'who put the emit in charge of the cream?' and 'hang on, ratio of cream to crumble isn't quite right there!' I couldn't remember the last time I had laughed so much and almost had to stop myself from groaning in protest as everybody started leaving the table to pitch in on the big clean up. Karen and Sarah started clearing the table, making a start on the massive pile of dirty dishes currently dominating the kitchen counters. Unable to sit and watch, I joined them, donning the yellow Marigolds, and filling the sink with hot, soapy water.

"Emily, go and sit down. You're not doing the dishes," Karen cried.

"I insist. It should be you sitting down after preparing such a delicious meal," I said, firmly.

Karen started wringing her hands, looking lost, as Tom offered his chair to her. "Emily's right, Mum. Sit down, have some more wine. Sarah, throw me a tea towel."

Mark excused himself from the room, his phone poised towards his ear, as I submersed my hands in the hot soapy water. I willed the heat of the water to distract me from the heat that seemed to be radiating from Tom as he took his place next to me, tea towel at the ready.

"You alright?" Tom asked me quietly.

"Me? Yes, thank you. How are you?"

Tom smiled. "Just checking after this afternoon's little squabble."

I cleared my throat loudly. "Don't know what you mean. Can you pass me that plate, please?"

Tom made a low disapproving grunt before meeting my request.

The dishes took a lot longer than I had bargained for and I was baffled that Karen didn't have a dishwasher in such a big kitchen. Everything was done in the 'good old-fashioned way', as Karen put it.

"Don't have time for all these kitchen gadgets," Karen had said. "Cost a fortune to run and don't do the job half as well."

"Would make clearing up a lot quicker though," Sarah had added, rolling her eyes and giving me a defeated look as she put away the last plates.

The kitchen cleared and a couple of pie bases in the oven, everybody retired to the living room with a replenished glass of wine. Tom got the fire roaring as Karen covered the coffee table with an array of different cheeses, crackers, and grapes. My eyes bulging, I wondered if every night was like this in the Trengrouse household or whether it was for the sake of having guests. Either way, it was wonderful. The only thing that stuck out was the obvious elephant in the room between Mark and Tom. They hadn't spoken a word to one another yet, which I found extremely odd between two brothers. I may not be an expert in the sibling front, but even I knew this wasn't normal. It was the ever-brash Sarah that pointed it out to Mark when Tom went to the bathroom.

"Are you two planning on completely ignoring each other for the entire week? Have you even said one word to him yet?"

"No," Mark snorted, shrugging to show his deliberate apathy. "He's not making any effort, why should *I* bother?"

"You know exactly why *you* should bother," Sarah hissed, giving Mark a meaningful look.

"Whatever. I'm going to bed."

Sarah flung her arms up in protest and looked at Karen for support. "Mum!"

"Darling, don't be like that," Karen tried to reason with Mark, gently.

"Relax," Mark sighed, his hands up in fake surrender. "I'm not storming off to bed in a huff. I'm just tired and need to do some more work before I hit the sack. No huffiness intended. Em?"

All eyes were on me again. I wasn't sure exactly what he was asking. If he was implying that because he was going to bed early, I should do the same, then he had another thing coming. This was the most content I had been in... well, I couldn't remember the last time. When no further hints came, I replied, "I'm going to stay up a bit longer, if that's okay."

"Fine," Mark sniffed, before addressing the room in a sulky manner. "Night all."

With Mark gone, I felt myself relax even more, sinking into the comfort of the armchair closest to the fire, one of the whippets curled in awkwardly under my hip. I was on my fourth glass of wine by now (or was it my fifth?), and with the glowing embers of the fire, my cheeks were blazing with colour - not from embarrassment this time. When Tom returned, my stomach did a weird, involuntary flutter to accompany those rosy cheeks. What was that all about?

"Where's Happy gone?" Tom asked the room.

"Bed," Sarah grumbled and Steve kissed her temple to sooth her. Gosh, they were such a cute couple.

Tom seemed satisfied, put a new log on the fire and sat down. His eyes met mine for a moment, causing my stomach to somersault so vigorously I thought I might vomit. Clearly, I'd met my match for the night, so placed my wine glass down and picked up a cracker in hopes of soaking up some of the alcohol.

"So, Emily. What do you do for a living?" Tom asked with genuine curiosity, popping a wedge of cheese into his mouth and leaning back into his chair. I was momentarily lost as my eyes wandered from his gigantic feet, his powerful legs, all the way up to his - "You seem to know your way around a coffee machine."

"I work at Blake & Co," I cleared my throat, giving myself a mental shake. "With Mark. But I used to work at a popular diner in Brooklyn. I still live above it, actually."

"See? So cool!" Sarah gushed, draped across Steve like a sleepy rag doll. Looks like the wine had defeated somebody else in the room besides me.

"Do you enjoy your job, Emily?" Karen asked, politely. "Must be a fast-paced industry in such a big city!"

"Yes, it can be. It's... it's good."

"That was convincing," Tom snorted.

"No, I do enjoy it," I frowned. "It's just, I'm not quite in the position I want to be within the company yet, but I'll get there."

I wished Tom would stop looking through me like that, like he was trying to analyse my every response. It was unnerving and made me feel hot and flustered.

"You seem hard-working. I'm sure you'll get where you need to be," Tom finally responded, leaving me a little flat. What kind of response was that? Well, what kind of response was I after? What was going on with me tonight?

"So, what made you go from diner to office work?" Tom continued. "You seemed in your element this afternoon."

What would he know? We'd just met. I bit my lip nervously as I realised how dangerously close we were to the taboo topic I never liked to think about, let alone talk about, to a room of strangers.

"Oh, you know... life changes, moves on."

Tom's eyes penetrated me as one of his eyebrows raised in anticipation of me extending my answer. Of course, I didn't.

"Anyway," Tom patted the arms of his chair and yanked himself up. "I'd best hit the sack. Got to be up again in a few hours."

"Oh gosh, this is late for you my love," Karen fussed, glancing at her wristwatch. "We should all head to bed now really."

Everyone said their 'goodnights' to one another and went their separate ways. I darted to the kitchen to put my pie bases in the refrigerator and it wasn't until I got to my bedroom that I realised how drunk and exhausted I felt. A prickling in the side of my head told me I had drunk way more than I should have as I grabbed for my medication, just as a text from Mark flashed on my phone screen:

'Remember who you work for. Stay professional please. M'

Exhausted as I was, I barely slept that night. Mark and The Beast made sure of that.

Chapter Eleven

Tom pondered deeply over his morning coffee the following day. The last couple of days had been unexpected. He hadn't anticipated feeling so in control of his emotions when in Mark's presence. Yes, anger pulsed through him like a volt, but he sensed weakness in Mark, a weakness that gave Tom an inner strength to be cool and collected.

Then there was Emily. The American girl. Exactly why was Mark with her? She wasn't glamorous. She didn't seem ditsy or idiotic. The features that made her attractive were real. She was plain, yet extraordinarily striking. She had taken Tom by surprise and he wasn't sure how to deal with it.

It was now 5am, the start of Tom's working day, and he was in his mum's kitchen making his first morning coffee. He always made his first coffee in his mum's kitchen, in habit of letting the dogs out so that Karen had that extra hour in bed before they demanded their freedom. It was a habit he had got into since his father died, whose job it used to be to set the dogs loose in the mornings.

On the way into the house that morning, Tom had noticed a light on in his old room. Either Emily slept with the light on, or she was awake. A small desire to go up and see if she was okay, if she wanted breakfast with him, came over Tom as his thoughts trailed off to how she had looked in his hoody yesterday morning. He batted those thoughts down straight away. Why was he so keen to be in her company? He'd known her for a day, and considering who she was associated with, he should avoid her like the plague.

It wasn't until he popped into the tearoom hours later for his Americano that he wished he had given in to the temptation and checked on her anyway. Emily was serving customers, taking orders at their tables. She was smiling politely, but Tom couldn't help noticing that her smile didn't quite meet her eyes. She looked unbelievably tired, her eyes looking dull and blood-shot. She had obviously attempted to conceal some scratch marks on the left side of her face, because her skin tone was patchy. What had happened to her? She looked like she had been beaten. Tom knew his brother was arrogant, a snake in the grass, but was he really capable of violence?

"Tom!" Steve thumped Tom's arm with his fist. "Were you even listening to me?"

Tom was dragged back to his senses, realising that Steve was trying to make conversation with him. He also realised he had been clenching his fists, hot blood pumping through his veins. He was furious.

Steve gave up getting a conversation out of him whilst Tom approached the till just as Emily finished with her customers.

"Morning Tom," Emily smiled. Tom thought he caught a small wince in her expression.

"Emily, are you alright?"

Emily seemed taken back by Tom's direct questioning, and suddenly seemed nervous, choosing her next words carefully. This raised Tom's suspicions even more.

"Yes, I'm fine. Thank you," Emily smiled again. "Can I make you another coffee? Do you want to try some pie? It's selling fast!"

"Don't change the subject."

Emily chuckled nervously, "I'm not. Thank you for asking - honestly, I'm fine. I didn't sleep very well last night. I'm just a little tired. Now, pie?"

Knowing that Emily wasn't telling Tom the whole story niggled him for the rest of the day. It was another cold September day and Tom's fingers were frozen at the end of a day picking apples, which didn't improve Tom's mood.

How they were going to pick three orchards-worth of apples by next week, god only knew. Harvest was always a tight schedule with full staff attendance, but Tom's employees had lacked the reliability he so desperately needed, especially with his sister's wedding acting as one of the many barriers. Trengrouse Cider Farm had never been the leading Cider company in Cornwall, nor the biggest, but they had a wealth of clientele, local businesses and companies who relied on their efficiency. Tom was not about to let the reputation of his father's business go down under his management.

Tom jumped onto his father's trusty blue Massey Ferguson tractor and shifted it over to the next tree, the engine chugging away tiredly. It was gruelling work but traditionally Trengrouse's Cider Farm had never used machinery in the process of apple-picking. Every last apple was picked by hand. With only himself, Steve and Ricky-the-Plonker on hand today, work was a little slow.

"Jesus, I can't feel my fingers. Is it really only September?" Ricky complained. He was good at that.

"One more hour boys and we'll call it a day," Tom said, checking his watch. It was five o'clock now. By the time the tractor was put away and the picked apples put into storage, it would be a long enough day after a 5am start.

"Is that Emily over there?" Steve pointed out from the other side of the tree. Tom peered around to where Steve was pointing. It *was* Emily. She was striding down the hill, seemingly unaware of her audience, making a beeline for the gates at the bottom of the sloping field which led to the back lanes.

"Where is she going?" Tom muttered aloud. He cupped his hands around his mouth and shouted down to her. "Emily! Emily!"

She couldn't hear and continued her strides to the kissing gates at the bottom. A few wipes of her face with her sleeve told Tom that she was crying.

"I better go after her. She looks upset," Tom told the others. Knowing that his large strides would be twice the distance of Emily's, he didn't bother running after her. It wasn't until he reached the kissing gates into the lane that he jogged to catch her up.

"Emily."

Taken by surprise, Emily whizzed around to face Tom, as if she had been caught doing something she shouldn't be. She had definitely been crying and was now doing her best to cover it by quickly wiping away the evidence. Tom wasn't fooled.

"Hi Tom," Emily croaked, putting on a weak smile. Why did she always feel the need to do that?

"I'm not going to bother asking if you're okay. You'll only fib to me again."

"Man, you're nosey," Emily chortled, wiping away another tear. "Look, don't mean to be rude but I don't want to talk about it."

"Lovers tiff?"

"Excuse me?"

"You and Mark. Have you fallen out?"

Tom thought he may have crossed a line and that Emily would bite his head off but after some frowning, she resigned and scuffed her shoes into the dirt. Her shoes, he noticed, were those flimsy fabric-type pumps. They were soaked through and caked in mud. Typical urban dweller. He would need to make sure the girl had some wellies while she was here.

"I don't think it's appropriate for me to talk about my argument with Mark to you, given the circumstances."

"What circumstances?" Tom replied, playing ignorant.

"Well... you two... you don't seem very close for brothers. Sorry, that's not me prying. Just an observation."

Tom smiled and nodded. "Your observations are pretty spot on. So where are you planning on storming off to? Do you even know your way around these lanes?" When Emily looked sheepish, shaking her head, Tom added, "You shouldn't go storming off in strange places by yourself. You're not even wearing the right attire. You'll freeze."

"Okay, okay," Emily rolled her eyes, a smile creeping in the corner of her mouth, before faltering into a look of defeat. A fresh batch of tears gathered in her eyes and it took Tom all his might not to wrap her up in a big bear hug. He'd never seen anybody look so downtrodden. Could this be the doing of his wretched brother?

"Come on. Help us pick some apples, then I'll take you back into the warmth. Here," Tom removed his outdoor jacket and peeled off the jumper underneath, passing it to Emily. He quickly replaced the outdoor coat before he lost his body heat. "Put this on. I know how much you like wearing my jumpers!"

This time a small chuckle escaped Emily's lips and Tom felt inflated that he had done that. He watched with odd pleasure as Emily climbed into his jumper and sighed in relief from the reserved body heat warming her through.

"Thank you."

"No problem," Tom said gently, momentarily falling into those emerald green eyes of her.

It wasn't long until Emily was smiling again, happily picking and asking about all the species of apples. It being a passion of Tom's, he was happy to oblige and told her all about the species of apple trees, the different measurements in root stock and the varied purposes for each. Tom always knew his talks on apples and cider-making bored his listeners, but Emily would continue to prompt him, asking more and more questions. Her enthusiasm was catching, and Tom was in his element. An hour flew by and he realised afterwards how much he had enjoyed spending it with Emily. She really was fun to be around, even with the ghost of those tears still visible on her slightly blotchy face.

Tom particularly enjoyed seeing Mark's thunderous expression when, later on, he and Emily walked into Karen's kitchen together, Steve following closely behind. They had put the apples into the press house and tucked old Betsy the tractor under her blanket for the night, still making it in time for tea.

"Emily! Have you been helping the boys with apple picking?" Karen asked in delighted shock. "Goodness, you are getting stuck in!"

"Yes, it was great fun!" Emily beamed. "Though my fingers and toes are quite numb now."

"Poor love. Go and stand by the AGA while I dish up. It'll soon warm you up," Karen turned on Tom and Steve. "You two should have made sure she was dressed appropriately."

"I told her she needs to forget about wearing those silly pumps around the farm while she's here," Tom winked at Emily to show he was teasing, delighted to see Mark squirm out of the corner of his eye.

"She can borrow my Hunters. I offered them yesterday," Sarah added. "I'll dig out some thick socks as well."

"You make it sound like she's going to be a regular apple-picker while she's here," Mark piped up. It was as if he was trying to be light-hearted, but his words only slithered out in bitterness.

"Well, why not?" Emily bit back. "Why shouldn't I help everyone out while I'm here? It's the least I can do."

"It's very kind of you," Karen patted Emily on the arm. *Good ol' mum,* Tom thought. Ever the peacekeeper. She heaved a large ceramic dish of chilli con carne onto the table, in between a mountain of rice and nachos. "Right, tuck in you lot. Emily, my love, can you prise yourself away from the AGA?"

Tom pulled out the chair next to him and offered it to Emily. This time it was Sarah giving him a funny look. He shrugged at her and started dishing chilli onto plates and handing them out.

"Emily, the bridesmaids and I are going into Truro tomorrow to collect the dresses. We're going to have a spot of lunch as well. Do you want to join us?" Sarah glanced at Mark, checking his reaction.

"Oh no, that's a bride and bridesmaid thing," Emily shook her head. "I can't gate-crash something like that."

"Don't be daft! I want you to come," Sarah scoffed through a mouthful of rice. "You can meet my girls before the big day. Mark, I'll bring her back in good time."

"I'll get those business proposals documented and sent off tonight," Emily added, obviously sensing Mark's irritation from across the table. "It won't affect my work."

"Shouldn't he be encouraging his girlfriend to relax when she's away on holiday?" Tom found himself arguing, turning to Emily. "I'd go for that lunch if I were you. Enjoy yourself!"

"What are you doing?" Mark snarled at Tom.

"He speaks!" Tom cried theatrically.

"For your information, Emily and I are still under contract. We're not on holiday; we've had to bring our work with us to be here."

"Well you're a real hero," Tom's words dripped with sarcasm.

"Boys, don't," Karen pleaded. Everybody's forks had stopped scraping the plates and were poised tensely as everybody watched the growing conflict.

"I'm just saying, Mum. We should feel privileged really. Every three years Mark is able to fit us into his busy schedule. He can even multi-task and bring his work with him."

"Fuck off, Tom!"

"Mark!" Karen cried.

"Yes Mark, language at the dinner table," Tom sneered.

"Enough! Both of you!" Karen barked at both of her sons, giving them equally frightening glares that successfully shut them up. "Not another word between you both until you can start being civil to each other. Now everyone, dessert?"

"No thanks, Mum," Mark spoke softly, with a little sadness. "Dinner was delicious. Excuse me." With that, Mark stood up, walked out of the kitchen, and went upstairs.

Sighing heavily, Karen said, "It was his favourite as well. Right, you lot. Don't just sit there. Help me clear up and make some space."

Chapter Twelve

It was never going to be an easy reunion, Sarah reminded herself. It would have been a miracle if they had got through the entire week without some conflict between her daft brothers. But it didn't make this evening's events any easier. Sarah felt sorry for her mum, exasperated over her sons' rivalry and worrisome over a wasted dinner. Of course, in Sarah's eyes - or anybody's eyes for that matter - it hadn't been a wasted dinner, the food had been delicious as always. But Karen had put on some of Mark's favourites in hope that it would cheer him up.

"He's just so serious these days," Karen had said sadly to Sarah that evening. "Where has my care-free, happy little boy gone?"

Her mum was right; Mark wasn't the same. Whether it had been years of climbing the corporate ladder in one of the biggest cities in the world, his lifestyle in Manhattan, or the way he had left things at home, Mark was an entirely different person whom Sarah barely recognised.

Another person Sarah pitied in this whole ordeal was Emily. Already a quiet and reserved person, she seemed to withdraw into herself after Mark stormed off upstairs. Almost out of obligation, Emily had taken herself to her room as soon as the clearing up had been done - no doubt to finish all the work for Mark that she had promised. So, at midnight, when everyone else had already gone to bed, Sarah sneaked into Tom's old room with two hot chocolates and a piece each of chocolate tiffin.

Setting the tray of goodies down on the bookshelf outside the room, Sarah knocked gently and peered her head round.

"May I come in?" Sarah asked in hushed whisper. Emily was sat up at Tom's old desk with her laptop, making Sarah's predictions correct.

"Sure," Emily said brightly, closing her laptop down. "I'm glad you've stopped me actually. I'm going square-eyed looking at this proposal."

"I come with treats," Sarah plonked the tray down on the desk and closed the door behind her, leaving them in total privacy. "How are you?"

"I'm great thanks," Emily smiled, sitting cross legged on the bed. "You?"

"No really, how are you? That couldn't have been easy for you earlier - the fight between Tom and Mark, I mean."

"Ditto to you."

"Oh, I'm used to it by now," Sarah waved her off. It was half the truth. It still hurt to see them be so foul to one another, but it was something she was used to by now - sadly.

She analysed Emily as they tucked into their hot chocolates. "I'm guessing Mark never mentioned the to-do between him and Tom."

"If I'm honest, he never mentioned Tom at all," Emily looked apologetic. "We never really talk about family."

"Does he get on well with your family?"

"Oh, I don't have any family."

Emily seemed so nonchalant over the whole thing, taking Sarah completely by surprise.

"You poor thing!"

"Oh, please. Don't show me pity. I hate pity. I've never known any different. I had a great couple of teenage years with a lady who fostered me. She owned the diner I worked at. She passed away, a while ago now."

"So sorry, Emily."

"Honestly, I don't handle pity very well," Emily tried to sound light-hearted, looking extremely uncomfortable all of a sudden. "It's why I don't talk about my upbringing very much. This is good hot chocolate by the way."

Sarah could take a hint and didn't push the subject any further. Emily seemed to have a very healthy, upbeat outlook on her unusual childhood, but it couldn't be easy to talk about it all the same.

"Please tell me if I am prying, but what happened between Mark and Tom? I'm guessing they haven't always been at war with one another."

Sarah winced, hoping it didn't reflect on her expression, "I'm not sure I'm the person to say. Mark has obviously kept it very private from you, though I'm not sure why. You should know really, but I don't want to be on the receiving end of Mark's fury if he finds out I'm the one who told you."

"Fair enough," Emily replied, not hiding her disappointment very well.

"Ask him."

"I'm not sure that's the best idea. I'm not his favourite person at the moment."

"What are you talking about? You're his girlfriend. Though, I admit, sometimes he doesn't act like it. Sorry."

Sarah always remembered Mark to be a bit of a hopeless romantic, a charmer. Sometimes he even came across as a bit of a sleaze-ball and Sarah would tease him for it. But she couldn't help noticing that he was almost cold towards Emily. Perhaps this was where the extra sympathy came from for the poor girl. She couldn't seem to do anything right.

Emily didn't comment and continued to take a lot of interest in her hot chocolate. Sarah, ever the nosey parker, was incapable of letting the question that was burning inside of her go.

"Are you and Mark okay?"

Emily's eyes widened and her cheeks burned - what was it? Embarrassment? She closely examined her mug and a couple of sighs escaped her.

"We're fine," Emily said, finally.

"Liar," Sarah blurted out.

A hesitant smile crept on Emily's face and she looked exasperated.

"He's stressed, I think. I've worked with him for nearly three years now; I'm used to him taking his stress out on me. It's all good."

"No, it's not. I mean, he's my brother - love him dearly. But don't let him treat you like crap and make you his personal punch bag. Metaphorically, obviously. Not literally," Sarah's eyes widened. "He doesn't... does he?"

"What?! No! Of course not!"

"No, I know... just checking. I don't feel like I know him

anymore. He's changed." Now it was Sarah's turn to sigh. "I thought, if I could get Mark here for the week... maybe the wedding atmosphere and all that - oh I don't bloody know. I was trying to play 'Happy Families' and clearly I was delusional."

"I think it's nice that you care so much about your brothers to want to... "

"Bash their heads together? Force them to kiss and make up? It's not going to happen... there's too much baggage between them. Argh! It's so frustrating. I want to talk to you about it, but it's really not my place."

"To be honest, I've been itching to know the details since I arrived. But don't tell me if it's not appropriate. I wouldn't want you falling out with either of them before your big day."

Emily was so nice and so level-headed, Sarah thought. She could see a friend-for-life in this one. It was a pity that after the wedding she would be on a plane, along with her brother, back to America. And goodness knows how many more years it would be until they saw Mark again. That final thought caused a threatening tear to form in the corner of Sarah's eye. She quickly wiped it away; no way was she going to start sobbing to this poor girl, who was already overwhelmed with her family's dramas.

"So, tell me about the wedding," Emily piped up cheerfully. Maybe she had caught sight of that damn tear.

"Oh, it's quite low-key. Nothing fancy like these hotel weddings. The marquee is going up on Friday. We're going to decorate the barns in front of it as well and make that whole area up for the evening do. There will be hay bales, bunting, a jazz band, fairy lights."

"Oh my god, that sounds way better than some hotel!"

"Do you really think so?" Sarah gushed.

"Totally! Some of these hotels can be so corporate and impersonal. Yours sounds beautiful and so 'you'!"

"Thanks, Em. I'm a bit worried that some people will be uncomfortable or moan about being outside. We're hiring in some outdoor heaters and there will be a couple of fire-pits going."

"Sounds magical. Screw the moaners, just as long as you're enjoying it!"

"You're a dream! Even some of my bridesmaids have had a

little quip about it being outdoors, whining that their hair will be so messy by the end of the evening or that they'll get muddy heels. You wouldn't think most of them play rugby!"

"Well, this is my first time in the countryside, and I think it sounds great!"

"We can make a country girl out of you yet. Sounds like you fitted right in with the apple-picking this afternoon. Tom said you were a trooper."

"Really? He said that?"

Sarah nodded and watched as colour flushed into Emily's cheeks.

"He's great. Knows a lot about apple farming. I learnt a lot."

"Mm-hmm," Sarah regarded Emily's face a little longer, considering her reaction. What was going on here then?

"Right, don't know about you," Sarah tiptoed out into the hallway to retrieve a bottle of wine. "That hot chocolate was good and all - but let's get to the good stuff. Sarah and Emily stayed up into the small hours of the morning, drinking every last drop of the wine, and when Sarah finally sneaked back across the yard, through her front door and up the stairs, the faint sound of her fiancé's snores escaped from the bedroom. Sarah carefully joined Steve under the covers, but her mind was racing, causing her to lie on her back wide awake, staring at the ceiling. She was unsure why, but a memory slipped into her mind. A memory of her father that hadn't surfaced for a very long time. For a moment it took her breath away.

It was a cold, harsh day in October, the last week of harvest. Sarah was eight, Mark ten and Tom sixteen. It was a day full of apple picking, frozen fingers and contagious giggles, and Sarah didn't want it to end. They had been picking apples now for hours and a mid-afternoon mist was settling over the top orchard. Mum had brought up a large pot of hot stew to keep them warm as they worked.

"Come on troops," Dad had shouted. "No more time to stuff those little faces. Let's get the last of these apples picked."

Sarah had skipped after her dad, placing her small hand in his large, calloused ones while Tom and Mark began fighting over who would drive the tractor.

"You always drive," Mark cried. "It's not fair, I want to drive."
"You're ten years old!"
"So? I know how to drive it. Daddy taught me."
"Grow up!"
"Boys!" Dad's voice thundered across the field. His voice always had the desired effect and the boys stopped bickering immediately. "Don't fight over such trivial things! You're lucky to have each other. When I was growing up I-"
"We know, we know," Tom grumbled. "You never had siblings growing up."
"Exactly," Dad gruffed. "So quit the bickering and love each other."
"But he's a pillock -"
"Thomas!" Dad growled. "Love-each-other. You hear me?"
"Yeah, yeah, we hear you," the children chimed, as Tom ruffled Mark's hair and reluctantly stepped down from the tractor.
"Don't crash it, squirt."
Mark had jumped in front of the wheel with glee, as Tom launched himself into the trailer with the apples setting off on picking some more from the nearest tree. Sarah had squealed with delight as her dad lifted her onto his shoulders so that she could pick from the highest branches.

"My little harvest troops," Dad cooed fondly, gently prising the apples from their branches and placing them into the trailer. "This is going to be the best year in the history of Trengrouse Cider! The best year!"

Her father's voice faded as Sarah was brought back to present day, Steve still snoring gently beside her. Her pillow was wet from the tears that had fallen from that unexpected memory. Her father had always been so passionate about the farm, and confident that each year things would get better. He never once gave it away that the business was actually in trouble, that one of the reasons he got them so hands on with the picking and the bottling was not just to spend quality time with his children, but that he'd had to make most of his employees redundant. It wasn't until her dad became too ill to work that Tom took over and broke down in front of

Sarah. Tom, her indestructible big brother, had broken down over the state of the business, over the pressure of it now being his responsibility to save, and later that very same month to find his marriage had failed tremendously, by the hands of his own brother. Sarah's chest heaved giant sobs at not only the memory of her father, but out of guilt for her eldest brother. He'd taken on so much, gone through hell and back, and still remained her absolute rock in life. She felt deeply disloyal towards him, and the alcohol now pulsing through her body made her feel an overpowering need to go and make amends with him. Right at that very moment.

"Sarah... bloody hell, do you know what time it is?" Tom mumbled, moments later. "What the hell is wrong with you?"
Sarah, still sobbing, snaked her way into Tom's torso and wrapped her arms tightly around his waist. Dazed and slightly confused, Tom then enveloped her into one of his big bear hugs, placing his chin on her head.
"I'm sorry!" Sarah sobbed.
"For what?" Tom sighed, amusement in his voice.
"For everything. I'm sorry that you had to take everything on with the business; I'm sorry that Catherine was a complete slut and screwed you over. I'm sorry that Mark is such a stupid... poo head-"
"I can think of better names for him right now," Tom interrupted, still amused.
"But he's still our brother... and as much as I hate him for what he did, I still love him as my brother - our brother."
Tom paused for a moment, holding Sarah out at full arm's length. "How much have you had to drink?"
"That's beside the point. The point is, you've had a really shitty time, and I feel like the shittiest sister in the world making you endure the next few days with Mark... but I need to have the whole family here for my wedding. I've already lost Dad, a little bit of Mark... don't make me lose you too."
Tom chuckled, causing Sarah to break into a fresh squeal of tears. "Why are you laughing?"
"Because Sarah Trengrouse - soon to be Sarah Bray - you are so ridiculous... and very thoughtful. I'm fine."

"Really?"

"I'm fine," Tom repeated, this time firmer. "It'll be a few days, then Mark will return to his little business land, your bleddy wedding will be done, and I can get this harvest finished. I - will - be - just - fine."

Sarah sniffed, feeling relief wash over her. "Okay. Just as long as - "

"We are also fine. Now fuck off to bed, I have to be up in two hours, and those apples aren't going to pick themselves."

Chapter Thirteen

I want to die. I want to die. Anything but this. Why won't it stop? Please, God, I want to die.

I woke with an agonising start Monday morning.

The birds were chirping cheerfully outside my window and a glorious strip of sunlight was beaming over the side of my face as I lay face-down on the bedroom floor. I was still in the same position from last night, the peak of my attack causing me to lose consciousness. My hands still gripped the duvet which had taken the plunge with me, and my knuckles ached from the intense strain they had formed all night. My mouth tasted awful, a mixture of iron and stale bed-breath. *Blood?*

I forced myself up; every part of me ached, as if I had dropped from a great height, miraculously without breaking bones. I stumbled over to the mirror and was horrified by who was looking back at me. Face drawn and gaunt, eyes sunken in with protruding dark circles. The worst part was the multiple scratch marks, like warrior stripes across my face and neck, where I had been digging and grabbing at my face with desperation. Perhaps I was hoping I could gouge The Beast out, find a release valve somewhere on my face that would allow the pressure to escape.

Gently, I pressed on the left side of my head, just above the temple. I hissed in protest as a shot of pain flew through every nerve in my face, setting my teeth on edge. I quickly licked over my teeth with my tongue, like I would if I had just eaten cold ice-cream. The pain lessened but the memory of the pain remained. I needed my oxygen. But it was thousands of miles away. The sound of the kettle rumbling to life downstairs told me that Tom was getting his first hot drink of the day. I listened intently as the back door was unlocked and the dogs scuffled through the kitchen and into the garden, their cat-like claws scraping the flagstone floor in excitement.

I longed to go downstairs, to chat to Tom. He was nice to talk to and didn't make me feel like a waste of space. That was a refreshing sensation. Then I remembered my appearance. I was pretty sure I had seen some of Karen's foundation in the bathroom the night before. I had my work cut out before I could show my face.

I was relieved, later over breakfast, that nobody mentioned anything about odd bangs and muffled screams coming from my side of the house last night.

The only person who was looking at me suspiciously was Mark. I avoided his piercing glares and focused on my breakfast as Karen, Sarah and Steve nattered about the day ahead. Tom was already on the farm, which disappointed me more than it should have. Then again, did I really want him seeing me in this state?

Mark nudged his phone over with his elbow, angling it towards me so I could read the screen.

'Don't ask any questions. We're leaving after breakfast.'

My insides turned to slushy ice as my heart hammered loudly in my chest. What had I done wrong now?

"We thought we'd try our hands at the pub quiz down the road tonight," Sarah prompted happily. "You any good at general knowledge, Emily?"

I didn't say anything, instead I looked helplessly at Mark who calmly finished his mouthful of cereal before speaking.

"Sarah, I'm afraid something has come up at the office... "

There was a loud clatter as Sarah dropped her spoon on the table.

"Oh no you bloody don't!" Sarah suddenly stood, almost knocking the contents of the table off. "You've been here for only a few days and already you're bailing!? My wedding is on Saturday!"

"I'm aware of that, aren't I?" Mark argued back. "But I've got a rather big responsibility in running a business that pays thousands of employees!"

"So what? You're not coming now?" Sarah cried, angrily.

"Mark, sweetheart, this is your sister's big day," Karen tried to reason, also looking upset. "Can work not manage without you for a little longer?"

"I haven't said I won't be coming to the wedding; I'll do my best. But only Sarah would stretch out one day into a whole bloody ten-day celebration! I don't actually need to be here!"

"You're such an ass-hole," Sarah burst into tears, pushing her chair back so hard it fell with a loud clatter on the tiled floor, as she ran out of the kitchen.

Karen tried to give Mark an assuring look, which soon faltered behind her hurt expression as she went after her daughter. Steve stood slowly, his shoulders tensing, looking thunderous towards Mark.

"Nice one, mate," Steve spat, before storming out of the kitchen as well.

Mark and I sat in silence at the vacated table, Mark with his fists clenched, looking ahead unblinking from the aftermath of his vagaries. I regarded him, my own anger building up inside me.

"Why are we leaving?"

Mark rounded on me like a hungry lion. "Because you have got too comfortable. Because you have taken this too far!"

It was as if he had slapped me. Unjustified and irrational rage pulsing from his every pore.

"Me? How have I come into this?"

"Exactly! How have you come into this? You've become Sarah's best pal! Tom is pining at your ankles like a pathetic puppy -"

"That's not fair!"

"Every chance he gets, he's goggling at you!"

"Hear yourself right now, Mark," I tried to reason, fighting back anguished tears. "You're sounding ridiculous. This was all your idea. I never got a choice; you threw me into this web of lies without my consent."

"You just remember what I have done for you. What I am doing for you," Mark spoke dangerously, jabbing at the air between us.

"Mark, please," I begged, tears streaming down my face. "Stop. I know I complicated things when I put that stupid post up, but you're so angry... I don't understand."

"Don't you forget where you would be right now," Mark

continued, ignoring my pleas, "if it wasn't for - wait a minute... "

I watched, incredulous, as Mark stomped furiously over to his mother's welsh dresser in the corner of the kitchen. He began investigating and searching for something that clearly wasn't there.

"Where the fuck....?" Mark muttered angrily, charging through the house to find his mum.

Feeling as if I was between two storms, that familiar sense of flight-mode kicked in and I started backing out of the kitchen, planning to remove myself from the storm entirely just as Tom's heavy-duty boots stomped into the kitchen.

"Emily? You alright?" Tom's deep voice rumbled through the quiet of the kitchen as he blocked my exit.

"Yes, umm, no. I don't know. Mark... something has really upset Mark. Can I just -" I tried to squeeze past Tom, my chest tightening from the need to escape, but he refused to budge.

"No, you're not going anywhere in that state. Where is he?"

"He's gone that way. To the living room, perhaps."

I followed Tom through the house to the living room where we found Mark confronting his mother about the mysterious something he had been searching for on the dresser.

"Where's Dad? Where's Dad's ashes?" Mark demanded. "Mum? Where are they?"

Karen looked nervous, frightened even, as she tried consoling an upset Sarah, who was sobbing dramatically into a cushion. She looked up at Tom for support, whilst attempting to answer herself.

"Darling... we thought... it's been... "

"Mark, you've been gone for three years," Tom boomed, coming to his mother's aid. "Dad needed to be laid to rest. You'd buggered off to America. We can't hold things off for your convenience."

"I could have at least been told about it!" Mark barked back. "I deserve to be informed."

"Mum deserves to know where in the bloody world you are. She deserves the odd phone call every now and again. But you didn't think of that, did you?"

At this point, both Trengrouse men were face on, Tom dwarfing Mark as he brought himself to full height in white rage. My feet seemed glued to the threshold as I cowered against the door frame.

"Boys. Don't," Karen quivered. "Please don't fight."

"I should have been given the opportunity to be there when my dad's ashes were being put into the ground. I should have been there."

"But you weren't, were you?" Tom snarled, his shoulders squaring. "You weren't there when he was ill. You weren't there when he died. And you were barely there on the week of the funeral. So, what difference would it have made if you were there to spread the ashes?"

"Tom, that's enough," Karen's voice carried a little stronger.

"No bloody difference what-so-ever!"

"Tom!"

A deathly silence fell over everybody, the air suffocating. I overlooked the scene, horrified at this broken family sat before me, everybody's grief bleeding out from their words, their actions, their bodies. It felt like the silence lasted a lifetime before Mark finally made a move towards the door, barging shoulders with Tom on the way out.

"Mark!" Karen sobbed, then to Tom, "Go after him!"

"Absolutely not!"

Everybody froze at the sound of tyres skidding on gravel and the unmistakable sound of Mark's car driving away and leaving the farm. It was then that everybody turned to me. Mark was gone. He'd walked out on his family at Trengrouse Farm for the second time in his life. But this time, he'd left me behind. And there was nothing I could do about it. I'd checked his room and his suitcase was gone. He must have done this before breakfast. He'd prepared to leave, one way or another.

There was a heavy atmosphere in the Trengrouse house that evening. Since the angry departure of Mark that morning, I had played every possible scenario in my head regarding what I was to do now, while The Beast antagonised me with small shots of pain through my jaw, like little electricity shocks.

An overpowering array of emotions coursed through me, like a toxic current. Anger, guilt, shame, anxiety: the list could go on.

Mark had left me completely in the lurch, but not before rearing an ugly side to him that I had never encountered before. I had always known he was short tempered and arrogant, and sometimes even a little chauvinistic, but he had never been nasty. What confused me the most was his accusations about me and Tom. Where had that come from? Why would he care? Our relationship was only an act, after all... wasn't it?

Now, I stood in the middle of my room, at Mark's family home, surrounded by people who thought I was Mark's girlfriend. I could almost laugh at the ridiculousness of the situation, had it not been for the overwhelming need to cry. What on earth was I to do? Should I leave? Fat chance of that happening; Mark had my plane tickets and I, sure as hell, couldn't afford to buy new ones. Should I find a way back to London in hope to find Mark there, or should I stay and hope Mark comes to his senses?

Considering the horrendous start to the day, the dress shopping and lunch with Sarah's friends had been bearable. The drive into Truro had been nothing short of horrible as Sarah had attempted to drive through thick sobs over her brother's dramatic departure, whilst giving me multiple near heart attacks as she threw her little red Fiat this way and that through the narrow country lanes leading to her local city. Her friends had swarmed around her loyally once we'd turned up at the Bridal Shop, Sarah's eyes blotchy and red.

"Oh, he's such an arsehole!"

"What a dick!"

"Give me his number? I'll give him a piece of my mind!"

As a group of friends, they were fiercely loyal. I had felt a pang of jealousy. Then I realised, with a hint of guilt, that I had something similar with Michelle. Perhaps I needed to appreciate my colourful, slightly unorthodox friend more. Perhaps I also needed to send her a message, check everything was okay. Check to see if *he* had been back.

A sense of dread hovered over me as I'd sat with these women, continuing to feel like an intruder. Most of Sarah's friends were welcoming and asked no questions as to who I was, and why on earth I was part of such an intimidate event. There was one friend, however, who I had immediately felt it necessary to avoid.

Her name was Katie.

Behind a sour-faced expression - which appeared to be stuck for the foreseeable future - there was quite possibly an attractive face. When introduced, Katie merely acknowledged me with a nod, her expression stony and unwelcoming. According to Sarah, she was always like that with new people and I was not to take it personally.

Now, back at the farm, Steve and Sarah were laying the dining table with cutlery and glasses, Karen was removing some plates from the AGA, and Tom was unwrapping the fresh fish and chips that Karen had bought from the nearest village. I scuttled into the kitchen like a socially awkward mouse. I really shouldn't be here.

"Emily, darling. Come and sit down," Karen fussed, smiling warmly.

There was a hint of pity in her eyes and she pulled out a chair for me to sit on, but this only made me squirm uncomfortably. No sooner had I sat down did I feel the urge to get up and help Karen, asking her if she was alright. I shuffled over to Karen in Sarah's fluffy bed socks, out of earshot and ignoring Tom's trailing gaze. Perhaps Mark had had a point.

"I'm sorry about earlier, Karen," I found myself saying. "I think it's appropriate that I leave tomorrow-"

"Nonsense, my darling," Karen cried, almost making me jump out of my skin and wrapping a comforting arm around my bony shoulders. "You've got nothing to be sorry about, and you have no reason to feel unwelcome here."

Karen said the last part with such fierceness that I truly believed it. I felt a compassion towards Karen and wanted to share all my truths and lies to her. But I was reminded almost immediately that I wasn't really the person they thought I was. I was a total fraud at this point. Karen's kindness warmed my heart but at the same time only strengthened my shame on tricking these good-natured people. The truth bounced dangerously on the tip of my tongue and I almost blurted it out as Karen handed me a plate of buttered bread to add to the table.

I'm sorry for lying. I'm not really your son's girlfriend. I'm his employee and I am doing this so I don't lose my job. There's also a pretty dangerous guy in Brooklyn waiting for a big pay out.

It all sounded ridiculous, not to mention completely implausible, so I bit my tongue, took the buttered bread and sat down at the dining table next to Sarah. Keeping my eyes down, I felt Tom's gaze burn a hole in the top of my head as he sat down opposite me. I really wished he would stop doing that, just for a moment. I was having trouble functioning enough, and yet my eyes threatened to stray in an attempt to lock on with his.

"Sweetheart, forget what happened earlier," Steve was comforting his sour fiancé quietly. "We can still have a nice time tonight. The others are already planning on meeting us there at eight. I bet Emily could do with a laugh, eh Em?"

"What's this?"

"Quiz night," Steve informed me, rubbing Sarah's back as she picked at her chips sadly. "Down in our local. Four rounds of ten questions. Winning team wins £50. Mini wins on each round wins us some drinks. You in?"

"My general knowledge isn't very good," I admitted.

"I shouldn't worry," Tom chimed in. "Can't be much worse than Sarah's. She once asked how far Edinburgh was from Scotland.

Everybody laughed. There was an instant change in the atmosphere and suddenly we all started eating our food with a bit more gumption.

"Leave me be," Sarah chortled, laying on her thick Cornish accent for comedic effect. "I rarely cross the Tamar Bridge into Plymouth!"

"Right, it's settled," Steve said, happily. "Quiz night is back on. Tom, you coming?"

"Nah mate," Tom waved his hand. "I've got invoices to sort out."

"You're going," Karen ordered, pointing a threatening finger at her eldest son, with a twitch of a smile. "This one, Emily. Biggest worker out there; doesn't know when to switch off and take some 'down-time'."

"Well, we can't have that," I teased. The sudden buzz for an evening out was contagious and the fact that Tom was joining us set off butterflies in the pit of my stomach. I pushed any thoughts of Mark to the back of my mind and summoned up a slightly more extrovert version of myself in preparation for tonight's antics.

The Smuggler's Inn, a cottage-like pub minutes from the farm through the winding lanes, was bursting with locals as the four of us arrived that evening. It was a pretty little white-washed cottage, with a thatched roof, and made more beautiful with the blooming flower baskets and window boxes, overflowing with colour. If it wasn't for my mood, which was growing darker as the evening drew in, despite my best intentions, I may have appreciated its charm a little more. I felt quietly overwhelmed by the bustling atmosphere inside and felt myself withdraw into myself, like I always did in busy places, craving the solitude I was so familiar with. I hid behind my company and eyed the exit longingly.

"Emily? Drink?" Tom shouted over the crowd, gesturing with his hand to support his words, his head bowed slightly to avoid the low bearing beams. I put my thumbs up in response and tried to act nonchalant and entirely comfortable in my current environment.

"Emily, come here," Sarah beckoned me over. "Come and meet these shit-bags! This is Luke and James. And obviously you've met Heidi, Toni and Katie."

Great. Katie. That's all I needed. Each of Sarah and Steve's friends raised their hands or nodded their heads in answer to their names being called out. All except Katie, who merely smirked. Go figure.

"Guys, this is Emily. She's A-mer-i-can!" Sarah shaped her mouth around each syllable.

"Hi Emily!" James leaned over to shake Emily's hand. "You survived the bridesmaid lunch today, I hear. This one," James gestured towards Toni with his thumb, "hasn't shut up about the wedding since she was asked to be bridesmaid."

"I'm Maid of Honour though," Katie added, quickly.

"Yes, yes," Toni said with a hint of impatience. "Don't forget, Katie is Maid of Honour. She'll remind you a thousand times, but don't forget."

Katie shot Toni a dirty look, quickly followed by a rude

gesture involving her middle finger. They were obviously close. I couldn't have felt more out of place, my infringement growing by the minute. Where was that exit again?

"So, Emily, are you any good at quizzes?" Luke asked in a raised voice across the table.

"Um, I don't know," I answered as several people negotiated around me to get to their seats. "I've never been to one."

"Oh! Well you're in for a treat!" Luke clapped and rubbed his hands together keenly. "I am the King of Quizzes!"

"He takes it very seriously," Heidi added, rolling her eyes and encouraging me to sit next to her on one of the bench seats.

"You didn't moan last time, when I won us £100," Luke pointed out, shooting a cheeky grin at Heidi just as Tom returned with our drinks. It was a cosy little alcove in which our table sat and my heart skipped a beat as Tom squeezed in next to me, his thigh pressing up against mine, his meaty arm resting behind me on the back of our bench chair, mainly down to the fact there wasn't a lot of room.

"So where did you two meet?" Heidi asked, smiling at me and Tom. There was a slight pause as we exchanged confused glances, passing the confusion over to Sarah.

"Wrong brother, Heidi," Sarah piped up, eyes wide.

"What... Mark?" Luke boomed across the table.

"I thought he was-" James' sentence was cut short as Toni elbowed him hard in the ribs.

"Makes sense," Luke shrugged, ignoring the awkwardness lulling over the table. "I was trying to work out how Tom would have come across something exotic like Emily. You don't leave the farm, do you mate?"

"Cheers, Luke," Tom grumbled over his beer.

"He'd find a girl if he wanted to, wouldn't you Tom?" Katie piped up, suddenly chirpy now it had been confirmed that Tom and I weren't an item.

"So, what are we calling ourselves tonight?" Tom sat up, seemingly ignoring Katie.

"It's sorted," Luke gloated. "We are... wait for it...'And the winner is!'"

"That's shit," Steve spoke, deadpan. Chuckles echoed around

the table.

"No it's not," Luke protested. "It's clever. Then when we win, matey boy over there will say, "And the winner is: 'And the winner is'."

"Yep... that's shit," Steve repeated. Everybody laughed, including Luke.

"Ladies and gentlemen," The quiz master's voice boomed through the sound system around the pub. "Get your pens at the ready. The quiz is about to begin."

I started to relax a little as the quiz master fired questions out to his listeners. He was amusing to listen to, cracking jokes in between questions in his broad Cornish accent. I was starting to see the appeal of 'Quiz night', looking around fondly as teams on other tables huddled around their quiz sheet like pirates around a treasure map. The wine Tom had bought me also started working its magic, giving me the confidence I needed to have a go at answering some questions. There really weren't many I could answer, as a lot of the general knowledge was Cornwall-based, but when the questions started merging into more global events I edged forward on my seat, listening with determination.

"Whose controversial US presidential campaigning greatly increased his popularity within his party in 2015, yet increased party fears that it would be unelectable should he lead it?"

"Ooh! Ooh!" I bounced up and down on my seat in excitement.

"The yank speaks," Katie muttered under her breath,

I chose to ignore Katie's snide comment and tapped the quiz sheet enthusiastically, "Trump! Donald Trump!"

"Nice one, Emily," Luke praised, scribbling my answer down.

"Who won the men's World Ice Hockey Championship in 2015?" The quiz master continued.

"Canada!" I whispered loudly across the table. Tom's chuckle rumbled through me and I bit down on the smile protruding on my face. "I'm a big ice hockey fan."

"Glad to see you're enjoying yourself," Tom muttered quietly so only I could hear, a wide smile meeting his twinkling eyes. Butterflies fluttered uncontrollably in my stomach. The desire to kiss those lips was suddenly all consuming. I ripped my eyes away, my cheeks blazing. Perhaps I needed to slow down on the wine.

"What is the most populated city in the USA, named after a general?" The quiz master boomed. I brought myself back to reality and focused on the question.

Luke and James were muttering cities under their breath as Sarah, Heidi and Toni chirped away happily, completely uninterested at this point in participating in the quiz.

"Houston," I eventually chirped up, the answer popping into my head. "As in General Sam Houston."

"Man! This girl is on fire!" Luke punched the air, victoriously. "Tom, I'd nick this one from Mark. Keep her for yourself."

I frowned a little at this comment, shifting uncomfortably in my seat as Tom silently downed the rest of his pint.

"Who's the one taking her home tonight?" Tom added cockily, shooting me a cheeky wink before heading back to the bar for another beer. My eyes trailed after him, my mouth wide open in disbelief. Talk about loosening up. I chuckled involuntarily, my brain suddenly foggy.

"He's got an eye for you," James chortled. "Here we go again. The Trengrouse brothers and their bloody love triangles."

Luke kicked James under the table, "Jesus mate, do you have a filter?"

"What do you mean by that?" I asked. By then, the girls had tuned in, Sarah regarding me cautiously, giving me a look that said, *'don't ask. I'll tell you about it later.'*

By the end of the evening, we staggered out of the pub in good spirits. Luke and James danced ahead, celebrating their victory. They had won the quiz and bagged the £50 prize. Even Katie was in high spirits as she linked arms with Heidi and Toni, attempting the can-can down the little village street, shouting their goodbyes as they parted ways.

I had been nervous before, at the thought of walking through the lanes in the darkness back to the farm. But on this particular evening, it couldn't be a more beautiful walk. The moon shone brightly through the trees above us and the crickets chirped away in the nearby hedges. The temperature was pleasantly mild and the smell of the earth warming in the sun all day still sat in the air.

Breathing in that heavenly fragrance and reining in the desire to skip down the lanes, I thought I could walk quite happily for the remainder of the evening.

"I'm so glad you're here," Sarah beamed, grabbing my arm. I giggled - like, actually giggled. "No, truly. You've just sort of... fitted in like a piece of the puzzle. And don't worry about my stupid brother. He'll come round, he always does. He's always been the dramatic one... awful temper."

"I've noticed," I replied sourly, for a moment sobering up. I had almost forgotten about Mark and his irrational disappearance. Not to mention his complete abandonment; leaving me alone with people I barely knew, in a place thousands of miles from home. To say it was a dick move was the understatement of the century. Despite this I couldn't deny that I had felt such contentment this evening. In fact, it was the most relaxed I had been for months, the most fun I had had in a very long time, and the first time that I didn't feel completely and utterly alone. At this very moment, with plenty of alcohol in my system, a part of me hoped that Mark never came back and left me to a new life in Cornwall. Away from corporate politics, and employability conundrums; just left to set up a new simplistic life in the country, where I could breathe easy and find a way to control or even defeat the Beast that had ruined my career, and my life.

Chapter Fourteen

It wasn't very often that the Trengrouse's held a big party but, after all, this was their parent's silver wedding anniversary. It was August 2013, and Tom and Sarah had planned a surprise anniversary party for their parents which was now in full swing. Mark, as always, had been too busy with work to help out, but he promised to make it in time for the start of the party.

"It started two hours ago. Where is he?" Sarah demanded, agitated at her brother's unreliability.

"You know Mark. He'll probably turn up at the very last second," Tom grumbled, pouring cider for the guests.

"Well, we need to do the cake soon. Poor Penny needs to go in a minute, and she worked so hard on that cake. She's dying to see their reaction."

"Okay," Tom gave in, wiping his hands on a towel. "Let's do it now."

Moments later, everybody at the party gathered around Karen and Roy as they prepared to cut their cake. There was a happy buzz in the air as family and friends joked and chatted amongst themselves.

"Oh Penny! You've outdone yourself," Karen cried, admiring the stunning two-tier cake in front of her. Penny had very creatively decorated the cake to look like a basket of apples and a bottle of Trengrouse's finest cider. "It's too nice to cut. Isn't it lovely, darling?"

"'Ansome!" Roy growled, taking a seat next to Karen in front of the cake.

"Glad you both like it," Penny smiled.

"Right guys, let's see you cut the cake!" Tom said, now holding a camera up ready to photograph the moment. "Where's Catherine?"

"She's coming," Sarah piped up. "She's just...Dad?"

It happened so fast.

Everybody turned to Roy as his limp body slid down onto Karen's side.

"Roy? Roy! Sweetheart, what's wrong?!" Karen cried frantically, trying her best to support him.

Tom dropped the camera as Roy's entire body began to jerk aggressively, his eyes rolling to the back of his head.

"Oh my god, Dad! Dad! What's wrong with him?" Sarah sobbed.

"Dad! Can you hear me?" Tom grabbed his shoulders to steady him.

Suddenly Roy's body went rigid, quickly followed by projectile vomiting. Out of impulse, Tom grabbed the bottom of his father's jaw, attempting to clear his airways, meanwhile being coated in his father's vomit. "Mum, move! He needs to lie down. Move!!"

Rendered speechless, Karen moved out of the way as Tom lay Roy down and yanked him into the recovery position. Meanwhile, guests around them either watched helplessly or tried to find ways to help. Multiple people were calling ambulances and within ten minutes one had arrived. By now, Roy had stopped being sick, his body worryingly still. Tom, his body trembling in shock, clutched his sister in his arms as they watched their father be taken away by ambulance to the hospital, their mother loyally by his side. Guests muttered their thanks and declared their hope of Roy's full recovery before departing one by one, just as Mark made his way slowly up the drive in his flashy company Mercedes.

Completely unaware of the evening's event and smiling ear-to-ear, Mark stepped out of the car and called over to his siblings. "You guys must have pulled off a seriously lame party for it to end at 9.30!" His smile faltered as he saw the expression on his brother and sister's faces. "What?"

Tom woke with a start, beads of sweat sitting on his forehead as he stirred from his dream. As the sleepy fog lifted, he realised it hadn't been a dream but a memory he had put to the back of his mind. What had triggered it to surface like this again?

That night had been the first sign that Tom's father was very sick, and things had only got worse from there. Only weeks after that awful night, Roy Trengrouse had been diagnosed with pancreatic cancer, and only six months after that, he passed away in his own bed. From the first sign of his dad's decrease in health, Mark hadn't been there. He'd been late, and as usual, he'd been absent. Through the hospital appointments, the taking in turns in nursing him and then finally the funeral arrangements, Mark had been absent - and Tom had always resented him for that. Mark could be selfish and egocentric, and yet a few weeks after the funeral Tom was hit with more hurt and betrayal than he thought he could ever imagine enduring.

His beloved Catherine, somebody he thought he knew so well, coldly told him that he wasn't good enough for her - that she deserved more than a small, meaningless life on the farm. Then she left, arm-in-arm with his brother, never to be seen again.

Mark had done irreversible damage to their relationship, and Tom would never be able to forgive him for that.

Now it was the morning after the pub quiz and 'the pot calling the kettle black' couldn't have been more relevant than it was at this particular moment. With a few beers down him, he had openly flirted with Emily, staying by her side all evening, that sense of protectiveness growing stronger. He groaned as he recalled the irrational sense of anger he'd felt towards a poor, innocent bloke, who had approached Emily at one point in the evening to offer her a drink. He remembered squaring up to the poor man, putting a protective arm around Emily and leading her away from the poor bugger. Why had he done that? Surely this made him no better than Mark!

Actually no, scrap that. Tom had been married. Mark and Emily had a very new, very dysfunctional relationship. What kind of boyfriend made his girlfriend cry, only to then abandon her in a strange place without any contact? No, Tom thought, I refuse to feel guilty.

A 5am start wasn't as easy as usual. Tom rarely drank the night before an early start and was usually much more sensible about his bedtime: certainly not 2am in the morning. There had barely been any point going to bed.

Tom chuckled as he approached an equally exhausted Steve

who had had a lot more drinks than Tom and was looking worse for wear.

"Mornin'," Tom whispered, his voice box a little hoarse. He handed Steve a coffee. Steve could barely form words and settled with a grunt. "Quiz night seemed like such a good idea last night." Another grunt of agreement from Steve.

They shuffled their way to the distillery. Loud machines pulping, squeezing and smashing apples did not sound appealing right now, but it had to be done. They were already scats behind.

"Emily certainly came out of her shell last night." Slowly, with the help of caffeine and a bacon roll, Steve had emerged out of his zombie state. "I like her. She's not a typical, loud American."

"Wow, that's major stereotyping. Don't let Emily hear you say that!"

"You know what I mean. Some Americans can be so over-confident."

"And Brits can't?"

"Good point. You and her get on very well."

Tom looked at his friend, attempting to keep his face neutral. Was it that obvious, his infatuation with Emily? This wasn't good. "Don't know what you mean, mate."

"Oh, come off it! You'd be great together - much better than her and your twat of a brother. What kind of a dick-head boyfriend leaves his girlfriend behind in a strop like that?"

"I'm not my brother," Tom grumbled simply, focusing on the bottle capping task he was currently on.

"Didn't say you were, mate. I'm just saying, you would treat her a lot better than he seems to."

"It doesn't matter - after this week I'm sure she'll be heading back to America. I'm here. I don't do long-distance relationships."

"So, you admit that you like her," Steve smiled victoriously, which was returned with a rude gesture from Tom.

Later on, they were back in the field picking apples, the light breeze soothing their heavy heads. There was nothing better than being in the great outdoors with the most evil of hangovers. With Steve's constant comments regarding Tom's feelings towards Emily, Tom had refused to go into the tearooms for his lunch.

Instead he sent his sister a text, who later brought out fresh sandwiches, looking equally as delicate.

"Emily's not in the tearooms. She wasn't looking well so I sent her back to bed," Sarah had explained without either man asking the question. "She's obviously not used to drinking as much as we are."

By the end of the day Tom's hangover had subsided but Steve looked defeated. Tom sent him off to spend the evening with his wife-to-be, which would probably result in both of them falling asleep on the sofa, and Tom stayed behind to finish boxing-up some orders.

While labelling some boxes for local companies, Tom considered the conversation he had had with Steve earlier on. Clearly, it wasn't just Tom suddenly noticing his growing feelings for Emily. Then again, he had such a reputation for being a man-of-little-words that he supposed the warmth he had shown Emily last night would really be quite a contrast from his usual mannerisms. It wasn't his fault. Tom had always prided himself on being a one-woman man, a man who would find his rightful partner and spend the rest of his life devoted to her - one of many disparities between him and Mark, who was known to be a womaniser. He thought he had something special with Catherine. Catherine and Tom had gone to college together. Then a few years down the line Catherine had worked on the farm whilst studying for her degree - just in between terms and mainly taking phone orders and stock-taking. She was never hands-on enough to do any of the gruelling work. They had started dating, then were married the year after Catherine graduated as a fashion designer. Two years they were married - then next thing Tom knew, she and Mark had moved to America together, almost immediately after demanding a divorce. Tom neither knew, nor did he want to know, how long the relationship between his wife and his brother had been going on behind closed doors, but he had turned his back on dating women since and spent his life focusing on the business. Until this week, he hadn't spoken a single word to his brother for three years. He had planned to keep it that way, but it was inevitable that a family event such as a wedding would force him to face it sooner or later.

It was only through Sarah that he knew that things between Mark and Catherine hadn't lasted long, and that she had dumped him for a richer, more successful man, moving to California with him in a matter of weeks. This should have made Tom chuckle with glee, should have made him say "serves him right", but his misjudgement of Catherine had only hurt him more. How could you get somebody so terribly wrong? How would a boring, grumpy cider farmer like himself ever compete with a successful businessman in New York?

The same was true with Emily. Why on earth would she waste time with him? She was beautiful, kind, and exotic, the complete opposite to him. She was intelligent and had a promising future as a business consultant in Manhattan. No way did he stand a chance while he was picking apples in a muddy field for a living. No, last night had been fun, but he was putting his fragmented heart on the line here and it was sure to get stamped on. He needed to take a step back.

Of course, all those good intentions went out of the window when he stomped his way across the yard to his front door an hour later. He wished he had trodden a little lighter now (which is impossible in steel-caps) because there, outside his mum's front door, sheltering under the porch was Emily. She looked distressed and was on her phone. She turned at the sound of Tom's footfall and tried to plaster on a brave face. At this point he should have left her to it, minded his own business and taken himself inside to have some dinner. Instead he found himself approaching Emily and standing beside her as she attempted to steer the conversation away from its heated topic.

It was clear that she was talking to Mark.

"I understand that," Emily continued. Even in the poor light of the porch, Tom could see Emily's face turning crimson from embarrassment. There was a pause as Mark ranted down the phone at her. "But Mark... Mark... what am I supposed to do now? Mark! Listen a minute." Her voice became thick as she tried to hold back tears. Automatically, Tom placed a steadying hand on her shoulder, his fingers close to the nape of her neck. She tensed for a moment, then seemed to accept it and sank a little in her exhalation of breath. He took a step forward, his body towering above her, the sweet scent of her hair making him lean in.

She seemed to give up reasoning with Mark and fell silent, taking in his rant; she began rubbing her temple vigorously. "Fine. Just - whatever - email it to me. See you Friday."

Emily hung up. Tom didn't dare say a word. He was remarkably calm, though anger festered in him from hearing Mark talk to Emily in such a way. He hadn't picked out exactly what Mark had said, but his tone was pretty clear. Tom and Emily stood in the porch in silence for a moment, Tom's hand now fully working its way to her neck, her breathing irregular, as if she were on the verge of a panic attack. Seconds seemed like minutes and Tom didn't know whether to break the silence or not. She turned to face him, locking her bottle green eyes on his chocolate brown ones.

"Emily... "

Before Tom knew it, and through Emily's initiation, they were kissing. Emily had to stand on tip toes to reach him, her arms around his neck to keep her balance. When the initial shock had subsided, Tom sank into the kiss and lowered himself slightly to relieve her from stretching. He wrapped his arms around her waist and lifted her slightly into him, deepening the kiss. She smelled deliciously natural, a hint of coconut from her hair, and her lips were irresistibly soft. They sank deeper and deeper into the kiss; breathing became almost impossible. All the guilt and doubt Tom had initially felt dissolved as his heart swelled, reminding him what it had felt like before it had been broken into a million pieces. This - what they were doing at this very moment - was right, and he felt a rush of hunger towards it.

Suddenly Emily ripped herself away, wriggling out of his arms. She looked at him in horror, bringing her fingers to those beautifully soft lips, where his had just been.

"I'm so sorry," Emily weeped.

"Don't be," Tom spoke gently, edging towards her as if she were going to run away any moment now. He chanced another step. "Emily... "

"Don't say my name like that."

"Like what?"

"Every time you say my name... you have no idea the effect you're having on me," Emily closed her eyes and appeared to be inwardly battling with herself. She tapped the side of her head again and began rubbing it fiercely.

"Are you okay?"

"It's just my head. I'm okay. I'm just really stressed right now. I'm so sorry... I've messed things up so much. Like I always do. I think it's best I go back to bed. I-I came down for cell service."

"Come in with me for a moment." Tom was semi-aware that he was backing Emily into the corner of the porch but couldn't seem to stop himself. He didn't want her to go. "I'll get you a cup of tea and we can talk."

"You're so lovely," Emily sighed. "Thank you, but no... I should lock myself away for the evening before I mess anything else up. Good night."

Before Tom could say any more, Emily slipped into the house and left him in the yard, his chest on fire and his brain whirling.

Chapter Fifteen

Giving myself a stern talking to this morning, I had planned to keep my hormones in check. Last night had been a mistake. A beautiful, heart throbbing, breath-taking mistake. I couldn't stop thinking about that kiss. The way our lips had felt against each other. The feel of his tongue on mine and the way his arms had enveloped around me, making me feel the safest I had ever felt. It was as if his strength glued all my broken pieces together, leaving me feeling complete for just a moment.

This week had also been the strangest week of my life, and it was about to get stranger as I helped Sarah load the gator with sports bags and a big net of rugby balls. I was starting to think this whole week was one big, bizarre test and I was waiting for somebody to jump out and say, 'surprise!'

"I'm not going to be expected to play, am I?" I asked, dubious, as I struggled to fit the net of balls into the trunk.

"It's only a friendly match and the girls will go easy on you," Sarah replied, a pleading tone in her voice.

"Sarah, I've never played rugby in my life! Honestly, I'm not the sporty type. Can't I just stay here and help with the tearooms or something?"

"I've closed the tearooms for the rest of the week now," Sarah reminded me. I didn't say that I was beginning to see why the tearooms wasn't doing very well, with the sporadic opening hours I had witnessed so far. "Come on, Emily. At least have a go at chucking the ball around at the beginning. It's such a laugh!"

"I thought rugby was a man's sport, anyway."

We were now clambering into the gator, Sarah giving me a look of horror as she put her key into the ignition.

"I'm going to pretend you didn't say that," Sarah whispered dramatically, causing me to suppress an amused smile. "I am the captain of Truro Ladies, and I am here to tell you that women are bloody awesome at rugby and that men could learn a thing or two."

"Not doubting that for a second," I chuckled, as Sarah started pulling out of the yard and up the long, bumpy drive in the direction of the north side of the farm. Naturally, my eyes started to scan the distillery area and nearby orchards for signs of Tom - I really needed to get a handle on this crush.

If I wasn't already nervous and completely uncomfortable at the idea of *giving rugby a go*, I was now one hundred percent ready to bail from the field as we approached a large group of both men and women chucking an oval, white ball between them.

Sarah and Steve were hosting a friendly game of Touch Rugby - whatever that was- in the only field that wasn't currently filled with over-laden apple trees, and for some torturous reason I was being asked to play.

I tugged, self-consciously, at my borrowed shorts, while the wind cut through my bare skin like knives. I groaned under my breath seeing Katie looking more ferocious than ever as she launched the ball across to another girl I had yet to meet. The men really were enormous. It was the only way to describe them - though Tom's physique would probably dwarf some of them by at least half a foot. It was then that I suddenly realised I was scanning the field for a sign of Tom again and inwardly scolded myself for being so needy.

"Where's Steve?" Sarah shouted, boisterously, as she dragged the bag of bibs into a coned-off square of the field. Everybody shrugged in response, their eyes fixed to the ball. "Fuck sake! He'll be late then. Right you lot! This is Emily! It's her first time, so be nice!"

"Nice to meet you Emily," a man with a flow of curly blond hair jogged up to me, with a surfer's tan glowing in contrast to his white rugby top and shorts. I practically whimpered as a gust of wind cut through me a second time, the shorts riding up into undesirable places. The man's warm handshake was a welcomed gesture as he enclosed my cold hand with both of his. "I've heard all about you from Steve."

"Good things I hope," I replied lightly, through chattering

teeth.

"Oh dear, you're not used to the cold, are you?" the man smiled in amusement.

"Oh, New York gets cold enough! I just don't tend to voluntarily wear shorts in this temperature."

"I'm Jake by the way," Jake announced, a boyish grin plastered on his face.

"Nice to meet you," I replied, suddenly struggling to make eye contact. He was attractive and confident - very confident.

"Careful who you're chatting up there, Jakey-boy!" Steve suddenly called from the gate.

"Don't know what you mean, mate!" Jake retorted back, his eyes still fixed on me. "Just getting to know the lovely Emily here!"

He was being nice enough, but I felt exposed by my ridiculous outfit, and his wandering eyes, and started squirming uncomfortably.

"Whatever you do Emily, keep clear of this one," my heart stalled at the sound of Tom's voice as he strode over. He wasn't smiling. "He's had more dates than hot dinners."

A glitched smile formed on Jake's face as he put a bit of distance between us.

"Alright, Tom! Long time, no see. Haven't seen you at rugby for a while."

"Make that three years," Tom muttered, standing behind me and placing his large, hot hands on each of my shoulders. That seemed to be enough and Jake nodded in understanding, drifting off to find a ball to chuck.

"That was rude!" I muttered to Tom under my breath.

"How was I rude? Saved you a lot of trouble there."

"Be careful that you don't sound jealous," I teased, my mouth moving before reason.

"Perhaps I am."

It was Tom's turn to flash a boyish grin but this time my insides melted with desire. I was semi-relieved for the distraction when Sarah got everybody's attention to split us into teams.

"Dammit, we've got an odd number," Sarah scolded. "Somebody will need to sit out of the first one."

"That's fine by me," I jumped in, quickly. "I'll watch from the side-lines, get an idea on the rules."

It wasn't a contact sport, I was glad to discover - unlike the game of rugby I had heard of - just a matter of the players passing the ball down the line, past the opposing team until somebody crossed the edge of the square.

Okay, perhaps I could do this.

I quickly found myself on the balls of my feet, willing Sarah to reach her destination as she skilfully darted between players and dodged people's touch, whilst noting the rules that if somebody did tap you on the shoulder the ball must be dropped for the team player behind to retrieve.

Then the ball was suddenly in Tom's arms. He was a machine. I watched with admiration as the quiet, reserved Tom transformed into an unstoppable force. Fast, agile, but solid. I began cheering him on, whooping and punching the air as he slammed the ball down for a try.

"Right, you! Your turn!" Sarah bounded over, nudging me on to the pitch. "Now that you're getting into it."

Regretting that last whoop, I ambled over to take Sarah's spot. Heidi gave me an encouraging nod and passed me the ball.

"Just tap the ball on to your foot, then pass it when you're ready," Heidi explained kindly.

"Go for it, Em," Tom called from somewhere behind me.

I could have cried at the pressure of having so many eyes on me, but I did as instructed and gave a feeble pass to Heidi, my new safety net, and from there, the game assumed its fast pace chaos. I jogged around in awkward discombobulation, attempting to look useful until the ball was in my possession once again, thanks to Toni.

"There's a gap! Take it, Emily!" Heidi shouted.

I prepared myself to run just as Jake darted in from nowhere and tapped me on the shoulder.

"Don't worry, just pop it on the ground and take a few steps back. You're doing great, Em!"

I didn't know who the encouraging words came from, but I appreciated it quietly, as I followed the instructions. The game resumed once more, and Heidi swooped in to retrieve. I held back, not wanting to get in the way. Just when I thought the art of holding back was my thing, I was suddenly Katie's only choice in player to pass to and just as the ball left her hands, I knew this was going to hurt.

The ball made impact with my stomach and I felt the wind leave me with great force. I coughed and spluttered, the ball trickling away from my feeble grip.

"Bloody hell Katie! Take it easy!" Tom yelled from the opposing end. "This is Emily's first go!"

Katie held her hands up in a weak apology and I took big gulps of air, trying to relax my lungs which were now aching from the cold and the ball's impact.

"I'm okay," I gasped, straightening up and picking up the ball. I offered it to Katie.

"It's your go!" she barked impatiently.

I wanted to just throw the ball in her face and walk back to the safety of the farm, but something told me this would only make Katie's unjustified disapproval worse.

Remembering to tap the ball on my foot, albeit awkwardly, I then passed the ball back to Heidi who took off down the pitch, leaving me to gasp for more air without the attention of all the players.

The match carried on for another three minutes and then the ball was in my hands again - dammit.

Without thinking about it, I tucked the ball under my arm and ran as fast as I could. I stifled the rising feeling of panic as players turned on me and charged, looking to reclaim the ball. Suddenly the gap was closing as Jake, Toni and Steve formed a barrier, my breath suddenly ragged and my ears hammering from the adrenaline pumping around my body. The last time I had needed to run like this, the situation had been a lot more sinister. Something shifted in me as I recalled that horrible memory, and a flight mode kicked into gear. I faked a manoeuvre left only to quickly reroute right, dodging my shoulder from Jake's outreached hand and sprinting straight through to the try line. A small rupture of applause could just be heard, but my hearing was muffled, and my vision tunnelled. A bead of cold sweat trickled down my forehead and my heart pounded in my chest and in my ears. I was vaguely aware that Tom was talking to me, asking me if I was okay.

It wasn't until he placed his hand on my shoulder that I jolted to my senses again, sending a knee-jerk swipe in his direction.

"Whoah, Emily?"

"I need a moment. Sorry," I mumbled, unable to look at anybody but well aware that all eyes were on me. I stared into Tom's wall of a chest, trying to control my breathing.

"She alright?" Sarah asked anxiously from behind Tom, who was now scrutinising my face.

"Yeah, she's fine," Tom replied, not taking his eyes off me. "Think she just pulled something on that last hurdle. Didn't you Em."

Barely audible, I simply nodded in agreement and stuck my thumbs up.

"Ah, bloody hate pulling a muscle - hey! Ro's here!" Sarah bellowed, distracted by a friend jogging across the field. "You're late Ro-Go!"

"Right, your numbers are even again now. I'll take Emily in for some Deep Heat."

"Beg your pardon?" I squeaked, suddenly snapping out of my mute state.

"Oh, take your head out of the gutter, young lady. I meant a cream to sooth sore muscles. And you wipe that sulky expression off your face, Sarah. We'll be back in one game."

Tom and I didn't speak as we clambered back into the gator back to the yard. Our comforting silence continued as we entered the welcoming warmth of Tom's cottage, Tom inviting me to sit down on the sofa closest to the wood burner.

"You're not going to start asking me questions about what just happened, are you?" I asked the back of Tom's head as he started making coffee.

"Not if you don't want me to," Tom replied simply, stirring loudly, and tapping the spoon against the rim of the mug.

"Good. Because I really don't want to."

"Then don't," Tom handed me a mug of hot coffee and sank into the armchair opposite me. His sudden nonchalant attitude was a little infuriating, so I occupied myself with staring at the flames in the wood burner, tucking my feet under me to warm myself up and my chest heaving with ragged breath. It was then that the damn tears started falling.

I had bottled all of this away, so why was it coming back to haunt me again? Why in the middle of a ball game, of all places? This place, the people, the love that surrounded all of it, was stripping me of the guard I had built around me years ago, and I was left vulnerable and raw.

Tom remained silent but his presence was enough. I put my coffee down on the table next to me and let the tears consume me for a moment, hiding my face in my hands in an attempt to maintain some of my dignity. I was pretty sure I'm an ugly crier. Once the sobs had subsided, Tom passed me some tissues and sat back down to return to his coffee.

"You're good at this," I commented, my voice thick.

"Three years of grieving with my mother and Sarah. I'm used to tears."

I winced, "I'm sorry. You guys have been through so much."

"So, have you, it seems."

Tom watched me patiently as I fiddled with the tear-soaked tissue in my hand. I really didn't want to talk about it but something in the way Tom waited, with no expectations, made my barriers quiver slightly.

"For a small, very shit, period of my life I... " I paused. I had never shared this with anyone - not even Michelle. Only Gwynne had known. Not very proud of a lot of things in my past, this particular patch brought me deep shame and fear of how people would perceive me. I faltered, suddenly worried at how Tom would see me if I told him.

"Go on... you can tell me," Tom encouraged, his eyes soft but his brow furrowed in concern.

"I lived on the streets of Brooklyn. For six months."

Tom's nonchalant approach suddenly dropped, and he sat forward to the edge of his seat, a look of horror on his face.

"Shit, Em. You poor thing."

There it was. A reaction I had always dreaded to hear after sharing that part of my life. Except Tom's reaction wasn't of disgust or the judgemental disapproval I had always expected. For some reason, his reaction made me feel better in a way and my barriers were at risk of crumbling all together.

"Fuck. I am so sorry. Come here."

Tom moved to sit next to me, gathering me into him gently and enveloping me into the deepest, warmest hug I had ever received. I snuggled into the nook of his arm and let my head rest on his chest, the sound of his heart and the rise and fall from his breathing soothing me. Every ounce of self-loathing that had surfaced from that one crappy memory appeared to evaporate as I heaved a deep, healing sigh into Tom's torso.

"How come playing rugby triggered all this?" Tom asked me as he stroked my hair.

"I don't know. The chasing, I guess. I spent a lot of that six months running."

"Fuck," Tom whispered, mainly to himself. Again, this expletive outburst made me feel better and I found myself snuggling into the warmth of Tom's embrace. "Well, whatever you do, don't go doing a marathon or something."

An involuntary snort of laughter escaped me, despite myself and I felt his arms squeeze me gently.

"Please don't tell anybody. You're literally the only person I have told."

"Not even... Mark?" Tom frowned as I shook my head. "Of course, I won't say anything. You ready to go back."

"Can we stay here for a bit," I felt drained from the sudden emotional spillage and really wanted to finish my coffee.

"Of course we can," Tom smiled. "I'll put a log on the fire."

Chapter Sixteen

It was April 2004 and today was the day I was being fostered. Her name was Gwynne. She seemed nice and she owned a diner which meant, hopefully, I'd be getting a meal tonight. She'd just picked me up from the station, the cops waving me off with a friendly smile. They weren't smiling earlier that day when they interrogated me from my stoop, picking up my bag of belongings and barking at me to get in the car.

Gwynne tried sparking up conversation as we walked to the subway. She was an older lady, plump and with a slight limp as she waddled next to me.

"You doin' okay there, doll?" Gwynne said as we settled on to a seat on the L-Train, her Brooklynese accent somewhat reassuring and maternal. I nodded in response and hugged my biffy. "Boy, I can't wait to get some food down you. When was the last time you ate?"

I shrugged and busied myself, looking out of the window.

"Well, when we get home I'll show you around and then you'll be able to just help yourself to anything you fancy from the diner. I made key-lime pie this morning - you're gonna love it!"

Home. She just said home. She had to be kidding if she thought I was going to call it home.

Once on foot and unable to stand seeing Gwynne strain under all the bags, I prised them from her hands.

"Ah, you're a good girl. Thanks, doll. The diner is just a couple more blocks away."

We were in South Williamsburg now, the Williamsburg Bridge towering above us and the corner of Bedford Avenue dancing in colours of red, yellow and grey. A large grey-scale mural of a girl, with her face in her hands, looked forlorn and lost in thought, covering the entirety of the side of a red block of flats.

"That's the 'Mona Lisa of Williamsburg'. Isn't she a sight?"

Gwynne beckoned me to follow her down a much less colourful street, the bars becoming fewer and shops becoming less hip. "I'd like to say that my diner is in the thick of it all, but it's been in our family for a couple of generations now. Things have changed. Your papers say you're from Brooklyn originally?"

"Apparently so," I replied, eyeing up a group of youths on the corner as Gwynne's Diner came in to view.

"Which side?"

I shrugged, "I don't know."

"Well, here we are!"

"You named it after yourself?"

"My Pa did actually," Gwynne smiled up at her sign with great affection. "I couldn't change it now, God rest his soul."

Gwynne's Diner was the beam of light on an otherwise grotty street. White, plastic patio furniture sat on the curb, with large stripy red and white beach umbrellas swaying in their stands. Inside was a bustle of hungry locals getting their coffee and pie fixes. The food smelled incredible and my stomach grumbled and ached in protest from months of hunger.

"Let's get you that pie," Gwynne waddled to the counter, washed her hands and gestured towards the pie cabinet. There was at least eight different pies to choose from, each one with a mountain of toppings. I chose a slice of pumpkin pie shyly and clambered awkwardly on to a stall.

"Is this the foster kid you were saying about, Gwynne?" an elderly man spoke, his voice rough and hoarse.

"Her name's Emily," Gwynne called over the cabinet, as she skilfully manoeuvred a wedge of pie on to a plate. "Emily, this is Joey. A regular. You'll see him daily."

"Can't get through my day without a Gwynne special!"

"Don't call it that! It don't sound right in front of a young lady!"

Joey and Gwynne shrieked with mirth and even I felt a twinge of a smile, a muscle that hadn't worked in a long time.

Life with Gwynne became a reassuring pattern. I got up at 6am to help with preparations in the diner. I went to school. I hurried back again. I did an evening shift in the diner. I did my homework. I went to bed.

It was the most stability I had had in my short life so far, and it did me good. Even when my teenage hormones got the better of me, Gwynne seemed only relieved.

"Thank god! There was me thinking you didn't have a personality," Gwynne clamped me in one of her side hugs after I bit her head off about wanting to just go upstairs and watch some television. "It's crucial for a girl these days to have a temper. It's how you get your way around men."

I didn't know what she meant by that, but I smiled all the same.

Five months past and I soon became settled and somewhat content in my new life with Gwynne. I considered myself almost converted to home life.

Then Gwynne's son came home.

His name was Sal. He was a long-haul trucker and had returned home to take some annual leave before setting back on the road. I eyed him suspiciously from behind the counter as he dropped his bags down in the doorway, letting Gwynne fuss over him and plant kisses all over his prickly cheek.

He had jet black hair, slicked up with wet gel and an engorged stomach which disproportioned his 5ft 6inch figure. He wore greying joggers and a dirtied black sweater, his patchy beard unkempt and framing a cruel looking mouth. It wasn't until he looked up at me, that his lips curved into a smile which marginally improved his appearance.

"Emily, this is my son - Sal Hernandez. Son, this is Emily. She's part of the family now."

Gwynne was clearly smitten with the return of her son and was flustered in excitement as she dragged his large bags to the stairs leading up to the flat above. I noticed, with instant dislike, that Sal had no intention of helping his elderly mother with his own bags.

Finding ways of avoiding Sal for the next couple of weeks became a new project, but when living in a small three bedroom flat above a diner, options became pretty thin on the ground. Particularly one evening when Gwynne announced she was going out with a friend to play Bingo and that I was to stay in Sal's sight for my own safety.

"Sal, make sure Emily stays in and does her homework. She's not allowed out on school nights."

"Can't I come with you?" I pleaded as Sal sank into the sofa with a groan.

"Sal will take good care of you, doll. Don't worry yourself. I'll be back before ten."

The door closed behind Gwynne and I stared at it in growing panic.

"Get me a beer, Em," Sal ordered from the sofa, switching over to today's game on the box.

"I've got homework to do," I retorted, edging my way towards my bedroom.

"Get - me - a - beer - and sit down," Sal barked, softening his tone as he tapped the sofa next to him.

Recoiling from the idea of spending the evening with Sal and grabbing his damn beer from the refrigerator, I focused on keeping myself calm and poised. I didn't want Sal knowing that he made me nervous. He'd probably like that. I handed him his beer and sat on the far edge of the sofa. This was where more furniture would come in handy right now.

"We don't gotta watch the game, y'know?" Sal was suddenly sweet and generous, his bipolar manners giving me whiplash. "We could watch a movie?"

"No thanks," I muttered. "I really do have a lot of homework."

"What homework you got? Perhaps I can help you? It's been a while, but I can probably recall some of my school years."

Emily guessed that Sal was in his late twenties, maybe even early thirties. She muttered, "Math."

"Math? Oh hey, I'm great at Math! Go and get your books, I'll help you out."

Maybe if I just slipped out of the door, I could catch up with Gywnne. I'd get an ear-full for not doing as I'd been asked but it was better than this. Whether Sal was genuinely trying to be helpful or not, I didn't like his company. He made my skin crawl. He didn't have an ounce of Gwynne's warmth and his temper was unpredictable, dangerous. Whether it was fear of the consequences or not wanting to spoil Gwynne's evening, I grabbed my algebra books and set them on the coffee table in front of Sal.

"Good girl. Let's have a look." Sal set his beer down and scanned the equations, a frown set on his brow. His eyes shot up at me in annoyance. "You gonna sit with me? You can't see the equations sat all the way over there."

I edged reluctantly along the sofa so that I was able to see the books but with a safe distance between us. Sal quickly closed that gap, pressing his meaty thigh against mine. It took all my strength not to recoil at his touch.

"There's a simple method for these equations really," Sal began, his boozy breath invading my nostrils. "I'll show you the method I use, then you can follow."

I politely listened, meanwhile my eyes darting to the door. To my surprise, Sal was good at algebra. He passed me the pencil and I copied his method on another equation. I was starting to relax, focusing my mind on the mix of numbers and letters in front of me, when Sal's hand brushed my hair to one side. My blood froze and my skin crawled as his hand then traced my back, down to my hips and along my thigh. I gripped the pencil in my hand, judging the sharpness of the lead, but my mind went foggy with fear as his hand wandered up my thigh to the rim of my skirt.

My saving grace was the doorbell, which brought me out of my terrified haze. I plunged the pencil into Sal's leg before darting out of the room, through the apartment door, stumbling down the flight of stairs and wrenching the front door open. A spotty and bewildered pizza delivery boy jumped to the side as I bolted, down the street and out of sight.

I must have been running for over twenty minutes before collapsing on a bench outside of a laundrette, my lungs burning a hole through my chest. My face was damp from tears I hadn't realised I was shedding, and I was trembling ferociously. I realised quickly how hopeless my situation was. I was fourteen, it was ten o'clock at night and I had nobody to turn to. I was entirely alone. I also had no money and barely enough layers to see me through the night. I wasn't unfamiliar with sleeping on the street. I had been doing it for six months at least before the cops handed me over to the system and Gwynne came along. But I'd at least had plenty of layers and my trusty biffy to keep me warm.

I turned my attention to the laundrette behind me, my brain scolding me for what I was already planning to do. I found that usually if I acted quick enough, my mind didn't have enough time to process too much of what I was doing, which meant unwanted emotions such as shame, guilt and self-loathing didn't seep in until after the task was done. I slipped in through the door of the laundrette and approached a basket of clean clothes, the owner preoccupied with their back turned and headphones in. I quickly located a grey sweater and tucked it under my arm.

"What are you doing?" the woman was taking her headphones off and looking at me, bewildered. "That's my husband's sweater."

"I'm sorry, I need it."

I left behind the woman's cries of protest and continued my jog down to the next block, slipping the freshly laundered sweater over my head, the warmth cocooning me almost immediately. That was better. But what to do now?

I couldn't go back. Not with him there. He had ruined everything for me, and I hated him for that. My brief time with Gwynne had made me soft as well, so if I was going to make it through the night, and the next few after that, I'd need to undo all of that and bring Street Emily back to the surface. She was there, ready to pick up where she left off.

Chapter Seventeen

To my relief, nobody mentioned a single thing about my strange behaviour later that evening. I found myself deep in thought over the memories that had surfaced from this afternoon's antics. I recalled the night I had run away from Sal and kept invisible from the cops for a grand total of two hours, before being cornered at the subway where I had attempted to break into one of the public toilets. I had been taken straight back to Gwynne, her disappointment in me cutting through my heart like ice picks. I remembered Sal playing the victim, stating to the cops that he had tried to reason with me, that I was irrational and aggressive.

"She's a foster kid - she's been through a lot, so I get that she's angry," Sal had droned on with his insincere sincerity. "I just wish she'd let my mother and I help her, y'know?"

Gwynne and the cops had believed him of course. I was the ungrateful stowaway. I was the angry foster kid who had lost her way.

A heavy draw of breath opened my lungs as I clenched my eyes shut for a moment, trying to will the thoughts away, back into the little dark corner of my brain that I preferred to keep under lock and key.

I'd told Tom far too much as well, like an idiot, and had regretted it almost as soon as I had returned to the safety of my room. I'd have to make it my main priority for the rest of the evening to avoid him entirely.

"Oh my god, Miller! A week in Cornwall and you're dressed like you should have a pitchfork with straw hanging out of your mouth!"

Michelle's tinny voice over my ancient laptop speakers intruded my bedroom as we finally squeezed in a Skype chat. Her usually bright hair was dull and dusty from the clay dust and she had a few smears of the clay on her cheek.

"I'm a land girl," I retorted, indignant. "It's Sarah's bachelorette party."

"So, Sarah is Mark's sister? You've infiltrated yourself nicely."

"Please don't say it like that," I hissed at the screen. "It makes it sound like I'm undercover or something."

"Aren't you?"

"Helpful as ever. You're supposed to be calming my nerves."

"Oh get a grip, Em! You're on a business jolly in the sunniest part of Great Britain when you should be tucked away in the dustiest corner of the office fighting for your job right now. You're making it sound like such a hardship. I need a jolly like that, I think. I'm meant to be finishing a commission for that damn consultant lobby and all I keep doing is sculpting penises - unintentionally of course."

"It's just complicated."

"How so?" Michelle straightened in her seat, smiling at the thought of gossip. "Things between you and Mark levelling up?"

I sighed and tapped a pen on the document files beside my laptop, something I would need to tackle tomorrow on Mark's orders back in London.

"Actually, Mark is in London. Like I said, it's complicated. Can I explain it all another time, when I'm not in the thick of it and we can somehow laugh about it all?"

"Sure," Michelle nodded, looking both concerned and disappointed at my unwillingness to share. "Look after yourself. You're the most boring person to have ever attracted so much drama. It's really quite sad."

"Gee, thanks," I responded, deadpan.

We signed off and I relished in the silence that followed in disconnecting from that part of the world again for a moment. Michelle was right of course; I probably did need to get a grip. But then she also correctly pointed out that trouble seemed to find me, and I never sought it out - so maybe I was just hoping for a bit of a break.

When we started getting ready for Sarah's bachelorette, suddenly there wasn't enough time to worry about anything else. I now needed to worry about finishing my outfit off for tonight, of all things. So here I was, feeling strangely comfortable in a set of borrowed dungarees and heels, my hair now fashioned in a 1940's style under a red head-scarf. I examined my new look, a frown set on my brow as I gave myself a stern, internal talking to.

Emotionally, I felt unguarded and exposed, sensing I was on the verge of losing my nerve all together. No longer protected by my mundane, monotonous life back in Brooklyn, the spontaneous nature of this trip, bolstered by the mix of acquaintances I was fast counting as good friends, was stripping me bare from the thick armour I had attempted to build over the years.

I realised also, as I heard Sarah's trademark slamming of the front door and heavy-footed ascending of the stairs, that this was the longest time I had not been entirely alone for a while, and the constant interaction was becoming exhausting.

Sarah came bursting in, buzzing with excitement and looking regal in her ensemble, her hair in rollers under a maroon red headscarf, similar to mine.

"Emily, you look great!"

"So do you."

"You need more makeup though. I have some red lipstick and liquid eyeliner here. Give me your face."

I braced myself patiently as Sarah applied lipstick to my chapped lips. I really wasn't one to wear makeup, but when Sarah was done even I had to admit it finished the look off, my eyeliner flicking delicately in the corners and making my green eyes pop out under my mousy brown hair. I stared at myself longer than needed, somewhat satisfied with what I could see - for once.

"You look well," Sarah suddenly said, her voice unusually calm.

I smiled in response, a small frown accompanying it where I wasn't sure how to take her comment.

"Girls, you look fantastic!" Karen's shrieks of pride echoed across the yard. "Proper land girls! Stand together, let me get a photo!"

Karen ushered Sarah and her bridesmaids in front of Tom's Land Rover, the Keswick Green paintwork complimenting the World War country image. Emily watched in quiet amusement as the girls straddled the bonnet of the vehicle vainly, Karen snapping away like some frenzied photographer.

"Emily, you should be in the photo!" Sarah protested.

I shook my head so violently that I winced as the Beast reminded me of his imminent existence. I rubbed my temple as I replied, "You don't want me in the photo. I'll cramp your style, honestly."

"Yeah, don't make her look any more uncomfortable that she already looks," Katie said, not kindly.

"Are we catching a cab?" I asked, ignoring Katie as Sarah started measuring out glasses of prosecco for everybody.

"Tom has offered to take us. Then he'll go back for the boys. They're doing the stag night on the other side of town."

I felt a ripple of relief over the news that Tom would be nearby tonight. After this afternoon, I just felt like I needed him close. Why that was - well, I didn't want to start dissecting those feelings just yet.

Moments later, Tom stepped out of his cottage across the way, zipping up his body-warmer and unlocking the Land Rover, at which point the girls clambered into the back inelegantly. This left me with the front seat.

Tom held the door open and gestured, in amused courtesy.

"My lady," and much quieter so that only I could hear, as I climbed into the front seat, "You look beautiful."

"Let's go!" Sarah bellowed from the back, cutting through the warmth that was currently trickling through me from Tom's compliment. "I want shots!"

"Classy as ever, Sarah," Tom tutted once he was in the driver's seat, starting the engine.

"Have fun girls, but please stay safe!" Karen's caring words carried off in the wind as we jostled up the bumpy lane.

Newquay was already buzzing with life when we pulled up outside a club crawling with people. I wrung my hands anxiously, suddenly feeling very disquieted with the idea of joining the crowds dressed in this way.

"You don't have to stay here, you know?" Tom whispered as the girls prepared their exit, gathering their belongings and finishing drinks. He observed me with quiet concern as my eyes darted frantically, my seatbelt remaining firmly buckled. "I can drop you home and you can join Mum in an episode of 'Escape to the Country'. Much more civilised."

"I'll be fine," though the offer was tempting.

"Right, have fun girls," Tom spoke to the whole car, giving me an encouraging smile.

We all clambered out onto the pavement - Heidi, Toni and Katie getting straight into the queue for the nearest club, but Tom beckoned Sarah over and started talking to her quietly through his driver's window. Sarah did a few nods before waving him off.

"You can go now!" Sarah demanded of her brother.

"Just take it easy," Tom spoke to his little sister like she was an out-of-control teenager, then turned to me and smiled. "Have fun Emily. Stick with Sarah, please."

"Just go!" Sarah booted the wheel of the Defender impatiently and with that Tom pulled away, disappearing around the bend. My safety net gone, I suddenly felt cold. Sarah linked her arm into mine, "Tom has asked me to look after you and make sure I don't lose you. What kind of dickhead does he take me for? I'm not going to lose you - we're going to have an amazing night and get sloshed!"

In comparison to the small pieces of Cornwall that I had seen so far, Newquay was a paradox - a stray puzzle piece. It had a sense of misplacement: a bright, lively contrast from its tranquil country surroundings - an oasis of noise in a sea of calm. I wasn't sure I liked it very much.

The night began as it had meant to go on - loud, messy and unpredictable. Four more of Sarah's friends joined us whose names I didn't catch. Trays upon trays of shots were purchased, and many other drinks consumed.

The streets were a confusing mix of carousers in skimpy outfits, surfers in their wet suits cutting through town to get to the beaches, and locals with a simple pint in their hands.

By the time we reached our fifth destination, there wasn't a sober person left in the group. Everything seemed faster. Everything seemed louder. The drum and base of the music pounded through the floor, sending vibrations through everyone and everything.

A small trickle of euphoria set in, a very dull feeling of happiness with no sparkle. I stumbled without purpose from room to room as the music penetrated my ears. A small part of my brain was telling me to stop drinking as the Beast started sending warning strikes across my gums.

I finally found an exit out of the dark, suffocating atmosphere of the club and staggered out into the fresh, salty outdoors - tainted with cigarette smoke.

I gulped in the deliciously crisp air, willing it to cleanse me of all the alcohol I had just consumed. One of the local beaches was just below, quieter evenings being enjoyed by couples and small gatherings of friends. The sun had set hours ago, but a full moon flooded the beach with its brilliant white gleam, the light glistening on the water. The chaos of the club behind me faded into the distance for a moment as I focused on the dog having its late evening walk, the couple's hands entwined as they strolled along the water's edge. The gathering around the little fire pit echoed with laughter.

"I've been told to look after you," Sarah's slurring words cut through my moment of calm, the noise of the club crashing back into my senses. "So, look after you I shall!"

Slumping against the wall that I was leaning on, Sarah looked at me with hazy eyes. "D'yknow? I don't feel very drunk. D'you feel drunk?"

"Drunk enough," I answered truthfully. "Are you ok?"

"I'm getting married in two days," Sarah's eyes widened in realisation. "I'm no longer going to be Sarah Trengrouse. I'm going to be Sarah Bray. How weird is that?"

"Excuse me, love - got a cigarette?"

"No! And you just interrupted me in a very important conversation!" Sarah blurted.

"Alright, keep your knickers on!" The man scuttled off to find another supplier.

"Maybe we should have something to eat or some water before we move on," I suggested, eyeing Sarah warily.

"No! No, no. I'm not drunk. See? I'm not drunk. What we need is more shots."

"If you don't eat something, you're going to be so ill," I warned.

"No, I won't. Hey!! Look!! It's the boys!! Yew-hooo!!" Sarah screamed over the wall down to the pavement below where Steve's stag attendees were swerving side-to-side in equally drunken states, supporting a particularly messy Steve. I scanned the group. No Tom.

"It's my wife!! The old ball and chain!!" Steve hollered up to Sarah. "I love you!"

"I love you!" Sarah screeched back down to him, equally as loud, at risk of toppling over the edge.

"Where's Tom?" I asked, tugging the back of Sarah's top to keep her from falling.

"He's topping up the car park. He's stone-cold sober," Steve added unnecessarily.

"Come on Steve! Stop talking to your missus! Next pub - let's go!"

With that, Steve was dragged away by his fellow stags and disappeared around the corner.

"We need a drink," Sarah announced, dragging me back inside.

That contagious party feeling I had experienced earlier had quickly evaporated. Sarah's stomach finally gave in after one more shot, and suddenly Heidi and I were on hair duty as she vomited violently into a toilet. Her rollers had slowly fallen out one by one from such vigorous dancing, some still dangling on strands of hair behind her head scarf. Katie and some of the others had remained on the dance floor completely unaware and Toni was seeking out water for Sarah. To make things worse, my head had been pounding for the last half an hour. I was on the edge of an attack.

"Told you not to have that round of sambuca. That stuff will keep you pissed for hours now," Heidi scolded as Sarah wretched into the toilet bowl. She handed a fistful of hair to me and got her phone out of her bag. "I think we'd better call Tom for that lift. Call it a night."

I nodded in agreement, trying not to be sick myself - both from the smell and from the agonising pain I was experiencing.

"Hi Tom, it's Heidi. Are you alright to pick us up in a minute? Sarah's puking... Oh great. So is Steve. Okay, thanks very much.

Meet you outside Sailors in fifteen minutes."

It took a while to round everybody up and to get Sarah outside the club. Katie and the others - whose names I still didn't know - wanted to stay, so they said their goodbyes and slipped back into the club. This left Sarah, Heidi, Toni and me waiting on the pavement for Tom's arrival, each of us feeling as sorry for ourselves as the next.

"What are you lovely ladies meant to be?" a grubby looking man shuffled over.

"Land girls," Toni answered curtly, avoiding eye contact with this man.

The man chuckled, a cigarette hanging from his bottom lip. "The fuck is a land girl?"

"Women who worked on farms during the Second World War," I piped up, wishing immediately that I hadn't as Heidi elbowed me to be quiet.

"You a yank?" the man stepped forward.

"American, thank you very much."

"Hey! Stuart! Get over here! This girl is a yank. You like them!"

I felt myself coil as two more men walked over, looking equally as troublesome.

"Well, well. What do we have here?" Like his friend, he too wore a cigarette on his mouth. His hair was unkempt, his clothes equally so, and his trousers hung far too low around his crotch area. He had to be well into his thirties but stuck in his teen years as far as fashion was concerned.

"You like Americans, don't you Stuart?" his friend repeated, gleefully.

"Yeah. They're easy."

"Do you know what? You pricks can piss off!" Heidi snarled, just as Tom pulled up on the other side of the road. "Come on Emily. Let's get away from these ass-holes."

Toni and Heidi picked a half-conscious Sarah up off of the pavement and dragged her across the road. I picked up my jacket to follow.

"Not so fast, sweetheart. I haven't had a kiss yet!"

"You're not getting one. Leave me alone," I called over my

shoulder, wrapping my arms around myself for comfort. I suddenly felt cold and unclean, a dozen tainted memories seeping to the surface.

"Not until I get a goodnight-"

"You heard her. Back off," Tom snarled, appearing from practically nowhere, advancing on the man with frightening aggression.

Stuart stumbled backwards, quickly trying to recover himself. "It's only a bit of fun, mate."

"It's harassment," Tom squared up to Stuart, towering over him by at least half a foot. "Now, go back to your mates before I make you look really stupid."

"Fuck off," Stuart snarled, though he didn't seem as confident. He scuttled away, attempting a swagger back to his mates to keep face.

I simply stared at Stuart's retreating back, suddenly teary and defeated from the total mess that was this evening. Tom removed his jacket and cocooned me in its mass.

"Come on, let's get you home," Tom soothed, putting an arm around me and leading me back to the safety of his Land Rover.

The contrast between the journey to Newquay and the return home was extreme, with everybody subdued to silence from the night's events. Tom pulled us to a heavy halt in the yard and everybody clambered out, muttering their thanks as they did so. Heidi grabbed some keys from Sarah's clutch bag and started fumbling with the lock in the dark, whilst balancing a half-conscious Sarah on her arm. Toni, supposedly supporting the other side, didn't appear to be in a much better state. I'd have laughed if I wasn't so close to crying.

"Here. Let me help you," Tom insisted, taking the keys from Heidi who was now panting in her efforts. Tom unlocked the front door with ease and opened it to allow the tangle of girls into the warmth of the cottage.

"Are you staying here or back in the house?" Tom asked me.

I gestured to Sarah's cottage, still wrapped in Tom's jacket, and stepped inside, Tom following closely behind.

"I'd best make sure you girls get to bed safely," Tom tutted. "You've all gone way over-board."

"We won't disagree with you there," my head was spinning, the alcohol still circulating my system leaving my mind foggy.

"Emily, I'm going to put these lot to bed, then I'm hitting the sack too. Do you mind?" Heidi asked, already halfway up the stairs.

"No, you go ahead. I'm going to have a glass of water, then I'll be right up."

With some loud struggles, the odd swear word and even a giggle or two, the three of them were eventually upstairs, leaving Tom and I utterly alone.

"Thanks for dealing with those guys earlier," I started, filling the silence.

"That was the last bloody thing you needed after this afternoon," Tom growled. "I left you there thinking you were safe. It's bloody Newquay! What must you think of us?"

"Oh well, we have our fair share of tools in the US too. I have a pretty good right hook when needed, so don't worry about me."

Tom chortled; it was a low rumble that brought goose-bumps to my skin.

It was about two seconds before I realised that my green eyes were locked onto his deep brown ones. I tried to tear mine away but realised it was a little late for that. Tom was already edging towards me, backing me into the corner of the kitchen.

"I will worry about you," Tom spoke softly. "I get the impression no one else bloody does."

My lower back collided gently with the counter and Tom's large figure was shadowing me, his breath in my hair. He was so close, I could take in his scent. It was a heavenly, natural sort of smell - a mixture of cologne and something sweet, like the smell of the cider being made from the distillery.

"What are you doing?" I breathed into his chest, my heart pounding.

"Finishing off where we began last night," Tom spoke softly, bringing my chin up with his hands, claiming my mouth with his. Our lips completely locked in the kiss. Tom pressed himself against me before picking me up onto the counter. The calm, reserved Tom that I had met days ago was suddenly animalistic, passionate, and demanding and I had no intention of stopping him. His lips left my mouth and migrated to my neck; I closed my eyes, mapping out the path he was creating from my neck, downward. I began to lose myself in paradise when a noise at the top of the stairs caused us both to stop in our tracks, our heavy breaths mixing together as we waited for more movement. A toilet flushed upstairs and the person responsible for bringing me back to my senses returned to their bed, shutting a door behind them.

I wriggled myself out of Tom's hold and regained my balance on the kitchen counter, catching my breath. Tom's hands retreated to the counter either side of me, framing me in with his arms.

"We should go next door to mine," Tom spoke through heavy breaths.

I looked at Tom in disbelief. "We should take that as a close-call and call it a night. This is... "

"Wrong?" Tom looked hurt at the word.

"No, that's the problem. It doesn't feel wrong. But it doesn't stop it being... oh I don't know the word. It's naughty!"

Tom snorted a laugh and raised an eyebrow. "Naughty?"

"Shut up, that's not what I meant! Not like that, anyway," I brought my hands up to my face and rubbed the skin in exasperation. "Oh god, what are we doing? I'm so confused and so intoxicated." And in pain, I added silently.

"Are you okay?" Nothing seemed to be getting past him this evening. "You look like you're in pain."

"Yeah, it's nothing," I lied. "I just get these head pains sometimes. I shouldn't have drunk so much."

"Maybe you should go to bed," Tom advised, though he seemed sad at the idea. "I've got to play taxi one more time for Steve's lot. I'll come and check on you when I get back."

I melted a little at the offer. He was so sweet.

"Honestly, I'll be fine. I just need some water - maybe an aspirin - and I'll be right as rain tomorrow." This was a complete lie as well, but I didn't want Tom to fuss.

"Okay. Whatever you'd prefer. I'll see you in the morning."

I smiled fondly and my heart swelled as he lightly kissed my forehead. It was such a small, sweet gesture and yet sent the same energy through me as the previous, more passionate one.

Once Tom was gone, I was left stranded on the kitchen

counter, my mind fuzzy and warm, and yet sharp with an approaching shadow attack. I prayed that my lies of a simple water and aspirin would keep The Beast away tonight. I didn't have anything stronger in the way of drugs and I wanted to hold onto the memory of Tom's lips for a little while longer.

Chapter Eighteen

Karen had thought it was such a wonderful idea at the time, when she had volunteered to cater for her daughter's entire wedding. She was trying to be practical - Tom's and Catherine's wedding had been so extravagant, a sure sign that the marriage wasn't going to last. Catherine's taste and demands in things were thriftless; Tom was always much more idealistic and had found the whole wedding extremely stressful and strenuous on his pocket.

Poor Tom.

She thought about that wretched girl daily, and not in a fond way - not in the slightest. She blamed that girl for Tom's distant persona, his need to constantly bleed himself dry into his father's business. She blamed her for the broken relationship between Tom and Mark. Mark was of course responsible too, but she had been the main instigator in this whole horrible ordeal.

She shuddered to think what her dear late husband would say right now if he was around. He'd knock those boys' heads together, tell them to stop being so bloody stubborn and proud, and to make amends.

It was now 5am in the morning. It was rather early, and she knew there would be some guests in the house that would be worse-for-wear from last night, but she had woken in a state of panic thinking of all the things she had yet to do for the food before the wedding - which was now less than two days away!

Trying her utmost to be quiet, Karen dragged out saucepans and trays, mixing bowls and utensils and scanned her list of dishes that still needed making. Half of it had already been scratched off and dishes were now safely in freezers. She would take them out last minute tomorrow evening to thaw overnight ready for her to prepare the next morning. But the rest of it was dishes that she couldn't freeze, and that needed to be made fresh.

Her sister-in-law, Margaret, would be over later to make some

Pavlovas. Margaret's meringue was far superior to hers, so she was happy to let her lead on that one. She had also promised to come early in the morning and help her with final preparations. So, this was something Karen could count on to stop her going into complete disarray.

She checked the time on the clock wall above the AGA. How strange. It was now 5:15am and Tom hadn't been in for his coffee. Perhaps he had got in later than he thought last night and was chancing an extra hour in bed. Karen doubted it but wouldn't blame him for doing so. She had been a little vexed at Sarah and Steve for making him chauffeur when he had his usual early start. But Tom had said yes, as he always does when it's something his beloved sister wants. At least two out of her three children had a close relationship.

Karen was measuring out flour when Tom burst into the kitchen, nearly sending one of the dogs flying.

"Tom m'love, a little quieter - there might be people sleeping upstairs."

"No one slept in here last night, Mum. The girls slept in Sarah's, and Steve's lot slept at mine."

"Oh, well there's me creeping around this morning like a -" Karen realised, at a second glance, her son was looking a little frantic, flicking through the yellow pages.

"Mum, what's the name of that old friend of Dad's - the fireman?"

"Nigel Trevail - he's in the book. Why, darling? What's wrong?"

"It's Emily - she's not very well. She won't let me call the ambulance but said something about needing oxygen. Didn't Nigel provide a cylinder when Dad was ill?"

"Yes, he did. But he could get into trouble if he keeps taking oxygen from his workplace. Why does Emily need oxygen? What's wrong with her?"

"I don't know. She says it's chronic," Tom ranted, punching in Nigel's number. "Whatever she means by that!"

"Tom, sweetheart! You can't call him now. It's 5 o'clock in the morning!"

"Shit!" Tom slammed the phone down. "Well I'm going to

have to call the ambulance then."

"What symptoms does she have?"

"I don't know - she can barely speak. She keeps banging the side of her head, saying her head is hurting."

"She's not just a little worse for wear?" Karen aired the side of caution, trying not to sound patronising.

"No Mum! You should see her, it's not right."

"Okay, darling. Don't worry. You call the ambulance and explain the symptoms. I'll go out to her a minute. Where is she?"

"In Sarah's."

Karen didn't hesitate to put her shoes on, crossing the yard to Emily's aid. She'd been retired from nursing for nearly five years now and, going by the symptoms Tom was describing, she wasn't sure what expertise she could offer, but she'd do her best all the same.

Emily was lying on Sarah's sofa, with Heidi kneeling down on the floor beside her.

"Sorry Karen, hope we didn't wake you. Emily's really poorly," Heidi said nervously.

"I was awake already, don't you worry. Emily, my darling, what's wrong?"

"I'm... having... an... attack," Emily managed. Tom wasn't exaggerating. She looked like she was in agony and the side of her face appeared raw from where she was dragging her nails down the skin. It was as if she was trying to tear the pain out of her skull.

"Is this an on-going condition, Emily?" Karen asked firmly, her previous experience as a nurse beginning to show in her voice.

Emily nodded, closing her eyes, and tapping the side of her head, above her temple.

"What's it called? Have you been diagnosed?"

It took a while for Emily to answer and her voice was weak. "Sort of. They're called 'Cluster Headaches'... but it's not a headache. Trigeminal...something - argh!"

Karen had never heard of it. "Is there anything that helps to sooth the symptoms? Tom's calling the ambulance now."

"I told him not-"

"Emily, you are really unwell, and you need to be seen," Karen replied sternly, stroking the hair out of Emily's face. "Now, what helps sooth it?"

Again, there was a pause and a few grunts of pain from Emily before she answered. "Ice. On the back of my neck."

"Heidi, can you get some ice please? Bag it up in a tea towel."

Heidi went off to seek the items and Karen turned back to Emily.

"Anything else that usually works?"

"Oxygen... and DHE injections... I was on... verapomil, but... it was giving me heart palpitations and... making my blood pressure drop."

Karen was shocked. DHE, otherwise known as Dihydroergotamine, was an injection which supposedly caused blood vessels to narrow in the brain. Whatever Cluster Headaches were, it was obviously some sort of neurological condition. This was a lot more serious than she thought.

Heidi returned with a tea towel filled with ice which Karen applied to the back of Emily's neck. Tom came in just as the ice worked its magic.

"The ambulance is on its way. Shouldn't be long."

"Has she had some water? I'm not saying the alcohol caused this, but she'll be very dehydrated because of it," Karen advised.

"No, I don't think she has. I'll get her some." Tom rushed into the kitchen and came back out with a glass of water. Karen then ushered Emily up into a sitting position and urged her to take small sips of water.

"Is she going to be alright?"

Karen scrutinised her son's face, his usual cool, collective demeanour now jittery and anxious. Trying not to react, Karen stroked Emily's arm to keep her calm whilst calculating the unusual level of concern coming from her eldest.

It didn't take long for the paramedics to arrive. Same as Karen, they had never heard of the condition and had started doing routine checks on Emily, asking her a series of questions. As it was, she started to perk up after ten minutes of breathing through an open-air oxygen mask. Karen asked her why she hadn't brought these things with her from America.

"I didn't really know how it worked, flying with all these medical aids. I didn't want to make a fuss putting it all through declaration." Emily looked sheepish and very vulnerable. It made Karen want to take her under her wing, her motherly instincts swelling for the poor girl.

"But my darling, you should have at least said something. We could have got you some oxygen at least."

"I didn't-"

"Want to make a fuss," Karen finished off, nodding knowingly. "What are we going to do with you?"

The paramedic came over with his clipboard. He had already run the standard tests but had just come off the phone, enquiring about Emily's medication.

"Okay, we should be able to get a doctor to sign off a prescription for some of those sumatriptan injections and a cylinder of oxygen. The sumatriptan is self-injecting if that's alright. Can someone collect it from Treliske this afternoon?"

"Yeah, I'll collect it," Tom offered. "I'll tie it in with a delivery."

"Great. Now, because you're not a citizen we have to put charges to these prescriptions. These need to be paid in advance. Here's the number. Call and reference your details and you'll be able to pay over the phone. Is that all clear?"

Emily nodded at the paramedic, taking the number from him and looking extremely tearful all of a sudden. They allowed her a couple more minutes with the oxygen before packing up and leaving.

"That's why I didn't want to call them? I can't afford this," Emily sobbed.

Karen and Tom both exchanged concerned looks. Karen sat next to Emily on the sofa and tried comforting her. "It does make us appreciate our NHS services. Will it be very much?"

"Depends how many ampules they've prescribed me. I have to pay over $300 dollars for one carton of ten back at home."

"Gosh, that's a lot of money. How often do you have to use them?"

"Because they're so expensive I only use them when a severe attack comes along. But sometimes if the attack is really bad, I end up using three injections during one attack. I have no idea what they'll charge for my oxygen. I usually have my canister at home refilled to save money."

"Well can we not cancel the oxygen and just get some from Nigel?" Tom asked, hovering on the arm of the sofa. "It's 7 o'clock now. I'll go and call him."

"Sweetheart, why don't you start work after you've done that. You'll be so behind otherwise."

"Yeah, thanks for the reminder. Will do," Tom grabbed his coat and turned to Emily, looking torn.

"I'll take good care of her," Karen assured her eldest son, now wondering exactly what was going on between Tom and Emily. Surely Tom wouldn't be as foolish as his brother.

It was bad timing, she admitted, but Karen couldn't bring herself to show even the slightest hint of being inconvenienced. She may have missed out on two hours of cooking, but she really did feel so sorry for the poor girl.

"Right now, you take a seat at the breakfast bar and I'll get you something to eat," Karen said moments later, back in her own kitchen and bustling about for some eggs and bacon.

"What are you making?" Emily asked, looking around at all the pots and pans everywhere and the flour half measured into a bowl.

"I'm just finishing off the last of the dishes for the wedding. A few more quiches, some salads and the desserts and I'm nearly done."

"You're doing all of the catering on your own?" Emily asked, in awe.

"My sister-in-law is coming to help later as well. She makes better meringue than me."

"I'm so sorry Karen. You've got enough on your hands without me being a pain."

"I won't hear another word about it. You can't help being unwell, bless your heart!"

"Can I help at all? I can probably remember some of the recipes from working at the diner."

Bless her, she looked so keen. Karen wasn't one for having too many cooks in one kitchen, but she couldn't bring herself to decline Emily's offer. She was very good in the tearooms, perhaps Karen could make use of her spare pair of hands.

"You're a dear. That would be lovely. Let me fix you some breakfast first, then you can make up some of the salads for me. You're not to do too much though, not after this morning."

The morning passed by quickly, and Emily was indeed very handy in the kitchen. When Margaret arrived at 10 o'clock, late as usual, Emily was keen to learn how to make a meringue, so opted to separate the eggs carefully and precisely. Karen was pleased to see her perk up and even have a few giggles with her and Margaret. Margaret had a big personality which made her very likable amongst most people, but Emily's shy, reserved nature seemed to bounce off of her very well.

Sarah emerged from the depths of her hangover around midday and scuttled into Karen's kitchen seeking out food.

"Oh, nice of you to join the land of the living!" Margaret teased her niece from behind the counter.

Sarah winced, "Oh, I'm far too hungover to deal with your voice today Auntie Margaret. No offence."

"No offence ever taken," Margaret chuckled at the state of her niece as Sarah skulked around the kitchen, opening cupboards idly.

"For goodness sake, what are you after?" Karen huffed. Her kitchen was becoming too full and she couldn't work like that.

"I'm starving. The others are hungry as well. Any bacon going?"

"And I suppose you want me to cook it and make you lot some sandwiches as well?"

"That would be great," Sarah said, attaching herself to Karen's arm the way she did when she was creeping for something. "Love you, Mummy."

"Alright you creep. Get back to your guests and clean yourselves up. If they all smell as bad as you do, both cottages are going to smell like a stale bar. I'll bring the food over when I can."

"Thanks Mum," Sarah shuffled her way to the door, only just noticing Emily sat at the breakfast bar, filling vol-au-vents. "There you are Emily! Are you not hungover?"

"A bit, but not too badly," Emily looked up nervously. Heidi had clearly not said anything to Sarah about the episode they had had earlier that morning, and Karen had no intentions of doing so either. It would only embarrass Emily further and make Sarah worry.

"You're so jammy. I feel like death warmed up. Why didn't you tell me to stop drinking?"

Sarah left and Emily looked at Karen with amused exasperation. "I did tell her to stop drinking. Several times."

"I can believe that. And I can believe Sarah not listening to a single sensible word with a few drinks down her. Takes after her father for that," Karen chuckled knowingly. "Right. On top of everything else, I now have a dozen bacon sandwiches to make."

"Give me the bacon and the bread. I'll take it over and cook it in Sarah's kitchen. That way, it's done and it's not taking up valuable kitchen space," Emily offered, setting down the filling for the vol-au-vents.

"Is this girl a keeper or what?" Margaret said to Karen.

She certainly is Karen thought.

There was little that Karen took more pleasure in than spending a quiet sunny afternoon tending to her garden. She had always had what you'd call green fingers, since she was a little girl. But now, as a tired old widow whose heart was constantly aching from the grief and an absence of the last three or four years, it was a necessity.

It was over her rose bed, whilst pruning the heads, that Karen had wept out of worry for her husband's diagnosis.

It was whilst sowing some cosmos seeds in her potting shed that tears of realisation had streamed down her face, as she tried to come to terms that her husband would not be winning his battle against that horrendous disease.

And it was as she hacked away at her hydrangea bushes, decapitating each head one-by-one with anger and hatred towards her cruel, cruel world, she had grieved over the passing of her beloved Roy, trying to fathom how she would be strong enough to say goodbye, let alone do all the necessary arrangements for his funeral.

Every day, whether it be for ten minutes or three hours, Karen would put her heart and soul into the soil, nurturing her beloved plants - all of this in order to breathe, survive. Without it, she feared she would suffocate.

Today was a particularly good day to prep some beds for new annuals. The ground was wet, but not drenched and there was a warmth from the sun against the bitter wind. Karen planned to get some of her favourite autumn plants in, a tactic to keep colour going for longer, before winter stripped her garden of life. Cyclamens, marigolds and pansies always seemed to prolong the brightness of summer and deter the deadly prowl of winter.

Karen had finished everything she could with the wedding food for now, and so she had stepped onto her flag-stoned patio, immediately tearing up the odd cheeky weed that had protruded through the cracks, and was now drinking in the cold air.

It never took Karen long to get stuck in and lost in the labour of love toward her garden, and an hour had trickled away by the time she'd finished prepping the beds. As it always did when gardening, her mind wandered. Nowadays, her mind focused on her biggest worry. Her children. She supposed it was natural for a mother to worry about their children, no matter what the age. But Karen had had so many reasons to worry these last few years, it was any wonder she hadn't lost her mind over it all. And with the return of her youngest son, that ache in her heart that had only recently become bearable was fresher than ever: like a wound reopened.

Karen lent back on her haunches, suddenly short of breath. Daily, Karen felt like she'd failed as a mother. Was it while lost in grief Karen slowly lost that relationship with Mark? Had she failed him? What could she have done? The truth was - nothing. With that horrible girl's talons dug deep enough into his heart, there would have been nothing in this world Karen could have done. She could only hope now that things could get better and he'd return to her eventually.

Another half an hour passed by, and Karen was bending over the last of a bed of weeds, her thoughts interrupted by the sound of heavy footsteps. She looked up vacantly to see Tom peering over the garden wall from the nearest orchard. Karen eased herself gently to her feet and leaned slowly backwards. Her spine gave a soft cracking sound. She had overdone it.

"Don't over-do it, Mum," Tom grumbled, echoing her

thoughts a little too late. "I haven't got time to be peeling you off the front lawn like last time."

"I'm having little breaks here and there - stop fussing!"

"Looks good, though. Have you had lunch yet?" Tom asked.

"Not yet my darling."

"Can I get you anything?"

"You are a love," Karen smiled, tired from her labour. "A bowl of soup would be wonderful."

"I'll get Sarah to put some aside."

"Tom!" Karen called after her son. He returned and approached the wall again, this time cautiously. "You're being careful, aren't you?"

"With what?"

"Emily..."

Tom's sudden change of expression was all Karen needed. Suspicions of her anguished son finally showing feelings towards somebody was both a relief and a huge concern. A concern because, of all girls, it had to be his brother's. Those boys of hers! What was she to do with them?!

"Mum, I don't know what you're on about. Do you want the soup, or not?"

Disappointed, Karen considered pursuing the matter further, then seeing how uncomfortable Tom was, she decided otherwise.

"Never mind. Ignore your mother," Karen smiled. "I'll just take these weeds down to the compost, then I'll be there."

Chapter Nineteen

There was very little in Tom's small world that panicked him these days. There was the daily stress of the business, and the underlying worry of keeping his workmen paid each month. But never a reason for panic. Today however, a rising dread was working its way up from the pit of Tom's stomach, and he didn't like it at all. The worst part was he couldn't locate the main source.

There was this growing need to be around Emily that frightened him. He had almost vowed never to attach himself to another human ever again after his divorce, and now it frustrated him that his heart was giving his brain no chance to reason with the dangers that came with these new feelings. Worse still, his mum had started to notice his infatuation and her concerns only reflected his own.

With the traumas of this morning, a full day of apple-picking, on top of a trip to the hospital to collect Emily's medical aid, Tom felt positively drained. He dragged his weary feet into his office, Molly and Lula closely at his feet, and lit the small fire in the corner. It had been his father's office - a small section of the stone lean-to behind the distillery. Tom hadn't changed a single thing since the passing of his father Roy. It was exactly how he'd remembered it as a small boy, and he didn't plan to change it now.

"Settle down girls," Tom soothed. The dogs did as they were told and curled up together on a tatty rug across the stone hearth.

It was often a dark room, a single wooden sash window with the sun trickling in through the dirt and grime of the small glass panes. The same bunches of dried nigella pods still hung above the window, serving no real purpose, and the roll-top desk occupied the corner, along with the antique office chair that Tom now rocked on, back and forth.

Tom took great comfort in this little nook of an office and had taken refuge to it on many occasions during the turmoil of the last three to four years. On the days that had followed Catherine's dramatic departure, Tom had practically lived there, staring passively into the flames. And the day he had finally signed the divorce papers, he'd dedicated himself to hours of paperwork, barely taking himself out from behind the desk. Never had his accounts been so organised.

Recently though, it had felt like the business was running away from him. Every year's harvest seemed to get worse, and as he had been forced to make half his employees redundant last year, the pick took longer and longer. He had spent so much time out in the orchards recently, or late nights in the distillery doing the jobs that used to be done by at least three employees, so Tom just had no time to keep on top of the paperwork.

He threw his beanie hat on to the pile of invoices that needed to be faxed or filed, and peeled his gloves off his numb hands, attempting feebly to warm them by the fire.

The business was draining him. He could feel it ageing him daily, and there was nothing he could do. He couldn't let his father down, and he wouldn't see his mother disappointed. He'd had high hopes when Sarah had brought up the idea for the tearooms. He had felt sure it would bring in the footfall they needed, increase sales just enough to keep him up to capacity in workmen. At the moment though, it seemed the tearooms was going down with the farm.

Tom hadn't realised that he'd been holding his breath and released it with an exasperated sigh just as there was a timid knock on the old wooden door.

"Yep?!"

The door opened, letting in a bitter chill from the evening setting in, and Emily stepped in, popping her head around the door.

"Hey," Tom cooed, sitting up to attention, his stomach doing somersaults. "How are you feeling?"

"All good. Thanks for this morning. You were my hero."

A strange current ran through Tom, and he could do nothing in response other than clear his throat.

"Your mom asked me to get you. Dinner's ready," Emily smiled. "Hey, there you are, girls!"

Emily shut the door behind her and knelt down with Molly and Lula on the rug. Tom watched fondly as the whippets took in turns receiving ear scratches, their teeth protruding through silly grins, showing their appreciation.

"And to think I was afraid of these little guys," Emily said in a silly voice as she went to town scratching Molly's rear-end. Her laugh had a beautiful tinkling sound as she amused herself with Molly's strange butt-dance. Tom felt his heart swell as he drank in every beautiful feature of Emily's.

It was too late; he was falling for her.

"Are you alright?"

"Me?" Tom had been so busy admiring Emily; he hadn't realised she'd been scrutinising him through those emerald green eyes of hers. "I'm fine. Why?"

"You just seem really distracted. Like you're worried about something."

"Always something to worry about," Tom chortled wryly. "I'm alright though. Just got a tonne of paperwork mounting up, and no time to sort it."

It was mostly a scapegoat, but it spoke some truth. The mounting paperwork was getting him down.

"I can help sort all of that for you, you know?" Emily offered, shifting her weight to the other leg, and switching her focus over to Lula's chest. Tom frowned with disbelief. "No, seriously! I do this all the time back at work. It's basically my role. I can sort you out a filing system in no time."

Tom considered this for a moment. Was it strange that he liked the idea very much? It would give him more excuses to be around her. He tried not to deliberate how pathetic that made him sound.

"Urr, well, if you don't mind -"

"Of course not! Happy to help. I'll start it tomorrow."

Tom smiled, and offered his hand, pulling her up from the floor.

"Thanks. Come on, let's get some dinner."

The dogs sprang to life, as if this was their cue, and pushed their way past Tom's legs out into the darkening yard.

"Stupid dogs," Tom grumbled.

They crunched their way towards the house together, the familiar smell and feeling of another evening drawing in around them. It was fairly mild, but Emily was visibly shivering, her arms folded tightly across her chest.

"You really need to start layering up," Tom scolded. "Sarah's got plenty of jumpers and thick socks you can borrow. What's even the point of those shoes? What happened to the wellies Sarah lent to you?"

"Alright bossy!" Emily laughed. "I didn't realise how cold it was, and your office was a lot further than I had anticipated. Okay?"

"Yes. So far," Tom drawled. "I don't know how you managed to walk a whole five-hundred yards - ow!" Tom chortled as Emily punched him playfully on the arm.

"Horrible man!"

Their chuckles continued as they made their way into the main house, and into the warm kitchen where the usual evening bustle of dinnertime commenced. Tom's laughter faltered just for a moment as he caught his mother's expression - a look of concern and suspicion.

"You two are in a giggly mood!" Karen said, accusation in her voice.

"Your son is giving me grief for my dress sense," Emily made her usual beeline to the AGA, warming her hands by the hot plates.

"He has a point. You're freezing, child!" Karen tutted as she felt one of Emily's hands. "Sarah, lend the silly girl some clothes, will you?"

"I've already offered coats and some wellies! Not my fault if you don't wear them!"

"Wow, I'm getting it in the neck tonight!" Emily cried, though her cheeks flushed with happiness.

"I'll grab you a couple of jumpers later."

"Thanks Sarah."

"How's the food coming on, Mum? Did you and Aunty Margaret get lots done this morning?" Sarah asked as they all took seats around the table, chairs scraping loudly against the flagstone floor.

"We had a very productive morning. Emily helped as well."

"We're all going to be fighting for you soon!" Sarah chuckled. "You know you're not allowed to leave after the wedding, right?"

"Don't tempt me. I'm literally in love with this place," Emily sighed, looking down at her food. "I can't believe I'll have to leave in just a couple of days."

Tom didn't hear the rest of the conversations around the dinner table. Suddenly his mum's delicious food became bland and tasteless, and that rising panic he had felt earlier came back with painful force. He knew that eventually Emily would leave, so why only now did it seem to be really sinking in? That in just a matter of days he may never see Emily again. The very idea made him feel sick and he no longer had an appetite. In fact, he was suddenly finding it very difficult to be seated at that table at all.

"Sorry Mum. You'll have to excuse me for a moment."

To everyone's confusion Tom pushed his plate away and stood up.

"Where are you going?"

"I've just remembered I've left some of the machines running down in the distillery. You all carry on. I'll warm my food up later."

"Darling, you can finish your food first. Work will have to wait."

"No, I better... I had better make sure everything is turned off. Won't be long."

Before anybody could respond, Tom stomped his way back out into the yard and took a dragging breath of cold air. He rubbed his face over and over again, like he was trying to stimulate his skin into releasing every bad emotion he was feeling at that particular moment. With this panic came a fast build-up of anger and frustration, and the need to run his fist through something was suddenly all consuming. How had he got here? Why, whenever there was a woman involved, did he become this irrational ball of anger? He felt similar emotions with Catherine's departure, except he had no desire to stop her from leaving. He remembered feeling anger, yes - but mixed in with contempt and resentment. Now, with the anger came the panic, like he was running out of time and needed to find the courage to act upon... whatever this was. The whole thing seemed ludicrous. What exactly was he going to ask of

Emily? Leave your life in New York behind. Leave my brother! He doesn't deserve you. Move here, on an economically sinking cider farm, in the middle of nowhere. It'll be great, I promise!

Was he kidding himself?

"Sweetheart," the soothing, yet stern voice of his mother trickled through the darkness from the front door. Karen wrapped her cardigan tightly around her as she slipped her feet into the nearest shoes under the porch. Tom knew what was coming, and he didn't want to have this conversation. But he stood frozen on the spot, his mother's unspoken words already reverberating around his head.

"Thomas," Karen came to a stop in front of him. He refused to meet her eyes, and suddenly he was fifteen years old again, waiting to be scolded for something he had broken, or a profanity he had used towards his father out of juvenile frustration. He felt his anger bubble at a dangerous rate as tears smarted in his eyes. Seriously? Was he going to blubber in front of his mother, in the middle of the yard, over a girl?

Karen's stern voice suddenly shifted into alarm and concern, "Tom, sweetheart!"

A long pause hung between them, as Tom filled his lungs through his nose, trying with all his might to be rid of the tears. "Oh dear, you've really fallen for her, haven't you? Oh Tom. You silly boy. What about Mark?"

The tears vanished as quick as droplets of water on a hot plate. *What about Mark?* His mother asked. Like it wouldn't be fair to Mark. The one who stifled Emily's spirit. The one who had made Emily cry on more than one occasion just this week. The one who drove off, leaving Emily stranded without a word. The one who didn't deserve Emily, even for a second. His brother, who had ripped him of his happiness all those years ago, without the slightest remorse, now parading his own forged happiness right in front of Tom's face.

Karen ripped Tom from his toxic thoughts, "Tom! What about Mark?"

Tom's face contorted into a bitter grimace and he turned to his mother.

"What about him?"

Chapter Twenty

A gentle mist hovered over the front lawn and the sun was just beginning to peek over the distant hills. It was one more day until the wedding - early morning - the dew coating the foliage in Karen's garden below, which I admired through my bedroom window. There was a longing to get out into the fresh air which I would never have felt back in Manhattan. But being here, in the Cornish countryside, was good for me. It had been a very long time since I had woken up feeling refreshed or felt any desire to get the day started. But this morning, a new optimistic sensation rippled through me and it was an opportunity I needed to take advantage of. Right away.

The dogs scuffed around excitedly at the kitchen door, spilling over one another as I released them into the porch. Perhaps I should take the dogs with me for company. At least they would be exercised for Karen. I spent a few minutes searching around for a spare pair of wellies, a water-proof coat and a leash for each of the dogs. Feeling less than elegant but fit for a walk in the country, I zipped up my borrowed coat and followed the dogs out of the porch, through Karen's garden, heading towards the gate that backed out onto the fields behind.

The air was crisp and made my lungs ache, but I'd never felt so alive and free. Taking a deeper breath and filling my lungs to their full capacity, I stomped clumsily through the long grass. The dogs were running circles around me, barking at each other manically from excitement.

"Silly creatures," I tutted fondly as Molly rolled her back into the grass happily. "What a life!"

And it really was. What a life these dogs had. What a life, to wake up to this every morning. Breathing in fresh, fume-free air. Waking up only to the sounds of birds chirping, traffic barely audible. What - a - life.

Suddenly, the idea of returning to Manhattan, or London, or any city for that matter was something I didn't want to think about. Was it completely ludicrous that, at this very moment, all I wanted to do was remain here, and make this very view my permanent back drop?

The field, like most of the surrounding countryside, was sloped and overlooked a large river. It was a heavy descent towards the bottom of the field, but I could just make out a small set of kissing gates and wanted to investigate. The dogs read my mind, or perhaps they'd covered this walk a hundred times, and they led the way, lapping me in whippet-zoomies several times as they went. It was once I was through the kissing gates, and beginning a gentle stroll down the lane, that I allowed my mind to wander.

Perhaps it hadn't been such a bad thing, being ditched here. Perhaps it had been better not having Mark around. If I was honest, I felt more free, less judged. The longer I was away from the city and the further I was away from - well, everything - the easier breathing became.

I smiled to myself as I looked up to the trees arching over the lane, the sun leaking in through the gaps in the leaves and branches. The dogs trotted ahead, sniffing the ground vigorously, criss-crossing each other's path with contentment. The hedgerow was peppered with juicy blackberries, all hanging ripe and ready to be picked from their luscious green foliage. Licking my lips as I recalled Karen's delicious apple and blackberry crumble, I picked a clean poop bag out from my coat pocket and started filling it with the deep purple-black fruit. I was sure Karen could make use of them somehow. Popping a few in my mouth, I savoured the sharp, seedy taste.

The tunnel of trees finally broke out to a wider road, grass growing in the middle in a similar way to the one leading to the cider farm's entrance. I attached the leashes back on both dogs in case of a sudden car and descended down into another farmyard, the smell of cattle manure and hay putrid to my nose. I slowed and hesitated as I realised that I was walking right through a working farm.

"You're alright, m'love," an old farmer hollered over to me

from his tractor seat. "'Tis a public footpath through 'ere. You carry on. Oh, you got Molly and Lula with you. You stayin' with the Trengrouses then?"

"Yes Sir. Just until the wedding," I called back, shading my eyes from the sun as it rose higher above the cattle shed.

"Lovely job, lovely job. Well, we'll see you there, then! Our daughter Katie is bridesmaid and all."

So, Katie was a farmer's daughter. The warm welcome from her father bore no resemblance what-so-ever to her prickly nature. I jumped as one of the cattle nudged me from behind the galvanised field gate.

"She won't hurt you," Katie's father chuckled. "None of 'em will - daft as a bleddy brush they are. I hear Mark returned early this week?"

"Briefly," I replied, shifting slightly. "Hopefully be back again for the wedding."

"Core! I wouldn't want to be the one splitting him and Tom up when things get nasty," the old man chortled, drawing in sharp breaths in agreement to himself. "Though, best those boys just scrap it out now and be done with it."

"What do you-"

My attempt at getting answers was interrupted by Katie herself, who stepped out of one of the cattle sheds and heaved the sliding door shut. She had her long brown hair slicked up into a rough ponytail, wore a rugby jersey and leggings with boots and a thick layer of dried mud caked all over. She still managed to look fantastic.

"Hi Katie."

"Alright?" Katie grumbled. "Dad, what you gassing on about to Emily? She's Mark's bloody girlfriend, you daft sod."

"Ooh, bleddy hell - said too much then, din't I?" the farmer didn't seem sorry, more amused at this. "See you on Saturday, Bird!"

I beckoned the dogs to follow and headed back up the lane towards the cider farm, feeling thoroughly disappointed that Katie had come between me and answers about the brothers' dysfunctional relationship.

I tried to busy my mind again with more blackberry picking,

this time focusing on the opposite hedge.

Eventually, lost in thought, I became so distracted I barely noticed the herd of sheep that had descended down the lane and entirely blocked my path. I gasped, dropping a handful of blackberries on the floor as the dogs barked and danced amongst the woolly clouds on legs.

What the hell was I supposed to do? As I stood there, contemplating my next, very careful move, they had filtered out to both sides of the lane, meaning I was now stuck in that very spot, edging into the prickly hedge as the occasional woolly coat brushed up against me. Were sheep aggressive? Were they likely to bite or attack me if I dared to move? The dogs continued to bark and jump amongst the sea of wool; they looked like they were having the time of their lives. Meanwhile, panic was rising rapidly in my chest and I realised I was entirely frozen in fear. My rapid breath was quickening, and beads of sweat were forming across my forehead. It was beginning to feel like forever, and by now there had to be nearly a hundred sheep in this tiny, narrow lane with me and the two dogs. So much for them being my protection.

I was beginning to think I would need to resort to screaming for help when somebody from afar was calling my name. A mixture of relief and mortification came over me as I realised who the voice belonged to.

At the top of the lane, Tom was wading his way through the sheep, shooing them casually out of the way. So perhaps they weren't aggressive, I thought bashfully. But this wasn't enough to release me from my frozen stance; and so, I remained as still as a statue, my arms now aching from being held high in the air, as if I was surrendering to my ridiculous situation.

An outburst of laughter escaped Tom's mouth as he spotted me, beckoning the dogs down impatiently as they greeted him with excitement.

"I could hear the dogs barking from the top orchard. I had to come and see what the commotion was," Tom was doubled over in mirth. "Now I know."

"Everything alright?"

Oh great, now I had an audience, I thought, as I heard Steve shouting from the far end of the lane.

"Yeah, it's just Emily, and Pete's sheep from down the way!" Tom shouted over his shoulder, shrugging with laughter.

"Ah, escaped again? I'll give him a call."

"Okay, can you stop being a dick about it now? And help me?" I snapped, catching a squeal in my voice as a sheep gave me an inquisitive sniff.

"They're not going to hurt you. They're bloody sheep!"

"How am I supposed to know if they're harmless? There's a million of them and one of me... and they're huge!"

Tom waded his way through, finally reaching me. "They're not huge. Let's hope you never encounter a herd of cows. Which, for future reference, are harmless as well. Right, come on."

Tom held his hand out, beckoning me to follow him, but I still felt rooted to the spot.

"I promise you; they're not going to do anything. They're too stupid to do anything. They're more interested in eating the hedgerows... and your blackberries."

I squealed once more as Tom pointed out a particularly large black sheep which was eating its way through the bag of blackberries I had been holding. I groaned in protest. "My blackberries!"

Tom chuckled again, grabbing my hand with his large, warm ones. "Never mind. There's plenty of blackberries where they came from. Come on, you'll be fine."

"No, I can't. I can't!"

"A piggyback then," Tom suggested, turning around.

"What? You're kidding!"

"Well I could just throw you over my shoulder if you like. Carried bags of apples heavier than you. Your choice but hurry up and decide. I have apples to pick."

Tom folded his arms across his large chest, faking impatience. He really was a magnificent specimen. A nearby sheep made a loud, low-rumbling noise and I started clambering up Tom's front.

"Bleddy hell, girl. Here we go."

As if I weighed nothing more than a basket of apples, Tom hoisted me into his arms - a much more elegant option that the previous ones - and suddenly I was close enough to feel his breath and take in his beautifully earthy smell. I draped one arm over his shoulder, whilst my other hand rested shyly at the top of Tom's torso. I could feel his eyes on me, but I trained my eyes on my hand which now fiddled with the top button of his shirt.

Tom waded back through with me and eventually we made it to the edge of the sea of sheep. I eased myself down and out of Tom's arms before my heart literally raced its way out of my chest.

"Emily, I -"

"All sorted," Steve called as he approached. "Pete's going to come and get them now. He's fuming. Says his nephew left the gate open after their feed this morning." Standing between us, his hands on his hips, he took in the situation, completely ignorant to the heat bubbling between Tom and me. "Right, cuppa tea?"

Once the sheep fiasco had passed and my heart had stopped palpitating, it continued to be a wonderful day. I decided to help Tom and Steve in the orchard for an hour, making up for their lost apple-picking time to come and rescue me. The late morning sun warmed my back and arms as I reached for the apples, and a gentle breeze cooled me when I got too hot. It was hard, labouring work and I struggled to keep up with the men, but the repetitive nature of the task kept my mind and my heart at ease.

After an hour, Steve's stomach got the better of him, reminding me that I hadn't actually eaten yet, so the three of us headed back up the hill, laughing and chatting, towards Sarah's tearooms where we stopped for a spot of brunch. The tearooms, not surprisingly, was quiet, so she and Karen sat down with us to enjoy a bowl of sweet potato and chestnut soup.

"This is delicious," I groaned, dipping a piece of cheese scone into the thick, paste-like soup. Sarah had suggested sitting outside, sliding her two lonesome patio tables together and bringing out spare chairs from inside. Karen had brought a throw from the house and wrapped it around her legs for warmth, as well as mine. Stifling a contented sigh, I couldn't have felt more at ease right at this very moment. With the views of the farm and its orchards glowing in the sun, the soup warming my insides like a small furnace and the gentle breeze, combing its way through my hair, kept my senses alive. This felt like the perfect advert for country living and I felt that nothing could burst the perfect little bubble I was currently in - until I took myself off to Tom's office to start his paperwork, receiving a call from Mark.

"I've just been on Sarah's Facebook. I see you've been on a real jolly," Mark spat down the phone, his temper radiating through the receiver. I silently vowed to delete Facebook when I got a quiet moment.

"Well, what else do you expect me to do? You're the one who ditched me in the middle of frickin' nowhere!"

"I don't believe this. You've been there less than a week and already you've wriggled your way in as 'Golden Girl!'"

"Sounds to me like somebody is a little jealous," I challenged without thinking, biting my lip afterwards. I started separating Tom's invoices in to piles with my free hand, waiting with bated breath for Mark's response.

"Of course I'm not bloody jealous. Don't be so pathetic! You're just... complicating things!"

"Things were made complicated when you decided to pretend we were together," I reminded him, coolly. I wasn't going to let him win this argument. After my morning walk, the encounter with the local sheep and an afternoon only steps away from being heaven, I was feeling fiery.

"Just stop pretending to be best friends with my family and stay professional!"

"I'm not pretending anything! Your family are lovely, if you would just-"

"I'm warning you, Miller," Mark growled. I snorted, indignant at his attitude. What was his problem? "Things between me and my family are complicated enough as it is without you meddling. I wouldn't expect you to understand anyway."

Suddenly, my blood ran cold, and I gripped my cell so tightly to my ear I thought the screen would crack under the pressure. Placing a pile of receipts back on to Tom's desk, I rose from his chair.

"What the hell is that supposed to mean?" I breathed dangerously.

"Nothing, just-"

"No, what the hell did you mean by that? What, because I don't have a family - I couldn't possibly understand?"

"Emily-"

"No, you're right. I don't have a clue about family complications," I continued, my voice dripping with disdain. "I mean, how dare I enjoy spending time with your family, getting a little glimpse at what it feels like to be around a family like yours. Making the most of being ditched in the middle of a strange place while my boss and supposed friend sabotages any chances of me keeping my job."

"Sabotage? I'm trying to help you keep your-"

"Oh, bullshit Mark! I should be in London right now, rebuilding my reputation in a new workplace. But thanks to you, I'm on a farm. In Cornwall. Pretending to be your girlfriend. All because you can't get your shit together. I've had enough! Mark, if you're not going to help me - or if me and my job are a lost cause - then tell me now so I can stop wasting my time. Because I'm done. Not just with you - all of it."

There was a long pause, the only sounds being the drumming of my heart and heavy breath, pounding loudly inside my ears. I couldn't believe I had spoken to him like that. A little bile was building in the pit of my throat. For the first time, I had stood up for myself, saying all the right things without hesitation. I'd be lying if I said I didn't feel ever so slightly liberated.

"You're right," Mark finally said, his voice small. "You need to be here. I'll book you a train ticket. You can be in London by tomorrow."

I thought about this for a moment. I did need to be in London, for the sake of my job. I should have been relieved at this point that Mark had finally come to his senses. The problem now though wasn't that I needed to be in London. It was that Mark needed to be here, in Cornwall, sorting out everything between him and his family. Perhaps Mark was right - I couldn't possibly understand his situation with his family. But as somebody who grew up without one, then kind of had one for a short period before having it ripped away again, a part of me desperately wanted to see this wonderful, yet broken family make peace and heal the wounds. On top of this, after today I didn't feel I was ready to turn my back on Cornwall yet. In the short time I had been here I had made a true friend out of Sarah, and so I felt I needed to be at the wedding. I wanted to be at the wedding. My relationship with Mark may have been made up, but the growing friendship with Karen and Sarah was real.

And Tom. What was I going to do about Tom?

"Emily? Shall I book the train?" Mark's voice penetrated my frenzied thoughts.

"No," I found myself saying. "No, I can't leave now. Sarah's wedding is tomorrow, and I've got vol-au-vents to fill later. She needs me.

"You're kidding me, right?"

"No. Not at all," I replied confidently, keeping my voice steady. "Now, I can't tell you what you should do. As you pointed out, I couldn't possibly understand your situation. But I can guarantee Sarah needs you tomorrow. She needs her brother to be there on her special day. So... your call."

I hung up and collapsed back into Tom's chair just as my legs went to mush. It was now very uncertain whether I still had a job to return to and whether Mark would ever speak to me again - but despite all of that, I knew I had done the right thing. Perhaps for the first time in my life, I felt like I was actually in the right place at the right time, doing exactly what needed to be done.

Chapter Twenty-One

Tom and Sarah were shoulder to shoulder, hovering over Tom's tablet when Emily came into the kitchen to wash her hands before dinner.

"What are you two up to?" Emily eyed the pair up suspiciously.

"Show her," Tom nudged his sister eagerly, his eyes beaming.

"Okay, well Tom told me about your head condition - thanks for telling me that you were unwell this morning by the way! Anyway, we've found something that might help."

Tom watched nervously as Emily took the tablet from Sarah. "It's a community of people on that Facebook thing. People who have the same condition."

"You sound like an old man when you say that!" Sarah scoffed. "You're thirty-six! Our Uncle Dennis has Facebook!"

"I don't really like the bloody thing," Tom gruffed. "But we thought it might be good for you to get in contact with some of these people... "

"Yeah - and there's a group in Brooklyn apparently which meets once a month as a support network."

"Yeah - well, I'm sure there are support groups here in Cornwall as well," Tom grumbled, altering his face a little too late as Sarah scrutinised him with a frown. They were both very animated at their discovery and waited with bated breath as Emily scrolled through the comments. Tom and Sarah had read through some of them earlier. Some were light-hearted, offering a virtual hand-out to those who might be particularly struggling. Others were more sinister cries for help from those at the mercy of their attacks. Scattered in between these were informative articles giving the latest on the condition. A quick scan through some of these articles had informed Tom that currently there was no cure, there was a substantial amount of research out there and it was known to be one of the most painful conditions on record. This alone made Tom sick to the stomach for poor Emily.

"I can't believe you guys have done this," Emily whispered, her hair framing and hiding the expression on her face. Was she pleased?

"Only took a bit of Googling," Sarah waffled on, taking lead on the navigating, and showing Emily different features on the group page. "It was Tom's idea - he was saying that there must be other people out there suffering from the same thing. So, a quick Google search took me here. I joined the group last night and have been speaking to some bird named Bevel. She's from North Carolina, is part of the admin team, but flies up and joins the Brooklyn meeting occasionally whilst visiting her son. Seems nice... Em?"

Tom and Sarah looked at each other in horror as Emily burst into heavy, ragged sobs.

"Oh no - Em!" Sarah cried.

"You guys are so wonderful... so thoughtful - I can't believe you have both done this!"

"Come here, you Muppet." Relief washing over him and without thinking, Tom wrapped a comforting arm around Emily's shoulders and kissed the top of her head, so naturally that it took a beat for him to realise what he had just done.

There was a moment of pause.

"This really is wonderful. Thank you so much," Emily gushed, going in to hug Sarah who was now narrowing her eyes at Tom over Emily's shoulder. "I'm going to have a quick shower before dinner and send a request to join this group."

Tom braced himself for a quick exit as Emily took herself upstairs, but Sarah was too fast and rounded on him as soon as the kitchen door was shut.

"Jesus Bloody Christ on a bike, Tom! Really? Emily? You stupid twat! I thought you were dead inside when it came to women now. Fuck sake, I'm having a deja vu!"

"Are you finished?" Tom barked back. "I was just comforting her - it's a lot to take in."

"There's comforting and there's sniffing the girl's hair! How long has this been going on?" Sarah was now jabbing Tom's chest, backing him into the kitchen counter despite his 6ft-4 to her 5ft-5.

A million to one clever retorts danced around in Tom's head as he glared at his sister. Except, there was nothing clever about this and he had no ground to stand on.

"I don't have to explain myself," Tom growled, picking his keys up from the table and heading for the door.

"Yes, you do! Mark screwed you over, I get it - but it doesn't give you permission to do the same!"

"Sarah, back off," Tom warned, his temper rising from having Sarah in his face.

"No, you need to talk to me about this! Mark -"

"Mark does not care for Emily!" Tom spat, his temper hitting boiling point. "He treats her like crap, and she deserves better."

"This won't make you feel better about Catherine, Tom." Sarah's anger had subsided slightly, and her eyes drooped in sadness at her brother. "Tom, you can't use Emily to get back at Mark."

"What kind of prick do you take me for, Sarah? Jesus, I don't use women. I'm not that bloke!"

Sarah clapped a hand over her mouth, clearly regretting her flippant comment already.

"No... no, I'm sorry - I didn't mean... "

"The one woman I was with... the one relationship I poured my bloody heart in to... I was the one who got bloody screwed over. Don't I deserve something good to come from all of this?"

"I'm sorry, I'm sorry!" Sarah wrapped her arms around his middle, tears streaming as she apologised over and over again. Tom's breathing slowed and he reluctantly returned Sarah's hug, his limbs stiff from anger.

"Would have thought you and Mum were pleased that I wasn't bloody dead inside with my emotions," Tom muttered brusquely.

"Mum has her suspicions too then?" Sarah leaned back from the hug, one eyebrow raised.

"Yeah... well, you're both nosey and should be bloody detectives. I'm going to go and switch all the machines off in the distillery before you start giving me the third degree."

The machines switched off and the outbuildings locked up for the night, Tom's stress levels went down a notch. They'd made good headway this week, despite everything. The machines would still need to run tomorrow, wedding or no wedding. That reminded him - he needed to message Ricky to remind him to come in for nine tomorrow morning to man the machines.

Tom admired the marquee as he passed it in the yard. His mate Andrew had supplied it and he hadn't counted on it looking as impressive as it did right now, acting as an extension into the barn where Tom would set up in his bar area tomorrow. Still lots to do in the morning.

In his office, he immediately noticed that his desk area was substantially neater and there was a fresh vase of cut Dahlias in the window. A nice feminine touch that hadn't been present in this office for quite some time. Emily had made a start on his paperwork and had even left little messages on Post-its.

How do your employees get paid every month? This is a serious paperwork mountain!

Your receipts are categorised in months now - you're welcome!

You're out of Post-its now. This was your last one. I'm using it to say 'Hi!'

Tom chuckled as he pulled off a couple more Post-its from random places around the office, her decorative handwriting and signature smiley faces making his heart pinch a little. Great, he was getting sentimental.

The last Post-it was on the vase of Dahlias.

Karen let me pick these from her garden. This one is called 'Naomi'. Love the dark red - reminds me of a pom-pom.

He admired Emily's handiwork, the way she had divided everything up and categorised into a simple but efficient system. She may have just saved him hours of work, something that would have taken him three times as long and without the fancy stationary. She had clearly used her own stationary once she'd exhausted his Post-it supplies. He made a mental note to reimburse her.

Back in Karen's kitchen, his poor mother was flitting around the kitchen like a whirlwind, Steve was setting the dinner table and the girls were bringing some of Karen's pre-prepared dishes from the freezers for the wedding food tomorrow. Almost every counter space was taken up by every dish imaginable and bowls of salads could be seen in the utility, taking up whatever counter space was left over. Karen had outdone herself.

"Just to warn you now," Karen said, plonking a pile of cutlery in the middle of the table for Steve. "Mark is on his way back. Emily said he left early this afternoon."

Tom glanced over at Emily who sent a rueful smile back as she followed Sarah back out to the freezers. She didn't seem very happy about Mark's return either. He attempted an encouraging smile back, but it turned out more like a grimace. He was running out of time with her.

"Sarah told me about this support group, Emily," Karen said conversationally on Emily's return, as she carved the chicken. "That sounds very positive."

"Yes, I joined earlier. I've started speaking to a lady called Gillian who lives in Canada. She seems to post quite regularly and says that she's chronic, like me. Bevel - the lady you've been speaking to, Sarah - she's episodic." Emily shook her head in disbelieve as she loosened the foil on the quiches. "I've learnt more about my condition in one hour from this forum than I ever have in a paid session with my neurologist."

"Well, it'll make a world of difference having that sort of support behind you. Well done Tom and Sarah for finding it. Right, come and sit down all of you - I'm dishing up now."

There was a bustle and scrapes of chairs as everybody settled into their places. Tom watched as Steve and Sarah held hands across the table and wished he could do the same with Emily, her delicate little hands enclosed in his. He felt Sarah's appraising eyes on him as he settled into a seat next to Emily and decided at this point, he didn't care.

"What time are your friends coming over?" Karen asked, looking flushed as she finally tucked into her roast dinner. "Do I need to make up extra beds in the house?"

"They're coming for 9pm. Katie just messaged me to confirm."

"My lot are coming over for a similar time," Steve added.

"No, we don't need extra beds. Mum, you've done more than enough. Thank you for everything you've done," Sarah rubbed her mum's forearm in thanks.

"You're welcome m'love. Not that I don't mind you having this little gathering tonight, I'm not sure why you need to have another one. Thought that was what your hen and stag do were for."

Their mum always huffed and puffed like this when she was stressed, so Tom was relieved to see Sarah smile and take Karen's criticism on the chin.

"You're going to be awfully tired tomorrow for the big day," Karen ranted on.

"Karen, it's our wedding week," Steve assured her, kindly. "It's just nice not to be working or passing out on the sofa from a long, tiring day."

"You mean this isn't a normal week at the Trengrouse's?" Emily cried in mock surprise.

"No, we're boring old farts most of the time," Sarah huffed. "Hence why we're making the most of it. You're welcome to join us, Mum."

"No thank you. I'll be having an early night. Margaret's helping me with the last bit of food early tomorrow morning."

"Good old Auntie Margaret."

"Don't you stay up too late with this lot either, Emily. You don't want your head being bad tomorrow for the big day," Karen nagged, pointing her fork towards a nervous looking Emily.

A ripple of belly-laughter erupted from Steve. "You're part of the family now, Em - you're getting it in the neck and all!"

"No, quite right. I'll behave, don't you worry Karen," Emily played along, her tinkering laugh igniting that little flame inside Tom again.

Tom kept quiet through most of this exchange, enjoying this moment at dangerous levels. Emily fitted in so perfectly. Catherine had merely tolerated everyone's company - she'd said so herself.

Tom had lost count the amount of times she'd stormed off from dinner, taking the usual family banter to heart. Family time was strained and soon their relationship was strained as well, as he found himself more and more needing to defend his family from her ill words towards them. How had he got her so wrong?

Tom nearly jumped out of his skin as Emily placed a hand on his leg from under the table.

"Are you alright? You're very quiet," Emily whispered, the others occupied in conversation with each other.

"I'm fine," Tom smiled. "Thank you for sorting my paperwork out by the way."

"You're welcome. I'm not finished yet, but hopefully I'll find some time before I have to go."

A heaviness fell between them and they both exchanged a look of remorse and regret at the departure that was fast approaching.

This couldn't be it.

Chapter Twenty-Two

It was the rarest of moments when Mark Trengrouse genuinely felt guilty for something. This was one of those moments. It was rarer still for Mark to admit aloud when he was wrong. This was not going to be one of those moments.

Mark knew he had stepped over the line the other day - when he had stormed out of Trengrouse Farm, leaving Emily behind. It had become a bit of a habit of his, running away. But the very idea that he hadn't been part of that moment when they scattered his father's ashes made him feel sick to the core. He'd felt like he'd been punched in the gut before the doors to the family circle had slammed tightly shut before him, leaving him to flounder. Then again, had it not been him who had created those doors between him and his family, locked them and thrown away the key? He always felt he'd shut them out of his life, but perhaps instead he had shut himself out of theirs.

To add to his list of blunders, he had some serious damage control to do once he was reunited with Emily. Poor Emily. He should never have left her behind like that, he knew that the moment he'd hit the A30 on the way back to London the day he'd done a runner. But as always, he looked after number one. He was a coward. And he hated himself for that.

Mark was back on the road now. He had spent three pain staking days back in the London office. People questioned the absence of Emily, to which he replied:

"She's offered to stay in Cornwall, to pick up the pieces there."

He thought he at least owed Emily enough to keep her fresh, delicate reputation clean in her new workplace. He didn't want them thinking she was a slacker, like they do back in Manhattan.

The three days in the office were gruelling, involving heated conference calls with his bosses back in the US, pointless interviews with inefficient potential employees, and running through things with a fine tooth-comb only to discover they weren't quite ready for D-day. But those three days in the office were just what Mark needed to get some distance and perspective over what had happened since his return to Cornwall.

He wanted to be at Sarah's wedding, he needed to be there for her to make up for all the times he hadn't been. But it was inevitable that he wasn't going to survive an entire week there, suffocating under the unsaid words and the resentment between him and Tom. It just wasn't going to happen.

Begrudgingly, Mark had agreed with mostly everything Emily had said to him on the phone. He did need to sort things out with his family, once and for all.

Passing the 'Welcome to Cornwall' sign for the second time in the last three years, Mark's nerves began fluttering to the surface, leaving him a little nauseated. He had to face looking into his mother's hurt eyes again, the disappointment that Sarah hadn't even attempted to hide, and eventually he would have to face Tom again. Added to the equation, he would have to face Emily - she was probably still pretty pissed too.

This was going to be a long weekend.

The sun was beginning to set as Mark turned into the long bumpy lane leading down to the farm. A warm red sky glowed through the trees, creating perfect silhouettes.

"Red sky at night, shepherds delight," Mark muttered under his breath, a little relieved that he was alone in the car. It was an expression his mum always repeated on a beautiful red sunset and he felt it his obligation as he drove towards the house to honour his mum's tradition. Mark hoped the old wives' tale had some truth in it.

As soon as the engine was off, reinstating country silence, and Mark was out of the car, he was greeted with his first predator. Sarah thumped him hard several times across the arms, shoulders and chest before ending her fury on one final shove which knocked Mark back a couple of steps.

"Wanker - prick - asshole!" Sarah sobbed, before giving him a quick hug and storming back into the kitchen.

Mark couldn't help but chuckle despite a small drop of fear that he was about to be rugby tackled to the ground in his

Burberry suit.

"Take it I'm forgiven?"

"Don't piss me off anymore, I'm very hungover!"

This was a good sign, at least for his brash little sister. Smiling, he grabbed his bags and made his way inside the house. He dropped his bags at the bottom of the stairs before descending into the kitchen. Scrapes of cutlery on plates told him that he was interrupting dinner.

"Mark, sweetheart," his mum spoke with apology in her voice. "We didn't know what time you were coming home. I've saved you a plate."

Seeing everybody sat around the dinner table like happy families suddenly made Mark feel like an intruder, and he felt an unexplained bitterness rise up from his gut despite his good intentions to be on his best behaviour.

"Not to worry. I'll go upstairs and unpack. Let you guys finish your dinner in peace."

"Don't be ridiculous. You must be tired. Take a seat and I'll put your food in the AGA to warm up."

"No, I'd rather-"

"Mark David Trengrouse. Sit down at once!"

Karen's sudden outburst stopped everybody in their tracks. Mark didn't argue - he knew that voice was saved for when his mother was at the end of her tether. You did not test that tether any further. He did as he was told and reluctantly took a seat next to Steve, opposite Emily, who had been avoiding eye contact since he stepped through the kitchen threshold.

Placing a hot plate of roast chicken in front of Mark a couple of minutes later, Karen broke the silence that she had created.

"We were just discussing usher duties for tomorrow," Karen began conversationally. "Sarah, would you like to update your brother on this?"

"Am I an usher?"

"Yep," Steve said, sourly. "Sarah's request. Not mine."

Mark ignored the last comment. It wasn't necessary; he knew full well it would never have been Steve's request to add Mark as a groomsman.

"You weren't here to get measured properly, so I hope I have the right size," Sarah continued. "But I wanted all groomsmen matching."

"What do you mean?" Mark prompted his sister to be a little more specific.

"Kilt! In the Cornish Hunting tartan because the Cornish National would look stupid with the bridesmaid dresses. Don't huff! You're wearing one. It's family tradition."

"Since when? Just because Dad wore a kilt at -"

Acknowledging the piercing glare Sarah was sending him across the table, Mark backtracked. "I'll wear it, I'll wear it. Of course I will." He was suddenly glad he hadn't mentioned that Tom never wore a kilt for his wedding. But he knew how badly that reminder would go down and was glad he had, for once, kept his mouth shut. He was silently grateful that nobody was interrogating him over his disappearance and that conversations were continuing as if he hadn't just returned from a three-day tantrum.

"So, what are my duties?" Mark prompted, trying to sound interested.

"Before the ceremony, give people a confetti cone and let them choose a side to sit. Then afterwards, help organise everybody for photos. Kelly, our photographer, isn't very authoritative when it comes to organising people. Then help guests find their seats for the main lunch."

"Sounds simple enough. What are you in all of this then?" Mark turned to Tom. He meant it as an attempt to exchange some pleasant words between them, but his voice was far from friendly and only sounded aggressive. He winced a little, waiting for Tom's response.

"Best man, of course," Steve interjected, allowing Tom to return to his roast in a deadly silence. "What else would he be?"

Dinner had been arduous, nothing less and nothing more than Mark had expected. Karen sent Sarah away, giving her a free pass on dishes for the evening, encouraging Emily to go with her and start up a bottle of wine in front of the fire. She also sent Tom and Steve away as they had some final heavy-labour things to do in the marquee and barn ready for tomorrow evening. This left Mark alone in the kitchen with his mum - he was not granted a free pass.

They tackled the dishes together in silence at first. If Mark was a dog, his tail would be retreating further and further in between his legs. Finally, when they were nearly finished clearing the kitchen, he couldn't take the silence any longer.

"Sorry I missed the beginning of dinner. The office is cr-"

"Sweetheart, I need to say something."

Mark looked at his mother, unable to hide the anxiety from his eyes. She never spoke to him like this.

"I think it goes without saying that this week and weekend is a very special moment for your sister. It is her wedding day tomorrow."

"I know that, don't I? That's why I'm-"

"You see, I don't think you do, my darling. You know consciously that tomorrow is your sister's wedding day. But I don't think you fully grasp that tomorrow is going to be one of Sarah's most important days of her life. I think - I hope - she only plans to do it once. So, it's important we make it a good one for her."

Mouth opening and closing like a goldfish, Mark was, for once, rendered speechless and with nothing to say. He struggled to look up at his mother, while Karen stood strongly beside him reading his expression upon her every word. He'd been cleaning the same plate for longer than was necessary now and forced himself out of his temporary trance, placing the clean plate on the draining board.

"You're right-"

"That means, my son," Karen continued. She wasn't done. "You need to put away any conflicting emotions you have that have caused you to be absent for so long. You need to put away your rehearsed office excuses and you need to be 100% there for your little sister. No more being selfish, my darling."

Mark felt numb all over as his mother's painfully true words pierced into him. He absorbed them like tiny needles in his pores and he suddenly felt breathless, tight chested. Tears smarted in his eyes as his mother's, full of years of hurt and grief, looked into his.

"Mum," Mark sobbed, his voice thick from holding back tears. 'I'm sorry', he wanted to say. But it was stuck in his swollen throat, clogging up his tears and making it painful to swallow.

Karen closed the gap between her and her son, hushing him

like he was a distressed baby and held his head to her shoulder, running an affectionate hand through his hair. Mark's tense body melted into the comforting embrace of his mother, something he hadn't experienced in a long time. A shuddering sigh released deep within him, and it was as if a process of healing had begun, and all the toxic energy Mark hadn't realised he'd been containing was making a slow exit out of his rigid body.

"Once Sarah has had her perfect day, this weekend would be a good time to make amends in all the right places. I already forgave you the minute you walked back through that door, and I love you for being so brave. I know it couldn't have been easy."

"Thanks, Mum," Mark sniffed into his mother's shoulder, ignoring the aching pain going through his neck from bending down so awkwardly to his mother's height.

"Final thing. I think you owe an apology to Emily. Poor girl. She's been fine, really helpful in fact. But it might be nice."

At the mention of Emily's name, an urge to begin his cleansing of wrong doings had already begun.

"Mum, about Emily. She's not actually my girlfriend."

"I see. Please explain."

Karen listened calmly and without interruption as Mark explained, from the beginning, why he felt the need to pretend he had a girlfriend and how Emily had been the perfect candidate for the job. Saying it out loud confirmed it - he had feelings for Emily. When he finished, Karen fell into a thoughtful silence. She didn't seem angry or upset - a frown fixed upon her face as if she was trying to work out a difficult maths equation.

"Well, I wouldn't say you've done the best job in wooing her, sweetheart," Karen finally said. A smile twitched in the corner of her mouth. "Poor Emily. What were you thinking? Honestly!"

"I know, I know. One cock up after another," Mark ran a hand through his thick hair. "I am working on getting her a promotion at work though."

"Well you had better get her one then. No doubt she deserves it! She's been invaluable this week just helping us here."

"I'm going to try. But it's not up to me. There are a few things standing in her way from being kept in a job, let alone promoted... that's why I tried to give her a fresh start in London."

"Does this have anything to do with her illness?"

"How do you know about that?" Mark asked.

"She had an attack early this morning. We had to call the ambulance. Poor girl was so upset about the price of her medical bill... "

"I think she's already in debt with her medical bills back in the US," Mark was reminded guiltily.

"I'm not surprised. It's awful! How one person can keep up with such expensive medical charges on such a permanent basis. People have been known to go bankrupt, lose their homes you know? We're so lucky to have the NHS."

Mark suddenly felt a fresh new wave of remorse. He had never thought about the struggles Emily must go through daily to keep up with her bills and medication. How short-sighted he had been.

"How much did the bill come to?"

"We managed to knock some money off by cancelling the oxygen. Tom picked some up from Nigel - you remember Nigel - so in total it was... £380. I've put it on my credit card for now - the poor girl was so distraught over it."

"I'll pay for it. I'll transfer the money now," Mark whipped his phone out. This seemed to be the only way he felt useful right now.

"Well, I'm sure she'll appreciate it. I think you need to have a good long chat with her. Sounds like she's burying her head in some very deep sand. You might not be her partner, but you can be a good friend at least."

Mark left his mum's kitchen feeling a little lighter. She had promised not to say anything about his and Emily's fake relationship but had urged him to tell the truth sooner rather later. In exchange, Mark had promised to be nothing but the perfect brother on his little sister's big day and to patch things up where they needed patching. This, of course, involved a conversation with Tom which he wished he could avoid at all costs, but he couldn't. No longer.

A mixture of surprise, hostility and anger flashed across Tom's face a few moments later when he opened the cottage door to his anxious brother. Mark's hands were sweaty despite the cold evening chill in the air, and he suddenly felt very nervous and unprepared.

"May I come in?" Mark asked in his politest voice, doing his absolute best to leave out any hostility. Tom didn't reply, nor did he show any signs of opening his front door to let Mark in. "Please. There are some things I need to say, and I think it's best to get them said tonight before Sarah's big day tomorrow."

Perhaps the thought of it being for Sarah's sake sold it for Tom. Reluctantly and silently he stepped to one side and gave the smallest of gaps for Mark to edge inside.

Mark had never been inside Tom's cottage since he had renovated it from its derelict state. He admitted reluctantly and silently that Tom had done a fantastic job. Given that he hated rural interior, even Mark had to admit he wouldn't quarrel at living in these surroundings. The kitchen was handcrafted and with solid oak worktops, the walls of the living space white-washed but still resembling the misshaped curves of the original stonework. A 60" flat screen TV, perhaps the only thing Mark could fully relate to as an essential in a man's bachelor pad, was mounted impressively, taking up most of the back-wall space. A small wood burner sat in the corner and was currently roaring with life, making the small living area cosy and warm. French doors led out into the garden and a spiral staircase gave access to upstairs.

In his quick glance around Tom's living room, he had almost missed Steve sitting on the armchair nearest the wood burner, cider in hand.

"I'll go and get some more drinks," Steve excused himself.

"Make it quick," Tom began, when Steve had closed the front door behind him. "I need to be up early tomorrow to sort out last minute snags in the barn."

This was probably the most words Tom had uttered to Mark in three years. Mark had already accepted that Tom wasn't going to make this easy. He took a deep breath and got straight on with it.

The conversation had started reasonably well, with Tom waiting patiently for Mark to stumble his way through a speech he probably should have rehearsed before hand - like a pitch to his clients back at the office. As the discussion progressed, however, words became more tangled and chosen more brashly. A seated discussion around the breakfast table became a stand-off in Tom's living room, eventually making its way out into the yard when Tom had attempted to chuck Mark out of his property. Mark was having none of it - he needed to finish what he had left to say.

"You've always been the favourite. I've always felt like I'm competing against you for their love, their approval," Mark continued, dramatically. East Enders had nothing on this right now.

"That is hugely unfair to say," Tom snarled, jabbing the air towards Mark. "Mum and Dad always showed that they loved you. Dad loved you. Mum still loves you! It's you that's always thrown it back in their faces!"

"I will never doubt that they loved me. But proud of me? No, not like they were of you."

"Oh, please," Tom began to walk away.

"It's true. Don't forget," Mark advanced on Tom once again, "I was the son who turned my back on the family business. I was the 'stupid' one who wanted to do something different. When Dad was ill, all I kept hearing was, 'we are so lucky to have you, Tom. Thank goodness we have you to pick up all the pieces, Tom. We're so grateful of you, Tom.' What do I get? 'Mark, must you keep disappearing off to London? Your family needs you here. Mark, I don't see what is so important about your job in London that would stop you from being here. To help your dad. Like Tom is.'"

"Dad was dying, Mark. You were never here."

"IT WAS MY JOB! I worked for a big corporate firm, I could hardly pop down to Cornwall."

"How can we forget about your big corporate job, in a fancy office-"

"There was only so much compassionate leave I was able to take. I wasn't self-employed like you," Mark thundered over Tom's words, not allowing himself to be interrupted.

"Oh yeah, and I could just take all the time off I needed," Tom spat sarcastically. "Compassionate leave? Sick pay? What's that?"

"That's not what I mean! God, you're making this impossible!"

There was a pause. The heavy breaths of the two brothers, as they stood yards apart from each other, lumbering over the silence of the late evening, as if it was waiting with bated breath at the unspoken words yet to come.

"I've always felt like a failure. In Dad's eyes especially. No matter how hard I tried, I wasn't a natural countryman. I was like a fish out of water. Mum and Dad never understood why I wanted a job in a 'fancy office' as you call it. Do you know, when I told Dad that I had received a place at university to study business he asked me, 'what do you want to go and do that for?' And when I told Mum, all she kept worrying about was who was going to help you around the farm."

Something shifted in Tom and he was suddenly very still, like Mark's words were seeping in.

"-and when I graduated, there was no 'well done Mark'. I don't think you even breathed any form of a congratulations my way. And that job in London? My first job as an associate consultant... it was only a huge inconvenience to the family because it was so far away, and I wouldn't be here to support the farm. Selfish, inconsiderate Mark. Following his dreams at the expense of his family."

For the first time, Tom looked at Mark directly in the eyes. He didn't argue, he didn't snarl. He just looked at him. Mark almost thought he saw remorse cross his face. In Tom's silence, Mark decided to continue.

"You have every right to hate me," Mark's soft voice broke as tears threatened and a painful lump formed in the back of his throat. "And I never expect you to forgive me. What I did...trust me, there is nothing you can say that can make me feel more guilty - more ridiculously stupid - than I already do. But with it, I carry resentment."

A light flicked on somewhere upstairs back in the house and Mark felt like he was out of steam. Tom continued to stand silently in the yard, the moonlight shining across his face as he battled with a mixture of emotions. The anger, though still there, seemed to be dominated by some other emotion that softened and yet aged his features.

"I see now that it was a mistake coming back here. I'm still that fish out of water." Mark started to back away, making his way towards the house. "All I can say is, I'm sorry for all the hurt I have caused you, brother. I'm sorry."

Before Tom could respond, Mark had reached the front door and closed it behind him, feeling as if every weight he had borne on his shoulders for the past three years had just doubled over night. He'd been foolish to think he could make amends with Tom after all these years of hurt and resentment. Years of unspoken words, finally out in the open, cutting into both brothers like hot knives, leaving irreparable wounds. Mark's searing anger shifted over to the day he'd met Catherine, the day she'd first made him feel special, the day they'd first started the affair, tiptoeing around his brother as if it was a thrilling game. Mark then recalled the pain he felt the day Catherine left him for Jack and ran to the utility toilet to vomit up his raging guilt.

What a despicable brother he was.

Chapter Twenty-Three

"Are you kidding me?" Sarah fumed. "Are you having a bloody laugh? On the night before my wedding and all!"

Sarah and I had been huddled under the curtains of Karen's living room window, looking out to the yard where Tom and Mark had just finished their shouting match. Mark had stormed back into the house and eventually Tom retreated back into his property, Steve following close behind with a crate of ciders. It had been horrible to watch, with Sarah getting more and more distressed beside me, cussing, and muttering under her breath. It wasn't always possible to make out the words being said between them, but the parts I had heard only strengthened my need to know - what exactly had happened between them for there to be so much hate?

Growling, Sarah fought her way out of the tangle of curtains, poked the fire in frustration, and drained the contents of the wine bottle into her glass.

"Those two! Honestly!" Sarah downed her wine in one. "It's my wedding tomorrow. Can't they just pretend to get on? Is it really that hard to just shut up and plaster a fake smile? I'm sure Mark does it in work every day!"

I winced at how accurate Mark's anguish was about his family's attitude towards his job. He had literally just been saying it in the yard to Tom, that part she did hear.

"Don't get me wrong - I'm so unbelievably relieved that Mark braved it back down," Sarah ranted, now helping herself to my untouched glass of wine. "I didn't think he would actually. But I swear, if those two make a scene at my wedding tomorrow I'm going to throttle them both to the next century!"

I smiled sympathetically, lost for words to comfort Sarah. I was silently grateful that Sarah's friends were on their way over - even if that did include Katie. I really wasn't good at this.

I battled in my head for a moment as to whether I should ask Sarah again to explain what had happened between them. Mark was clearly feeling guilty for something - guilty enough to actually apologise. I'd known Mark long enough to know that apologising and admitting he was in the wrong didn't come easy for him. Would I be crossing the line to interrogate Sarah for a second time? Before I could make a decision however, Sarah had made it for me.

"This is all over one bloody girl, you know?"

"It is?" I took a seat next to Sarah on the sofa.

Sarah nodded. "Yep. Tom's wife."

My heart pinched and lurched forward into my rib cage, up into my throat. Tom was married?

"Her name was Catherine. Well, is Catherine. She isn't dead, or anything. Although, she would be if I had my way - little bitch. Anyway - her and Tom were only married for about a year, but they'd been together for over three. To be honest, I was never that keen. She expected a lot out of Tom and threw the most horrific tantrums if she didn't get what she wanted. But Tom loved her for some unknown reason, so I had to keep my mouth shut. Of course, we were all a bit blind to Mark's infatuation towards her, so you can imagine the shock we all had when he ran off with her to America to start a new life together."

My chest, already tight from the news of Tom's previous marriage, suddenly felt so restricted it was hard to breath and my mouth fell open in shock to what I was hearing. I'd met Catherine. I'd seen the state Mark was left in when she'd run off with Jack from upstairs. I saw all the women that came and went as a result of a broken heart - I, too, had allowed myself to be a comfort rebound, mainly to satisfy my own loneliness.

God, I felt so stupid.

"Poor Tom," I found myself muttering, bringing my arms around myself, suddenly feeling cold.

"Oh Emily, it was bloody awful," Sarah went on. "The divorce had to be done over the phone. Tom locked himself away for months, only coming out to do his duties on the farm, not saying a word to anybody. Mum didn't stop crying for months. She'd lost Dad, her youngest son and mentally she'd lost her eldest son because he wouldn't talk to anybody. It was shit. Shittedy-shit-shit-shit!"

There was a heavy, elongated pause. Sarah drank some more wine. I stared into the fire as it crackled away, absorbing what I had heard.

"It was about a year until I started talking to Mark again. Managed to finally get some replies on Facebook and eventually we would have the occasional phone conversation. Took me longer again to convince him to have a conversation with Mum. I think, secretly, he was so ashamed of what he had done that he couldn't face talking to us. But when Catherine fucked off and moved on to her next victim - slut! - he became lonely and reached out to us. Never agreed to come back and visit us though. You must have done wonders to him, getting him back here for my wedding."

"Me? No, it had nothing to do-"

"Don't be daft. He's still a selfish prick of a brother, but you got him this far. You actually got him to cross that Cornish border. That's huge!"

I didn't reply. I refused to show any signs of agreeing or accepting to it for fear of being an even bigger fraud than I already was. It had nothing to do with me that Mark was here. Sure, my status on Facebook had set off a few sparks. But that didn't make me responsible for it all. I wasn't sure now whether I was glad that I finally knew the truth behind the brothers' quarrels. Right now, my heart was heavy for all of them. Poor Tom. Poor, stupid Mark. Poor Trengrouses. It seemed that everybody in this family were broken, in their own ways.

A new concern rose within me like bile. With all the fraternising between me and Tom in Mark's absence, was I any better? Surely my being here, the unstable foundations in which I was forming relationships with these people, was only going to add to the deceit that these poor people had been exposed to.

"You've done wonders to Tom as well, since you arrived."

Every inch of me froze, giving me away. It's as if she was echoing my concerns. I tried to recover, helping myself to a handful of roasted peanuts that Sarah had put out on the coffee table.

"Oh, yeah?" I squeaked, trying and failing to sound nonchalant.

"I don't think I've seen him so much in one week since the divorce. He'll always make an effort to have dinner with us all, but most of the time he just locks himself away in the cottage. If I didn't know any better, I'd say he likes you. Like - likes you, likes you."

"You and Steve have a wonderful relationship," I suddenly found myself saying, as a way of distraction. I felt sorry for Steve in a way, sitting under the radar of drama and only seeming to be there to pick up the pieces, never involved in shedding them.

"He's my rock," Sarah said dreamily. This made her smile.

"Sarah, there's something I need to be straight with you about-"

A car pulled up in the yard, the headlights flooding through the curtains and wiping out any chances of me continuing my confession. Now was not the time. Now was all about Sarah.

"Right, the girls are here," I grabbed the second bottle of wine and topped Sarah's glass up yet again. "This is the night before your wedding. No more bullshit family crap. Forget your stupid brothers and enjoy your evening. Why are you giggling?"

"I've never heard you swear before!"

"Well I don't do it very often, so this must mean I'm very passionate about you having an awesome night. Come on, get off your fanny and let's take this party into your place."

Sarah giggled and allowed herself to be pushed out of the door with her wine, laughing at the word 'fanny', pointing out unnecessarily that it didn't mean 'butt' in the UK. I rolled my eyes - this was going to be another long night.

With me not drinking, and an abundance of alcohol being consumed by the roisterer bride and her bridesmaids, the evening soon felt like babysitting duty. It turned out these girls were even more loud and troublesome in the safety of Sarah's home, but with their share of comical moments. Later in the evening, Sarah insisted on cooking everybody pancakes to which I was forced to intervene and finish cooking the pancakes for her, before anymore ended up on the ceiling. Once pancakes were consumed, a roaring game of Gin Pong was underway - Sarah's invention, apparently. The game became so rowdy that Steve came knocking on the door asking if he and his mates could join in. Of course, Sarah took the childish approach and launched herself behind the sofa, shouting at Steve for nearly jinxing them.

"The groom can't see the bride the night before the wedding, you goon!"

By 11pm, I was exhausted and took myself out onto Sarah's little patio with a cup of tea. It was a beautiful clear night, the full moon illuminating the garden beyond the patio. Insects chirped away in nearby bushes and a barn owl hooted somewhere in one of the nearby trees. There was a slight chill in the air, but with my hands clasped around my warm cup of tea and my cardigan wrapped around me tightly, I felt quite contented to just sit back in my chair to soak in the peace.

It was mostly quiet in Sarah's now, with the girls lying dormant for the night under duvets and watching chick flicks. Next door, in Tom's place, only the low rumble of male voices could be heard. It sounded to me as if a game of cards was underway.

I took my moment of solitude to digest what I had found out about the Trengrouse brothers this evening. The slight familiarity of this story was still bothering me.

The brothers had fallen out over one girl. Was I now the new Catherine? Was I now coming between the brothers and making it even more impossible for them to make amends? I still hadn't spoken to Mark alone since he'd returned and probably wouldn't now until tomorrow. What was I going to say to him? Did I still have the right to be angry at him for abandoning me in Cornwall? Or had I given up that right when I had allowed myself to fall for Tom? I should tell Mark everything, but the thought of telling him what had gone on between me and Tom terrified me to no end - especially with what I now knew.

Then a new fear came to me. If exposed to the truth, what would Sarah think of me? I had found a real friend in Sarah. A friendship I could see lasting a lifetime. I was sure Sarah would never forgive me if she found out that I too had wedged myself between the brothers, just like Catherine had. Well perhaps not quite like Catherine. There wasn't a marital status involved in this version of the story.

I sipped my tea in deep thought, nearly falling off my chair as a voice called out to me from the darkness.

"Emily?"

"Shit!" I gasped for air as my heart felt like it jumped into my throat, hot tea spilling into my lap. It was Tom, and he was chuckling to himself.

"I've never heard you swear before!" Tom chortled from the other side of the wall. He had taken himself out onto his own patio, perhaps with the same idea as me.

"You're the second person to say that to me this evening. I do swear when it's necessary," I replied, indignant, wiping myself down from tea spillage, my crotch burning from the hot liquid.

"Sorry, didn't mean to startle you. What are you doing out here on your own?"

"Getting some peace and quiet from those party girls in there. They're exhausting. You?"

"The same. My place has turned into a social club. One of Steve's numpty friends brought a dartboard with him. Going to have to fill in the holes and repaint my wall - those guys can't aim for shit."

"They'll all be sore in the morning. Not sure I'd want a hangover the morning of my wedding."

"It's not a good idea. I can vouch for that," Tom cleared his throat after that. I didn't reply, remembering that I wasn't supposed to know about his failed marriage. "Do you fancy going for a walk?"

"What, now?"

"Yeah, now. It's a beautiful evening and no need for a torch. The moon is huge tonight." Tom leaned on the wall, waiting for me to reply. Even in the moonlight, and in a dark T-shirt, his muscles were defined and inviting.

"I don't - I don't know," I stuttered lamely. "The girls are going to wonder where I am. I've already been out here for a while."

"A tenner says they're all passed out from too much wine. Come on, we won't be gone for long."

Biting my lip and considering the many reasons why going on this walk was a bad idea, I nodded in agreement anyway, not wanting to be rude. I also didn't want to let on that my perspective on things between Tom and Mark had changed drastically in the last four to five hours.

We were halfway up the long lawn that led from the two patios before the path steered them into Karen's walled garden. The silhouette of a sundial sat in the middle of a perfectly formatted garden; the flower beds sectioned off symmetrically to form a sort of geometric shape. The garden was enclosed in four high red-bricked walls, with arched entrances on each side. Tom and I had come in through the top entrance, in front of us Karen's house was in complete darkness. I felt a rush of guilt as I thought of Mark in one of those top bedroom windows, segregated from both parties with no chance of an invite. My thoughts with Mark, I didn't mean to be quite as startled as Tom enclosed my hand in his.

"What are you doing?" I demanded, my immediate reaction to try to rip my hand out of his grip.

"Holding your hand," Tom replied, not letting go, though his voice sounded a little doubtful. "Emily, there's something I need to tell you. I'm going to take a wild guess and say that you don't know the reasons why Mark and I can't stand to be around each other. The reason I need to tell you is because I don't want to be like Mark and pursue you while you're still with him."

Oh no. Suddenly everyone was all for the truth. Tom was about to tell me the secret. But if he told me his secret, surely I would have to tell him mine. I really wasn't prepared for this.

"About three and a half years ago, Mark ran off with my wife. Her name was Catherine," Tom began. "We'd been together for three years and Mark... "

Tom paused, analysing my excruciatingly forced reaction. I shifted on my feet uncomfortably, suddenly unsure where to look.

"You already know, don't you?" Tom's shoulders deflated.

"I do. I'm really sorry. Sarah and I heard you and Mark arguing in the yard earlier, and in her drunken state she told me. Please don't be angry with Sarah though."

"I'm not angry," Tom's hands retreated into his pockets. "A little relieved that you know already. Means I don't have to retell it."

"It must have been awful," I spoke softly, wanting to close the gap between us.

"It was," Tom replied gruffly. "I'm learning to come to terms with it. One day I may even forgive my brother, but in my own time. I don't want to be like Mark. I've already taken things too far. But there's something about you Emily. I can't shake the feeling that you're just with the wrong man."

Unable to breath, my first reaction was to take a step back, my second was to fold my arms around myself to form a barrier. I felt so caught up in this web of lies, I didn't know which way to turn next. How could I answer for myself, make the decision that was best for me whilst upholding the lies I was tied to? Well, that was just it. What was best for me was and had never been an option.

"Tom, I-"

"The relationship you and Mark have - it's not what you deserve. I mean, if I didn't know any better, I'd say you weren't together at all. There's nothing there, from either of you."

"Tom-"

"Do you love him?"

How could I answer that without giving Tom a seed of hope? My head was spinning from considering every aspect and impact of my answers.

"Do you love him?" Tom asked again.

"No," I answered truthfully. Of course I didn't love him. Did I used to have feelings for him? Very much so - we'd worked closely together for three years now. Did those feelings still exist? In a way. More or less. But Tom was asking if I loved Mark. I could only answer truthfully.

"Then why stay with him?"

I remained silent, afraid of the damage I could do if I opened my mouth again. The evening chill pierced through my cardigan and I wrapped my arms tighter around me, willing this conversation to end. Tom released a defeated sigh.

"Sorry. Come on, let's get back. You're cold and I've upset you," Tom said, an apology in his voice.

A million to one things that I wanted to say sat on the edge of my tongue, but I bit down.

Tom and I returned to the divided patio doors of both cottages. The lights from Sarah's TV still flickered through the curtains, but there was very little life inside which told me that the girls had indeed passed out.

"Think about what I said, won't you?" Tom asked, standing over me in a way that made my knees buckle.

"I will."

Tom kissed me on the cheek, the roughness of his beard tickling my skin as I breathed in his scent. As soon as he jumped the wall, returning to his own deflating party, I longed for his return. Emotions were so confusing.

Once back inside, I'd allowed myself to believe that my absence had gone unnoticed. How wrong I was when I found Katie standing in the kitchen, wide awake and pouring herself a hot drink, looking extremely gleeful.

"Well, well," Katie leaned on the counter, grinning as I stood frozen to the spot. "You've been a naughty girl, haven't you?"

"What do you mean?"

"I mean, sneaking around in the night with the wrong brother. You realise you had the wrong brother, right?"

"Tom and I were just talking," I grumbled, locking the patio doors and grabbing my phone to leave the room. "I think you've got the wrong end of the stick."

"I don't think I do. I saw Tom kiss you goodnight."

"Can you keep it down?" I hissed. I looked over at the slumbering bodies of Sarah, Heidi and Toni. Sarah's mouth was wide open, confirming that she was in a deep, drunken sleep. "I suppose you're going to run off to Mark now and tell him what you saw."

"What makes you think that?"

"Because, for some reason, you've got a problem with me. You've shown nothing but hostility towards me since we met, and because, by the looks of your face, you'd take great pleasure in screwing me over."

Katie's smile faltered a little at my uncharacteristic aggression, but I continued, now tired of everything.

"I'm dealing with a lot of crap here, okay?" My whispers were fierce as I jabbed my finger at the air between us. "It's not what it looks like - at least, it's not completely what it looks like. I didn't ask for any of this, but I'm dealing with it, okay?"

Again, Katie looked surprised and her face no longer looked smug, but creased in a frown.

"Alright, I get it. I won't say anything. Just as long as you're dealing with it."

"Th... thank you," I was equally surprised at Katie's back step.

"Don't take it personally by the way. I don't like most girls when I first meet them."

"Okay. Noted."

"I also generally care about the Trengrouse lot. My family and their family are very close. They've been through a lot and I didn't trust you."

I nodded with understanding.

"You and Mark aren't actually a couple, are you?" Katie blurted out, as if the idea had just come to her.

I groaned and buried my face into my hands, utterly defeated. "Is it that obvious?"

"Mate, it's worse than watching First Dates. If you are a couple, you're a highly dysfunctional one. I've known Mark for a long time. He's much more passionate with his girlfriends. No offence."

"Well, there you go. Truth is out. Just give me a chance to speak to everybody myself first. Please?"

"Alright, keep your hair on. I won't say anything," Katie chuckled as she stirred some sugar into her mug. "Bleddy hell, and there was me thinking you were a boring old prude. Turns out you are far more interesting than you let on. You want a cuppa?"

"No thanks," I replied, scrunching my nose up at Katie's backward compliment, but accepting it all the same. "I'm exhausted. I'm going to get ready for bed and go to sleep. Think I'll take Sarah's bed as you're all camping out down here. Not a word?"

Katie held her hands up in mock surrender. "Not a whisper!"

Katie and I said our good nights, hostility surprisingly reduced from our strange conversation. It had been an odd evening. Secrets had emerged out of their dark hiding places and it was inevitable that tomorrow more would rear their ugly heads to put things right. I wasn't sure just how strongly I felt for Tom. Strong enough to face Mark tomorrow and tell him everything? Tom didn't quite know the relationship between Mark and I, but he was still right. I needed to cut those confusing ties between us. If not for Tom, then for myself. It wasn't just Mark. I had always allowed myself to be tangled and suffocated and perhaps this week had shown me that enough was enough.

I prayed that I would sleep well tonight, and that the Beast stayed far, far away. I was going to need every ounce of energy for tomorrow.

The Wedding

Chapter Twenty-Four

Sarah

When a bride wakes on the morning of her wedding, she expects to feel glamorous, royal, and utterly radiant. It's safe to say this was the opposite for Sarah Trengrouse. Horribly hungover, her face peeling off the pillow from the dried saliva, she was anything but glamorous. Why, oh why, had she drunk so much the night before her wedding?

"Morning!" Her annoyingly chirpy bridesmaids sang from the breakfast table.

"Bugger off," Sarah groaned, burying her head under her duvet. The sun was beaming through her patio curtains, which was a good thing really - for her wedding day.

"Get up you lazy shit!" Toni chuckled. "Emily made us waffles - proper American style!"

"Well, not sure if they're 'proper American style'," Emily added, modestly. "But made by an American, yes."

"Well, they're bloody good," Heidi scoffed through a mouthful.

So far, the female members of the wedding were doing a great job at being delicate and lady-like. She had to admit, the waffles smelled amazing, even with her iffy stomach. Forcing herself up, she indulged in her waffle breakfast and a large glass of champagne.

"Best cure for a hangover - more alcohol," Katie had advised, unwisely.

After a less-than-healthy start to her big day, Sarah spent the next hour soaking in her mum's roll-top bath. This was a huge luxury as her mum, not usually a possessive woman, was particularly overprotective about her ensuite.

The morning flew by and it wasn't long until Sarah's hairdresser arrived to beautify all of them - including Emily.

"I want you to feel glamorous as well," Sarah insisted, when Emily fussed over the cost. "If only I'd met you sooner, you would have been in one of those bridesmaid dresses as well."

Emily had waved her off as if she was crazy, but Sarah spoke the truth. Emily seemed to fit the mould of the family so effortlessly that it made Sarah wish she <u>had</u> met her sooner. If only her daft brother had got his arse in gear. She had found a real friend in Emily.

Sarah wasn't the kind of person to get gushy. Nor to consider herself blessed or anything like that. But something about the day of your wedding, seeing your loved ones contribute to your wedding in their own special way, even made her a bit sentimental. From her bedroom window she could see Tom, her dear brother, slaving away in the barn next to the distillery. As promised, he had decked the marquee with strings of lights, dotted a couple of half barrel fire pits around for the evening, and was now hanging the last of her bunting which she had painstakingly made out of hessian for that vintage country-look. It was one thing she had really enjoyed when planning this wedding - getting creative and finding ways of making her expensive taste stretch further in her small budget. Many things that would be featured today had been hand-made either by herself, her mother or Tom. Poor Tom. Like he didn't have enough to do.

Even though there would be a large hog arriving that morning from a local pig farm, Sarah knew that her mum's expertise in the kitchen, and her skills in creating a feast fit for a king, would overshadow anything else.

There was one sight however that had really choked her up. No, it wasn't the sight of her soon-to-be husband pacing the yard, clearly practising his speech - though that did have her smiling. It was the sight of her other brother Mark, with his sleeves rolled up, carrying chairs from the tearooms to the distillery. Mark - who practically lived and slept in a suit - was dressed down to smart trousers and a shirt. He had his sleeves rolled up and was doing what would be considered in Mark's eyes as heavy labour. This was enough to bring a lump to Sarah's throat, because deep down she knew this meant he cared. It surprised her how peacefully Tom and Mark appeared to be working together. Granted, from where she stood, they were only passing chairs between one another, and very little words were probably being exchanged - but hell! It was progress, and she couldn't be more grateful of her brothers.

Tom

Something Tom had promised himself he would never do was to forgive Mark. And though it was not forgiveness that fell between him and his brother, perhaps understanding took its place.

He had to hand it to Mark. Last night they had hollered and shouted at one another, an argument loud enough and ferocious enough to send Mark back on the road again, sulking his way back to the nearest city. But not this time. The stubborn git had even come to see him early that morning, hands in the air like he was surrendering to a relentless battle, offering a hand with all the things that still needed doing. It had taken Tom by surprise, mainly because Mark never usually lifted a finger towards manual labour. But Tom was tired of being a dick about it all - so he accepted. And to be fair to Mark, he worked like a Trojan all morning.

"Right," Tom spoke up at midday. The pig farmer had arrived with the roast hog, setting up in the marquee. "Mark, you go and get ready now. Guests start arriving at one and you'll need to be around to show people where to park. Don't, for god sake, let people park along the hedgerow at the bottom. It's always waterlogged down there."

"Okay," Mark panted, setting down a table he had carried from the tearooms. He was definitely not used to this, Tom thought. "Got to say, this is a better workout than the gym."

"A whole lot cheaper as well, I expect," Tom replied, immediately annoying himself with his sarcasm. Sometimes he just sounded like a complete prick.

Mark made a small noise in agreement, gave out a final

hoofing pant, then made his way back to the house, declaring that he was now craving a hot shower to 'de-stink'. Tom chuckled reluctantly. It was becoming harder and harder to hate him. Perhaps this was because, and no matter how hard he tried to deny it, he now felt like the biggest hypocrite with his growing feelings for Emily. This wouldn't do. He'd need to come clean. He needed to remain the bigger person here.

Karen

A strange mix of emotions trickled through Karen like a gentle current, a few of the more dominant emotions coming in waves. One of the many days she had been dreading, since the death of Roy, was finally here. A day she should have been getting ready for with Roy by her side, asking her to fix his tie or put on his cufflinks, because he was always so useless at dressing up. Instead, she pulled on her dress, and fixed what little makeup she could bring herself to wear, in between deep heaves of unsteady breath. On top of everything she was feeling, little jolts of panic would ripple through her every time she thought she had forgotten something vital in her preparations for the food. Seconds later she would realise the thing she thought she had forgotten was indeed sorted, and she would go back to her disorientating battle with her emotions. Really, it was exhausting. She would be worn out before the wedding had even started.

Karen had caught a glimpse of her daughter in between transporting food to the tearooms that morning, and she looked absolutely radiant. Sarah and her band of bridesmaids had commandeered Karen's living room, along with the hairdresser and make-up artist that they had hired for the morning. Karen had smiled at the busy, excited sounds that came from the room, and couldn't resist taking a peek at her daughter, the beautiful bride. A simple pearl grip fastened her veil to her perfectly pinned hair, which flowed down in soft, golden ringlets. Her makeup was so naturally done that it was just enough to accentuate her beauty, rather than hide it. Sarah had always been tall, and squarely built - and she had always been more interested in suiting the jeans and t-shirt look than anything else. But today, she wore a vintage-style dress, with a lace Sabrina neckline, so well that it would have made Audrey Hepburn look drab. Karen beamed with pride as Sarah practically radiated with goddess beauty.

Karen wondered if Roy's absence would be playing on her daughter's mind this morning. Whether she felt robbed of the father-daughter wedding traditions she would not be able to uphold. She hoped that her father did, at least, cross Sarah's mind enough for him to be part of the day, but not at the expense of her happiness.

"Karen!" Margaret shrieked as she marched through the kitchen door. She'd caught Karen making unnecessary final adjustments to some of the desserts, breaking her train of thought. "What did I say? You should finish getting ready, spend a little time with Sarah before she heads down the aisle. I'll deal with the last of these dishes. Go on! Shoo, shoo!" Karen had heard her sister-in-law loud and clear, but she didn't do as she was told. Instead she continued to titivate with the positioning of the raspberries on her Pavlova.

"This was Roy's favourite dessert, you know?" Karen sighed. "He was never fond of cake, so I always made him a birthday Pavlova."

"I remember," Margaret soothed, her voice notched down many pegs as she sensed the change in mood. "Roy had always had a raging sweet tooth, even when we were children. I'd adopted the savoury tooth like Dad, and him and Mum the sweet tooth. Seems slightly mixed up, doesn't it?"

"Do you remember - the night of Roy's 40th - he'd raided the fridge after a few too many with Gerald and scoffed the entire Pavlova I had made for his party?! He was so poorly."

"Daft sod!" Margaret hooted.

"Oh, Margaret. I miss him dearly."

"I know. So do I."

"I don't know what I'd do without you here to get me through it all."

"Oh, sis. Don't get all sentimental on me now. We'll ruin our makeup," Margaret dabbed at the corner of her eye and cleared her throat. "Now, let's give that dear Sarah of ours the day she deserves. Roy is looking down at us, smiling proudly, and probably tutting at the state of the front lawn - I told Gerald to put the grass box on."

Karen chortled, the looming tears keeping at bay for now. "That's okay. It was one less job for poor Tom to do. Now, let's get the rest of these desserts down to the barn."

Emily

I looked at myself in the mirror. It had been a long time since I had felt pretty or even reasonably well-presented. My illness had robbed me of that feeling, and my exhaustion and forced lifestyle had taken a toll on my skin, my body, and my hair. But today, I could quietly admit to myself that I looked and felt pretty. Not beautiful. I would never be able to feel that, but I could confidently use the word 'pretty' for today.

Looking back at myself, that long-lost twinkle in my eye, my mousy-brown hair once flat and dull bounced with life, curled into soft waves which fell elegantly over my shoulder. I hardly recognised myself as I turned my head left and right, taking the transformation in. Toni had insisted on doing my makeup and I was now glad that she had, despite my reservations, as she had done it so naturally that it only highlighted my eyes and my high cheekbones. And a week at the Trengrouse's, living on Karen's cooking, had already added some healthy pounds to my emaciated waistline, my hipbones no longer protruding. Instead my skinny frame had a slight softness to it, the cream chiffon dress that Mark had bought me in London as a quick purchase for the wedding clinging to me in all the right places. My skin was still pale, almost translucent, but that wasn't going to be cured in a week - though the Cornish sun had certainly improved my complexion and had put a bit of colour into my cheeks.

"You look... beautiful," Mark exclaimed, creeping into my bedroom. Was Mark Trengrouse nervous? He was wearing his Cornish kilt - on Sarah's orders - but it was clear he was extremely uncomfortable about the idea, unable to hide behind the power of his usual city suits.

"Thanks," I didn't look at Mark, but instead started fussing over the clasp of my bracelet.

"On a scale of one to ten, how pissed are you at me?" Mark edged towards me. It infuriated me that he was trying to be cute, trying to lighten up the mood between us. I looked up and attempted my best scowl before returning to my clasp. "Okay, so eleven? Look, Emily - I'm sorry."

"Forget it, boss. No harm done - in fact, I had a blast while you were gone."

"Ouch! Okay, you are seriously pissed at me, and I deserved that. Look, I promise I'll make it up to you."

No longer able to endure watching my struggle with my bracelet, Mark gently took over, expertly securing the clasp as he continued with his apologies. I quietly scolded myself as ancient butterflies surfaced from the pit of my stomach and churned up old feelings. I averted my eyes as Mark took both my wrists gently in his hands.

"Once this wedding is out of the way, we can head back to London. The big chiefs are coming to the office to see the progress. We can get talking to them - start discussing this promotion. What do you say?"

I hesitated in replying, removing my wrists. What did I say to that? Mark was saying all the right things - in his eyes at least - but why wasn't it enough? It was almost like I couldn't believe him anymore. It wasn't until this very moment that I realised things had drastically changed between us. I struggled to look at him properly. A flurry of built-up anger and frustration towards him was bubbling to the surface, and I could hardly contain it.

"Emily? What do you say?" Mark repeated, concern creeping across his face. He was losing control, and he didn't like it. He wasn't used to it.

"I say - - I hope you're done using me as a puppet, because quite frankly, I'm getting whiplash from the way you treat me!" With that, I picked up my shoes and my shawl and stormed downstairs bare-footed, my heart in my mouth and adrenaline pumping loudly through my ears. Did I really just say that? I could only imagine the look on Mark's face, his mouth wide-open from shock. It partly made me gleeful and mostly made me feel instant nausea and regret. Enough to want to turn around and take it all back. But no - I had to stick to it and hold my ground. After all, it was about time he realised he couldn't keep 'using and abusing' me like this. As a girlfriend (fake or not), as a friend, as a colleague.

Enough was enough.

The wedding was getting into full swing as guests arrived in swarms. Mark, like a scorned puppy, had checked on me before heading to the field to help with parking, leaving me alone to wander over to the barn where the ceremony would take place. A contrast from the beginning of the week, where I had felt like an intruder, I was surprised to feel oddly relaxed and to even feel a twinge of belonging as I wandered leisurely across the yard, smiling at other guests as they caught my eye. Many smiled warmly back, some gave me an inquisitive look.

My cheeks burned ferociously when, as I entered the barn, Tom's eyes fell onto mine. He was supposed to be listening to Steve - who seemed to be giving him some important instructions about the rings - but his attention was faltering as he stared intently in my direction. Flustered by this, I took a seat in the back row of the mismatched chairs, all decorated with little wreaths of gypsophila.

"What are you doing, missus?" Tom demanded as he stomped down the aisle, his brawny thighs on show under his kilt, which I noted very quickly, from my racing heart, looked better on him than his brother.

"Why are you sitting back here? You should be at the front, with us."

"No, I shouldn't," I replied firmly. "I have no right to be sat up there. Before this week, I was a complete stranger to all of you. I'm okay back here, honestly."

Tom huffed, muttered something under his breath and an evil glint twinkled in his eyes. Suddenly I was hoisted onto his solid shoulders and carried to the front, kicking and flailing. I grabbed the hem of my skirt, desperately trying to keep my dignity in-tact as seated guests chuckled at the fun being had. Squealing and protesting and feeling completely ridiculed, I couldn't help giggling. Finally, Tom set me back down and ordered me to take a seat next to Karen, who gave my hand a squeeze and smiled reassuringly.

"That's better," Karen said matter-of-factually. "Can't be having you back there by yourself." Tom gave me a sly wink and my heart fluttered once again. I was definitely going to have a cardiac arrest if this continued.

It didn't take long for the barn to fill to the brim, an exciting buzz rippling through the building as everybody waited for the arrival of the bride. Steve was taking slow, deep breaths to calm his nerves and Tom was giving him strong words of encouragement, thumping him on the back occasionally. Mark and the other ushers returned from the fields. Mark looked windswept and cold as he took a seat on my other side. He leaned forward in Tom's direction and informed him that everybody was in and that Sarah was ready for him. With that, Tom gave Steve a final nod of encouragement and marched up to the back of the barn to give his little sister away.

Once the music, an angelic blend of Celtic instruments, strummed to life, I was immediately entranced and lost in the most beautiful and unique wedding ceremony I had ever witnessed. Sarah glided up the aisle, smiling from ear to ear in her vintage, laced sheath dress, grasping hold of an explosion of natural meadow flowers. She practically dragged Tom with her up the aisle, keen to reach her husband-to-be. Heidi, Toni and Katie followed closely behind in pale pink taffeta dresses that sat just above the knee. The style suited all three of them despite their entirely different shapes.

Sarah and Steve were having what was called a hand-fasting ceremony, something I had never come across and had to research on my phone the night before. The Celtic tradition of hand-fasting involved binding the hands of the couple with coloured ribbon, each colour symbolising a quality in their new marriage.

I listened intently as the priest welcomed everybody and gave her well-wishes to the new couple before clasping their hands together and delicately tying each ribbon around their entwined hands.

"Red symbolises your passion and your strength. Orange is

your bounty and mutual support. Blue is your patience, devotion and peace."

The entire barn was silent as the priest continued to layer the ribbons around Sarah and Steve's hands.

"Purple is power but also your humility and responsibility. Grey is balance, solidity, and unity. Black is your wisdom and vision for the future. Brown is your grounding in nature and home. Pink is your honour and romance. Yellow is joy and harmony. Green is your service and prosperity. White is your focus and purity of thought. Silver is your values and inspiration and finally, gold is your energy, intelligence and your wealth."

A sense of calm trickled through everybody and the birds in the trees outside sang away, their song filling the silence in the barn.

"Steven, I'd like you to repeat after me... "

The priest had Sarah and Steve repeat their vows, the ribbons binding their hands as they spoke of their promises to one another. I watched, tears prickling in my eyes as I witnessed two people who, a week ago, were complete strangers to me, but now were fast becoming very dear friends, bind themselves physically, emotionally and spiritually as one person. I watched as they exchanged loving looks, squeezed each other's hands under all the ribbon and wrinkled their noses awkwardly with deep fondness. Within minutes the ceremony was ended with a passionate kiss, an eruption of applause, and the sound of Celtic music burst to life once more. I followed the tide of guests outside into the yard, where the warm sun gave its blessings by shining down on the exchange of hugs and well-wishes. Canapes came out on trays; flutes of refreshing summer cocktails were handed out and the celebrations officially began.

Mark

It was hard to say whether it was the contagious atmosphere of a wedding ceremony or the particularly beautiful way in which Sarah and Steve had bound their marriage, but Mark was strangely glad he had been here today. Downing glasses of Pimms, wine, and later champagne, over toasts to the bride and groom, Mark felt a wave of calmness within himself as the wedding proceeded into the evening reception. Even he had to admit that the fairy lights, scattered lantern balls and the glow from the fire pits made for a particularly unique ambiance. It wasn't something he would choose for his own wedding, but he expected nothing less for Sarah. In the good spirit of things, Mark even found himself taking a small shift behind Tom's handcrafted bar to help serve out the famous Trengrouse Cider, which flowed in plentifully from the giant kegs that Tom had brewed specially for the day. From the bar, Mark took the opportunity to catch up with old acquaintances and family friends whom he hadn't seen for many years. He'd forgotten how infuriatingly good the cider was and found himself drinking far more than he had planned to, in-between drafting other people's servings. When the jazz band was in full swing, Sarah and Steve had their first dance and the guests formed around them, filling the dance floor. Despite recent events, Mark felt he was in for a good night.

Tom

Tom watched with growing concern as he witnessed his brother become more and more intoxicated. Mark had been drinking all afternoon and had had more than his fair share of cider come evening. Several times Tom had tried to prise him away from his next glass but could sense Mark edging towards the verge of aggression. He watched with embarrassment as Mark roared with laughter over something his friend Pete had said, overcompensating his reaction to what was clearly a mediocre joke. The people around them exchanged awkward glances over their pints as Mark threw his head back and released another roar of laughter, thumping his hand down on the bar to show his appreciation. Worse still, Tom cringed as Mark practically drooled over some of Sarah's old college friends, who Tom had always found to be cheap, loud, and exasperating. Tom would need to intervene, before Mark made a complete mockery of the evening and ruined it for Steve and Sarah. So far, they were oblivious to Mark's behaviour and he needed to keep it that way.

"Mark, mate. You've done well. Why don't you give this a rest now and grab something to eat," Tom suggested, placing a firm hand on Mark's shoulder.

"My brother, ladies and gentlemen," Mark slurred, swinging his arm around Tom's shoulders, albeit uncomfortably, as he had to go on tiptoes to reach. "Always making out like he's looking after me, but actually he just wants rid of me because I'm a fucking embarrassment." Mark snickered and looked at his audience for a reaction. They merely glanced at Tom anxiously, an awkward silence prickling between them.

"Sorry guys," Tom continued calmly, though inside he could feel his temper rising. "As you can see Mark has sampled a little too much of the booze this evening. Mark. Food. Now."

"Ooh, see? There we go. Tone has changed," Mark jeered, his balance barely keeping him vertical. "You must do what the boss says! He's the eldest, you see. Can do no wrong."

"Mark!" Tom barked, squeezing his hand on Mark's shoulder.

"I'm getting my fucking food! Back off!" Mark shook Tom's hand off his shoulder and skulked off, knocking some glasses off of the bar on his way.

As Mark disappeared into the crowd, Emily appeared from the same direction, looking concerned.

"What's wrong with Mark? He looks upset... and drunk!"

"That's because he is. He's practically had a keg of cider to himself," Tom said, picking up the fallen glasses.

"Oh god. I better go and find him...see if I can convince him to go back to the house and sleep it off a bit."

"Good idea," Tom agreed, relieved that he wouldn't have to deal with him, knowing it would end badly if he did. "But Emily, just be careful with him. He's a bad drunk."

"I've experienced drunk Mark before. Don't worry. I'll be fine," Emily smiled warmly and disappeared into the crowd. Tom's stomach did a flip and his head went temporarily fuzzy. He busied himself by pulling more pints, while thinking about Emily and how beautiful she looked today. A city girl amongst the country dwellers, and yet so suited to her surroundings.

Half an hour passed, Tom assuming that Emily had convinced Mark to return to the house. However, at that moment Emily approached the bar looking worried.

"I can't find him anywhere," Emily threw her arms up in the air in frustration. "I've asked lots of people and they say they haven't seen him. His car is still here so I can rule out that disaster. Why was he so angry earlier? Have you two fallen out again?"

"Emily, this is me and Mark we're talking about here. Let's assume we're always 'fallen out'."

"Well, I don't know where else to look."

It was then that Tom noticed that Emily was beginning to look tired, one side of her face looking blotchy and one eye looking slightly swollen.

"Emily, are you okay? You're not... you know... on the verge of another attack, are you?"

"I've got a bit of a throbbing pain behind my eye. It's just a shadow. It'll pass in a minute. I'm just getting worked up over finding Mark."

Tom signalled to Jamie - one of his employees - that he was coming away from the bar for a bit and led Emily away in the direction of the house.

"Come on, let's get you somewhere quiet for half an hour. Maybe have some of your oxygen. I'm not letting you get in the state you were in the other day."

Without thinking, Tom placed a protective hand on the small of Emily's back and walked with her to the house. They returned thirty minutes later, Emily feeling a little more renewed from some time on her oxygen. They were about to set back to finding Mark when the man himself clambered clumsily onto the platform where the jazz band were performing, the musicians giving Mark an affronted look for having their performance space breached by a drunk.

"There he is," Emily pointed. "What's he doing?"

Tom's heart sank as Mark gently pushed the singer to one side and grabbed the microphone. He had a glass of whiskey in his hand, and Tom wondered where he could have possibly got it from. They weren't serving whiskey tonight.

"Sorry to in'errup' your love'y evenin', but I have... a few things... I would like to say." Mark's words slurred into one another and his legs were barely supporting him as he leaned dangerously on the microphone stand. "Firstly, I wan' 'o say congratulations to my beautiful sister... where is she? Oi, Sarah! Ah, there she is... hiding, the little minx. Congratulations... could have done better... but congratulations. Secondly, I have a confession-"

"Shit, we need to stop him," Tom groaned, starting to negotiate his way through the crowd of people.

"I have been away for a while now... in America... three years in fact. I wasn't a very nice brother, you see. I went to America with Catherine. You remember Catherine, right? A lot of you here probably went to Tom and Catherine's wedding actually... so course you do. Yeah - well - me and her... didn't work out. Turns out she's a huge slut."

There was an uncomfortable murmur that rippled through the crowd as more and more of the guests stopped their conversations and paid attention. Steve mounted the platform and muttered something inaudible to Mark, attempting to get him off stage.

"Hang on, hang on. I'm not done yet. There's things to be said," Mark shouted loudly down the microphone. At this point every pair of ears in the yard were listening, including the people at the bar. "So, me running off with Catherine was a pretty shitty thing for me to do. Like seriously shitty. I don't blame Tom for hating me. I hate me. I'm a fucking shit. But do you know what makes me laugh the most? Tom? Where are you, dude? There you are!"

Tom stopped, just feet away from the stage, now frozen to the spot, unable to move.

"What makes me laugh the most is, everything we've been through together, you can't be truthful with me. Not going to lie, it's a little hypocritical," Mark chuckled, a little hysteria in his voice. Steve attempted again to get Mark off stage, but this time Mark shoved Steve away from him. "I said, I'm not done! Tom - why didn't you tell me you were banging Emily!"

Gasps and tuts rippled through the crowd and a wave of nausea rose in Tom as his feet rooted him to the spot.

"It's cool! I owe you! She's not even my real girlfriend. I lied about that too! I mean, I think it's just occurred to me that I've been secretly in love with her for the last two years, and for some reason I thought that making up a promotion for her at work and forcing her to play along to this fake girlfriend/boyfriend scenario would... I don't know! Like I said, I'm a shit. I'm a fucking shit and I don't deserve this family of mine... "

Tom stood horrified as he watched his little brother break down in front of Sarah's entire wedding party. He watched as his mum emerged from the side-lines and peeled her sobbing son from the microphone, leading him off stage towards the house, with help from Steve. Sarah was being taken away by her band of loyal bridesmaids; her sobs audible from across the yard. This was beyond a disaster. Tom felt many pairs of eyes on him, comments muttered under breaths, and it was a few moments until he felt he could move again. He looked around for a sight of Emily. She was nowhere to be seen.

Ignoring the unwanted attention from the people around him, he headed towards the house. His brother needed him and for once he was going to make sure he was there for him.

Emily

I wanted to scream.

A crippling sense of panic was rising rapidly in my chest as I haphazardly stuffed my belongings into my suitcase. I had to leave, right away. There was no way I could stick around now after that humiliation in front of Sarah and Steve's entire wedding party.

I had only myself to blame, of course. I had allowed myself to get caught up in this web of complication, this ridiculous love triangle between myself and two brothers. Best that I cut myself from the situation right away and leave this family to do some much needed healing.

I was just about to make headway, planning on slipping away without anyone noticing, when Tom's giant form blocked the doorway.

"Emily," Tom said, in that voice that made my knees weak.

"Are you okay? What are you doing with your suitcase? You're not leaving, are you?"

I didn't answer. I didn't know how to answer.

"I think Mark saw us going into the house to get your oxygen. He must have put two and two together," Tom continued. "Look, he knows now. This just makes things easier. Tomorrow he'll sober up, we'll explain everything -"

"Wait! Slow down! What exactly did we agree on and when? There's nothing to explain."

"What do you mean? Emily, I'm talking about you and me. I haven't felt this way about anyone since my marriage ended," Tom took a step towards me and I placed a cautious hand on his chest, pleading him not to get any closer. It would only make my departure harder. "I know you feel the same way, Em."

My voice was barely a whisper as the pain of what was about to happen restricted my throat. "I do. I really do. But I can't pursue this."

Tom looked like he was going to argue, so I stopped him with a hand signal.

"I will not come between two brothers. I will not be Catherine. It's already happened to you guys once. You need to sort things out with each other, without a girl getting in the way. Mark did a shitty thing. But it's time to patch things up. You can't do that with me around. I'm sorry."

Tom's eyes revealed sadness as he edged backwards. "So, what? This is it? You're just going to disappear?"

"I think I have to," I said thickly, a lump in my throat making it hard to talk. "I have to go. I'm sorry."

Before I could stop him, Tom had pulled me in and locked his lips onto mine. Enveloping me in his arms, we sank deeply in a kiss that spoke a thousand words. I was torn between the need to escape and the longing to stay in Tom's embrace, and when Tom tightened his hold on me, it only made my mind all the more fuzzy.

There was a commotion downstairs, and the sound of a distressed Karen calling for Tom. This was enough to break the spell between us, and I pulled gently away.

"I'm sorry," I whispered, my heart breaking into a million

pieces.

Before Tom had the chance to stop me, I grabbed my bags and rushed out, tears streaming silently down my face.

There was no time to say any goodbyes or to apologise for my fast exit. That sense of panic within me was rising, a sudden flight mode kicking in. I needed to get out of there as fast as possible. I could hear Tom calling after me, his voice a fierce roar as grief descended. A part of me wanted to go to him and the other, the part I would have to follow, needed to get far away. The taxi I had booked was sat in the yard. I jumped in, shoving my suitcase and bags onto the seat beside me, and grabbed for my seatbelt.

"Nearest train station, please," I choked, tears streaming down my face. My chest felt painfully tight. I was doing the right thing. It had to be the right thing. So why did I feel so terrible?

I chanced a look back at the house, as the taxi driver drove us down the long drive, regretting it immediately as my eyes met Tom's. He was standing on the doorstep, watching me leave. A fresh wave of overwhelming sadness clung to me painfully as I realised that I would never see Tom again. I would never be able to return to Trengrouse Cider Farm and I would never again see this family I had come to love so dearly. Once I handed my notice in at the firm - and I planned to do this on the plane home - Mark would never speak to me again. And the quality of life waiting for me back in Brooklyn... well, I couldn't bring myself to think about that right now.

Chapter Twenty-Five

Over the orchards, the morning sun gleamed dull, hazy hues of yellow and red. A chorus of birdsong welcomed a new day ahead as the sky awakened in the first grey light. The remaining apple trees were weighing down, pregnant with fruit and waiting to be picked - but Tom wouldn't be doing any of that today.

It was the morning after his sister's wedding, but members of the Trengrouse family woke with heavy hearts. Tom hadn't moved from his spot on the sofa since last night, the embers of the fire long extinguished after last night's events.

She was gone.

Tom said it over and over again in his head and still it didn't process. Last night should have been full of laughter and drinking and celebration, dancing, eating and smiles all round. Instead, the party had continued in the Trengrouse's absence as they isolated themselves to Karen's kitchen, nursing Mark's wounds. Tom had expected to hate his brother forever, but after seeing him broken and full of remorse in his drunken state last night, Tom's bitterness towards him had quickly subsided.

The creaking of the stairs brought Tom out of his sleepy state and he sat up, wincing from his stiff joints. Sleeping on the sofa wasn't such a good plan. As he stretched out, clicking and clunking in all the right places, a delicate version of Mark shuffled into the room, a blanket draped across his hunched shoulders.

"Morning," Tom grunted.

"Mmh," Mark grunted back.

"A sorry state we are this morning," Tom snorted. He glanced over at Mark who was now easing himself into an armchair. "Coffee?"

"Dear God, yes."

Ten minutes later, a warm coffee in their hands and the fire rekindled, the brothers sat in each other's company for the first time in years.

"What time is it?" Mark finally said once the caffeine had worked its magic.

"Six? Six-thirty?"

"Christ, no wonder we're both death warmed up! Why are we awake?"

"Because neither of us could sleep properly?" Tom reasoned, looking into the flames, and draining his coffee.

"Will Sarah forgive us?"

"Probably. But she'll bring it up occasionally for her convenience."

An amused smile broke out on Mark's face and silence fell between them again.

"I need to speak to Emily," Mark announced.

Tom stiffened in his chair and his heart began to ache, "Emily isn't here. She left in a taxi last night."

A mixture of panic, confusion and anger flashed across Mark's face as he scrutinised Tom's expression, hoping perhaps that he was joking, and she was simply asleep upstairs.

"What? Why didn't you tell - why didn't you stop her?"

"I tried. She wasn't having any of it and you lot were all in such a bloody state last night..."

Tom's explanation faltered and regret kicked in. He should have gone after her. He had given up too easily and he'd let her leave, just like Catherine. But Emily wasn't Catherine. He should have stopped her.

"What exactly has happened between you and Emily?" Mark asked.

A thick silence fell between them as Mark's question hung in the air, Tom holding back his response as he thought about the consequences of his answer. His mind drifted to three years previous when they had last sat together for a serious talk, Mark declaring his undying love for Tom's wife. How it had felt like Mark had run a white-hot blade through Tom's heart, twisted and ripped it from his chest, leaving him to bleed as he departed with Catherine.

"You heard me last night, I'm sure," Mark joked wryly. "Emily and I aren't really together."

"I think...I'm in love with her," Tom replied, simply. There, he'd said it.

Mark nodded, looking at Tom with - what was it, relief?

"That settles it then."

"What does?"

"We need to find out where she is. What time did she leave last night?"

"About 11pm. She'll be overseas by now," Tom slumped in his chair, defeated.

"Tom, our passports are in London," Mark looked concerned. "She won't have been able to fly."

Tom sat up, suddenly feeling sick with anguish, "shit. Fuck! I'm an idiot - I should never have let her go! I'm going to check the train station and the airport."

"Call the taxi company. See where they dropped her off!" Mark called over his shoulder.

"What is going on? Where is Tom going?"

Karen had edged into the room, her eyes red and weary. She'd had as much sleep as Tom and Mark then. Mark realised, with a hitched breath, how much his Mum had aged over the last three years. How her hair looked dusty with greys and her skin, wrinkled and paper-thin, hung looser. Her eyes had lost their sparkle and Mark knew this was from years of grief and worry. His heart ached with guilt and regret as he stood up gingerly and enveloped her in his best hug.

"It's Emily," Mark spoke over his mother's shoulder. "She left last night and we're trying to work out where she got to."

"Oh, the poor love. I hope she didn't leave because of everything that happened."

Mark unfolded himself from their embrace and looked down with shame, "I think she did. It's all my fault and I need to find her. Tom's going to track down how far she got by taxi last night."

"Make sure you do find her," Karen said. "That poor girl. She needs a family - and we need her."

Mark nodded and headed to the kitchen for better phone service. Meanwhile, Tom thundered in, slamming his archaic brick phone onto the kitchen table.

"Taxi company says they dropped her at St Austell train

station last night and that she jumped on to the sleeper. She'll be in London by now."

"Well?" Karen looked at her sons in exasperation. "Off you go then. The pair of you!"

Tom and Mark exchanged vacant looks as their mother huffed, shaking her head impatiently.

"Honestly! Pull yourselves together and work as a team, will you? My motherly instincts tell me that this poor girl is dealing with a lot more than just oxygen tanks and fusion injections. You two have had her bouncing between you like a bloody pinball, so you both need to fix this."

"What about Sarah?" Mark mumbled.

"She's ruddy ticked off and all, so best you're not here when she wakes up. I'll explain everything to her, send her and Steve off safely on their honeymoon. Meanwhile...fix this. And stop sulking, the pair of you."

Karen was cross and didn't hold back like she usually would, but a twitch of a smile played in the corner of her mouth to see her two boys, side by side, sulky expressions on their face from their being told off - like the good old days of their youth.

Moments later, Tom and Mark were on the A30 in Mark's swanky BMW rental, on their way to London. Mark had been trying multiple times to get through to the London office, but it had been too early for anybody to be there to answer the phone. Then Janet's name flashed up on the dashboard and Mark punched the green phone button on the hands-free to activate the call.

"Janet - hi! I've been trying to get hold of you."

"You alright, love? I've just got in," Janet's warm, northern voice filled the car. "Emily just called me. She's at Paddington and wanted me to get her passport ready. Said it's in the safe, so can you give me the code please love?"

"No, no, no! Don't let her have her passport just yet. Get her to the office and stall her, please Janet."

"Everything alright love? This is all sounding very dramatic. Emily seemed upset and all. You had a fall out again?"

"Just keep her there. We're on our way. We're just leaving Cornwall now."

"You want me to stall her for five hours?"

Tom ran his hands through his hair and tried to steady his breath.

"Please, Janet - just don't let her leave."

Mark rang off and the car fell in heavy silence as Mark crept his speed up, making Tom's knuckles white as he gripped the side of his seat.

"We're about to cross the Cornish borders. How do you feel?" Mark joked, turning to his homebody brother.

"Piss off you knob," Tom retorted, though he was smiling. "Went to Malvern show last year to promote our cider, so jokes on you."

Mark laughed and cranked up the radio. They may be making light jokes and holding conversations together, but neither brothers were denying the thick layer of unspoken words that still hovered between them. This was going to be a long process, rebuilding parts of a relationship that would never been the same, but this was a start either way.

"What are you going to do if we catch her in time?" Mark asked.

Tom drew in air and released loudly as he thought about his answer, "I really don't know."

"Well, you have about four hours left to come up with something good."

"After all your bloody tall tales and charades, you're going to need to catch me up on her current situation."

It was Mark's turn to release long, exasperated sighs as he explained how he'd met Emily, how she'd trained in-house and earned a promotion, how her attendance had slowly deteriorated. As he spoke, he realised how little interest he had taken in Emily's personal life, that actually he hadn't considered the financial trouble she'd be in whilst off sick - he'd only seen it from an employer's side.

"Mum said the other day that she reckons Emily has got into financial trouble," Mark continued. "I've never been to her place, but I'm pretty sure the diner she lives above is in a pretty rough neighbourhood in Brooklyn. I've never heard her mention any family."

"Did she tell you about her time on the streets?" Tom asked, instantly scolding himself for sharing Emily's secret. But he felt that Mark needed to know.

"No," Mark shook his head, ashamed that Tom already knew more than him from just one week. Swearing under his breath and hitting the steering wheel, Mark leaned his right arm on the window ledge, fuming with himself. "I hardly know her then."

"Is there nothing in New York for her then?" Tom sounded hopeful. "Is that why she agreed to take the job in London?"

Mark's shame grew as he contemplated filling Tom in on the truth behind the London arrangement. He decided that the bridge being built between them was far too new and fragile for that kind of load. That would have to be for another day.

"Catherine and I were never going to last long."

Mark glanced across at Tom who had just uttered that unexpected statement whilst staring out of his passenger window. Mark didn't dare answer - what could he say to that?

"I do realise that," Tom shifted in his seat and faced forward. "You didn't have to end my marriage so brutally, but I realise now that either way it would have ended in divorce. This doesn't excuse you. I'm just saying."

"I'm sorry," Mark spoke quietly, his eyes fixed on the road ahead. "I'll apologise for the rest of my life in hope that you'll forgive me."

"No need. That'll get on my tits after a while," Tom joked dryly. "I'll get there. Help me sort out this mess with Emily - that'll be a good start."

"You've got it," Mark nodded, a hint of sadness in his voice as he eased his foot firmer on the accelerator pedal.

Chapter Twenty-Six

Paddington Station was bustling with busy, purposeful lives as Londoners headed to work or reunited with loved ones. I came out of the public toilets, having finally changed out of my chiffon dress from last night and attempted to freshen up after a long night of travelling.

I was exhausted. I'd barely slept a wink on the train. Not surprising when I'd spent most of the night avoiding the ticket collector and jumping from one empty cabin to the next. I'd had no ticket and no way of paying for one either. It had been risky, but it was better than sleeping on a cold bench in St Austell train station.

I shuffled over to the coffee shop, buying a takeaway tea with the last of the change from the taxi money just so I could use their WiFi. I had used up my phone data and needed to locate the office to retrieve my passport.

My spirits lifted slightly after the warming tea and with the knowledge that the office was only a twenty-minute walk from the station, I set off at a tired, but meaningful pace.

"Y'alright love?" Janet greeted me at the front door before I'd even got past the little black iron gate leading from the pavement. Over a week ago, I had found the little London office underwhelming and a little dingy. After my time in Cornwall, where small and dingy translated more to charming and quaint, I appreciated the smaller features of the building so much more. I had also noted the little flowers that had been freshly planted in the window boxes and my heart instantly ached as I was reminded of Karen's garden back in Cornwall - bursting with colour and life.

"Hi Janet," I smiled, though my smile didn't meet my eyes. I tackled the gate, negotiating my suitcase around it inelegantly, Janet running over to relieve me.

"You look tired, duck."

"I am a little. How are you? The entrance is looking lovely, by the way."

"Ah, thanks Duck. I thought a bit of colour in the windows would do it wonders. The door has had a fresh lick of paint too. It's getting there. It's getting there. Come in. I'm the first one here, so we'll put kettle on and have a good catch up."

Janet was ranting and, if I didn't know any better, was acting a little skittish, but I was too tired to question it. Perhaps the launch had taken its toll on Janet more than anybody realised. For a moment I thought about raising it with Mark, then remembered myself.

"Did you manage to get the code for the safe?" I asked once we were sat down in the staff room with a cup of tea each. The staff room had undergone a transformation. Once dusty, damp, and full of boxes, now smelling of fresh emulsion, decked out with a new carpet and soft office loungers. "I'm hoping to catch this afternoon's flight."

"Oh, umm...er...no, love. But I'll let you know if I hear anything from Mark."

"Oh. You haven't been able to reach him?" I asked, surprised. Mark was never seen without his phone and was pretty much reachable 24/7.

"Nope. No. No answer," Janet sipped at her tea, muttering a few more noes in between.

I narrowed my eyes and was about to question Janet when she remembered something and jumped out of her seat.

"Oh, that reminds me!" Janet trilled. "A colleague from your office back in Manhattan called yesterday. Said they had a gentleman visit the office, asking after you."

My blood ran cold, and my finished tea threatened to make a reappearance.

"Who was it?" I squeaked, failing to keep the panic from my voice.

"Hang on, let me find the note. I wrote it down because it was an unusual name - well, probably not unusual over there. Where is it? Ah, here it is!" Janet held up a piece of paper that had been ripped out of a notebook, took her glasses from the top of her head and peered through them. "Sal Hernandez. That's it. Said he'd called in. Hadn't realised you were overseas but would catch up with you on your return. Lovely, well perhaps you can call him later and let him know. Use the office phone and save your data. Y'alright love? You're as white as a sheet!"

"Yes...I'm fine. Janet, would you mind if I excused myself a moment? Think I'll take your advice and use the office phone."

"Of course, Duck. Take yourself into Mark's little office. There's a phone in there."

"He's been stopping by the apartment, Emily. I don't appreciate the invasion."

"Your apartment?"

I rubbed at my head anxiously as Michelle's equally anguished voice rang through on the phone receiver moments later.

"Yes. My apartment. Demanding where you were and calling me a liar when I said you were overseas. Had to threaten to call the police in the end and told him to ask your employer if he didn't believe me."

I groaned, "that's how he knew where my workplace was!"

"Emily. You need to control this. I can't have him turning up at my door like that."

"No, I know. You're right. I know," tears smarted in my eyes and my hands began to shake. How ridiculous when there was a good three thousand miles at least between us. "I'll deal with it. I'll call him."

"Okay. Keep me updated. Stay strong."

Once I had rang off, I sat in solitary silence for a moment, attempting to compose my ragged breathing. He knew where my workplace was. The one place I had felt safe. He'd broken that invisible boundary and visited Michelle's in person. He had basically infiltrated the tiny little patch of life I had over there and the thought of returning suddenly felt terrifying. But what could I do? I had burnt my bridges here in the UK and my bridges were being burnt by Sal over there.

I was stranded.

Downstairs, I could hear the arrival of colleagues and the clinking of mugs in the staff room down the corridor as they prepped their first coffee of the day. I had to make that dreaded phone call, but I needed time to compose myself first.

"Hey, Em!" Harry roared from the kitchenette as I skulked in to grab my jacket. "How was Cornwall? Everything sorted?"

"Hey," my face nearly cracked as I forced a smile. "Yes, I think so. Mark's on it. Great to see you. I'm just going to pop out for some...flowers. I passed a florist on the way here."

"Doesn't stay still very long, does she?" I heard Harry mutter as I descended down the main stairs to the front door.

Outside, I filled my lungs with fresh air and wished more than anything that the air was the Cornish type I had recently become accustomed to, then I took myself for a stroll, past the florist and into the nearest park for some mulling over.

It was about an hour later, without the promised flowers in my arms, that I locked myself away in Mark's office again, a steaming mug of coffee in front of me for courage and made the dreaded call to Sal. It barely rang before it was cut off and relief was about to flood through me at the excuse that had been gifted to me not to have to speak to him, when a text message came through.

Use Skype. It's free.

Well, that was so much worse - and right on cue, the knots in my stomach returned as I reluctantly took my laptop out from its bag, placed it on the desk and turned it on.

"Well. There she is. The stowaway," Sal's disapproving drawl came through the speakers moments later. His large face took up almost the entire screen as he peered into the camera. Instinctively, I pushed my chair away from the desk, already uncomfortable with the proximity.

"Convenient that you should just take yourself off to another country. You know what day it is tomorrow right?"

"You didn't need to show up at Michelle's place. Or my workplace for that matter."

My voice was wobbly and breathless, but I urged myself to be more brave. After all, he was thousands of miles away and couldn't hurt me through a screen. This didn't stop my legs shaking violently from under the desk and my fingernails being ripped to shreds by my nervous hands.

"Ah, so that's why you're calling," Sal's face creased into a sly grin as he leaned back in his chair, his arms folded. "I was worried about ya, Em. You're always exactly where I need to find you, then I come back to the diner to be told you hadn't been home since you last stayed at Michelle's. Thought maybe you'd decided to overstay your welcome so came to get ya. Then I find out you've gone away without speaking to me first."

"What do you mean, speak to you first?" My nerves subsiding for a moment as irritation seeped in. "Why do I need to tell you where I am going? It was a business trip, for work!"

"You've never been on a business trip in your life," Sal sneered. "Then suddenly you choose to be on the other side of the ocean when you owe me money. You owe me money, Emily. The deadline is tomorrow."

His temper rose and he banged his fist on the table, making his screen jerk. Suddenly I realised that he mostly only lost his temper like that when he felt things weren't quite in his control. And at this very moment, things were entirely out of his control. For once, there was very little he could do if I decided to disobey him. I felt a sudden urge to giggle but stifled it with my sleeve. Then...

"Put it this way Emily. As soon as you've landed back in the US, I'm gonna be there waiting. And if you don't got my money, there's going to be trouble. OK?"

There was a faint commotion downstairs which I barely registered as Sal's threatening words paralysed me, my courage evaporating instantly.

"I'll pay for your ticket," Sal said, his bipolar temper turning sickly sweet. "You don't gotta worry about that side of things. Just get yourself to the airport and come home. Let's get this mess sorted, yeah?"

So many replies floated in my head and even dared to escape my mouth, but I pressed my lips together, unable to find my voice.

"Y'know, there's other ways you can pay me back," Sal's voice was like treacle now and made my stomach churn. "Wipe the slate clean, so to speak-"

"Emily, who the bloody hell is that man!" Mark boomed as he burst through the office door.

"Mark?" I croaked. "Tom!"

"Who the hell are you?" Mark demanded, wrenching the

laptop towards him and jabbing the screen at Sal.

"Tom," I gasped. "What are you doing here?"

"You're shaking," Tom knelt down in front of me, resting his large hands on my legs, then wiping my wet cheeks with his thumbs. I hadn't even realised I was crying. "Emily, who is this bloke?"

"This is...um...this is..."

"Guys, d'ya mind? I'm having a private conversation with my Emily here."

"What do you mean 'other ways to pay you back'?" Tom growled into the screen.

"This don't concern you. Leave me and Emily to talk, will ya?"

"Do you owe this twat money?" Mark chimed in.

"Who you callin' names buddy? She owes me money."

"He's my landlord," I finally managed. "Gwynne's son. I do owe him money."

"What kind of landlord harasses his tenant?" Tom continued, both him and Mark now squaring up to the screen. "I want to know what you meant by 'other ways to pay you back'!"

"There are laws against landlords harassing their tenants, you know?" Mark jabbed the screen again.

"Oh my god, will you both stop. Please! This is my mess. Let me deal with this," I cried, pulling the screen back towards me. "God, the amount of testosterone flying around right now!"

"Emily, end the call and let us talk about this," Tom pleaded quietly to me so Sal couldn't hear. "I've heard enough to know that I don't like this bloke."

"OK, I'm bored now," Sal announced. "Emily. Tomorrow. I'll meet you at the airport."

The screen went black as Sal disconnected the video call and my shoulders sagged as I released breath that I didn't know I was holding. My body started involuntarily shaking again - I felt cold to the bone. I turned to Mark and Tom who were both looking at me in horror. I was going to have to tell them everything.

It was exhausting, extracting everything about Sal from my memory and laying it out before me to piece together into some sort of explanation. Tom and Mark listened intently, without interruption. I cried. Multiple times. Tom's hands cocooned mine and Mark gave me the occasional reassuring squeeze of the knee. A growl occasionally ruptured from the bottom of Tom's throat as I spoke about the way Sal had treated me over the years. I skimmed over most of the detail but gave them enough information to justify my predicament.

"There's nothing I can do," I finally said, in defeat. "I let myself get into debt. I haven't paid my rent. Now I owe hundreds of dollars to him."

"Emily, you didn't allow yourself to get into debt. He's charging you extortionate money for a little studio in an area like yours," Mark informed. "You've been battling with medical bills as well. Fuck sake, Emily. Why didn't you tell me! We've been working together now for what - three years? Instead of letting the company think you're just being a pain in the arse with your attendance - you didn't think to tell me what's been happening here?"

"Are you seriously telling her off right now?" Tom said, incredulous. "Aren't you meant to notice when one of your employees isn't quite herself?"

"What, like I'm a bloody mind reader?"

"Oh, shut up! Both of you! Finally seeing you acting like actual brothers - don't start now. Tom, this was going on years before I started my job at Blake & Co. Mark won't have noticed anything different."

Then, as if I'd only just realised their presence, "What are you both doing here?"

Mark and Tom exchanged looks.

"Emily," my stomach clenched longingly, despite my affronted look, as Tom took both my hands. I looked directly at his chest, unable to look up all of a sudden into his eyes - particularly with Mark in the room. "You...I didn't want to..."

"Oh Christ," Mark tugged at his trousers before heaving himself into his desk chair, looking exasperated. "You're really shit at this. You mean you hadn't thought about what to say on our five hour drive up here?"

"That piece of shit on the video chat threw me off, alright!"

Tom looked bashful and utterly adorable.

"Emily," Mark took over, leaning forward at his desk, his hands clasped together as if he was closing a business deal. It didn't take long for Mark Trengrouse to recover then. "Tom really fancies you. You really fancy him. You both have my blessing to be boyfriend and girlfriend."

I scrunched my nose up at Mark's condescending tone, but my heart swelled all the same as Tom's hands tightened over mine. Then the breath was knocked out of me as Tom eased himself into a kneeling position.

"Or do that," Mark nodded approvingly. "Man of little words. More a doer."

"Will you shut up for a moment and let me speak, let alone think!" Tom growled, looking the most nervous I had ever seen him. I chuckled at the growing banter between these two, whilst my heart threatened to race so fast, I was sure it was fit to burst through my chest. I finally allowed my eyes to settle on Tom's, immediately glowing with warmth as I sank into them. His voice was low and gruff as he stumbled through his words. "Emily, I'm not very good at these long, soppy speeches so I'll just get on with it. Will you marry me? Will you start a new life with me, in Cornwall?"

I wanted to shout 'yes' a million times over, but my brow creased in worry, "what about the mess I'm in with Sal? As you've witnessed, I have baggage."

"We'll sort it. You don't have to do this alone anymore. Any of it," Tom soothed, squeezing my hands. Mark nodded, doing his best to keep his contributions silent. "Please, Emily."

"Your job here in London is secure," Mark chimed in after all. "You could commute occasionally or work from home. We'll make it work."

"There's so many things we can do, Em," Tom continued. "We'll sit down and put a proper plan in place. I'm sure Sarah would love your help in the tearooms as well."

Both of them were saying all the right things and I felt that hope begin to resurface, a perfect picture of my new life in Cornwall just within reaching distance.

"OK," I whispered, my eyes twinkling.

"OK?" Tom beamed.

"Yes! Yes, yes, yes!"

"Oh, thank god," Tom puffed, heaving himself to a standing position and enveloping me into his strong embrace. His lips found mine and we stayed locked together as Mark edged himself out of the room, muttering something about finding himself some decent coffee.

"Give me two more weeks to finish the harvest. Two more weeks is all I need. My visa should have arrived by then as well."

Tom and I were saying our temporary farewells in the yard. We'd been back in Cornwall for a week, mostly to recover from what had been an emotionally exhausting couple of days over the wedding period. I was heading back to New York one last time to wrap my old life up before starting afresh.

"You'll stay at Mark's place in the meantime," Tom instructed. "You're not to go back to your old flat without him, alright?"

"Mmm, I love it when you're bossy," I teased, wrapping my arms around Tom's middle as he planted a kiss on the end of my nose.

"Oh, get a grip you two, will you?" Mark complained as he finished his phone call. "It's all arranged to pick up Emily's things tomorrow afternoon, after we've landed."

"That'll take all of two minutes," I joked, bitterly. "I don't have a lot of stuff, so won't take long."

"Yes, but it's your visa we'll be waiting on after that. Once Tom arrives, you'll be able to set things up quicker and prove your engagement," Mark informed. "As for picking up your stuff tomorrow, you don't even have to go in there, if you don't want to," Mark offered.

"No, no. I want to say goodbye to some friends in the diner. Just as long as he's not there, I'll be fine."

"I doubt he'll have any reason to show his ugly face for a while," Tom added, his jaw set tightly.

"What do you mean?" I turned to Mark. "What did you do? Did you pay him off?"

"Of course," Mark nodded as if it was the most obvious thing in the world. "The piece of shit was owed money. But I did threaten to report him for breaking multiple landlord laws if he didn't walk quietly with his winnings and stop harassing people. Your annoying artist friend included."

"Mark," I gasped. I was touched and beyond grateful. "You have to be paid back. I have to pay you back."

"Don't be daft! Count it as two years of Christmas bonus that you never received because of your shit attendance," Mark winked. "And an early wedding gift."

"Thank you, Mark," Tom said, putting his arm around my shoulders and smiling warmly at his brother. "We really appreciate it."

"Right," Mark cleared his throat, declaring that it was enough sappiness for one day. "Shall we?"

"Two weeks," Tom sealed his promise, kissing me deeply.

"Two weeks," I smiled, holding him to his promise, and climbed into the passenger seat of Mark's car, waving to Karen from her kitchen window.

This time, as we descended down the bumpy lane, my heart didn't clench painfully at the thought of never seeing this special place again. This time, I knew I would be returning. This time, I was excited at the prospect of what lay ahead.

OK, so I was no closer to defeating The Beast, but I now had connections and people to reach out to the next time I found myself at its mercy, thanks to the very family I was marrying in to. Yes, I had lots to be thankful for and it was this alone that would make fighting The Beast ten times easier. For the first time in my life, I wasn't alone.

Epilogue

Three Years Later

It was a glorious summer's day at Trengrouse's Cider Farm and the sun was beaming down on the wedding guests as they arrived car by car into the neighbouring field. There wasn't a cloud in sight, only clear blue skies.

Nobody could have forewarned Emily Miller of an entirely different wedding to the one she had always fantasised in as a little girl. She would never have believed that she would be married on a little farm in the middle of Cornwall, thousands of miles away from her birthplace. Now the day had arrived, all was in place and she was ready to go down the aisle. The real deal had exceeded expectations.

Today she would marry her perfect man.

"Emily, sweetheart. Everyone's seated. Are you ready?" Karen entered the room and stopped in her tracks, taking in Emily's dress and her hair which was styled in simple little curls that fell just above her shoulder. Karen gave Emily a look that only a mother could give a daughter on her wedding day. For the last three years, Karen had treated Emily like a second daughter, made her feel like one of her own, and now she was going to walk her down the aisle and give her away. For Emily, it couldn't be more perfect.

"You look absolutely beautiful, my love."

"Thanks Karen," Emily smiled, embracing Karen before picking up her bouquet and hoisting her heavy train. "Okay, let's do this."

The barn had been transformed for the umpteenth time in its history. Seasonal flowers brought the walls to life, a sea of blues, pinks, and purples with clusters of large white lilies featured around the space. It was now a regularity to see the barn dressed for the occasion since Emily and Sarah had started their new business, hiring the place out for weddings and parties. An idea that had come to them both over a bottle of wine. In Emily's eyes though, the barn hadn't looked this beautiful since Sarah and Steve's wedding three years ago.

Excitement and nerves bubbled in Emily's tummy as they positioned themselves out of view behind the wedding guests, who sat chattering away, waiting for the ceremony to begin. As the gentle sound of Pachelbel in D Major began, the wedding party stood in unison and Karen turned to Emily with a smile, asking if she was ready. Emily nodded and they made their descent down the aisle to where her beloved groom awaited.

As Emily and Karen made their way down the aisle,
Emily caught sight of familiar faces amongst the wedding guests.

She smiled at Michelle, grateful that her friend had made the effort to travel all this way to see her marry. Even if her intentions had been to 'shack up with a British hunk'. In front of Michelle and near the front, Sarah and Steve beamed, their daughter Lily sat in Steve's arms, happily sandwiched between her parents. On the other side, Emily caught a glimpse of Gillian, Bevel and some other fellow Cluster Heads that Emily had become close friends with since joining the forum. People she regularly conciliated with and supported through episodes as they all found ways to live with their condition. Emily had even set up a Cornish group which was going strong with up to five members so far. They met once a month for coffee and cake in the tearooms. The Beast was much less threatening when you faced him as a group. Emily felt she had come a long way with dealing with The Beast in the last three years, having been in remission for over six months now.

If this wasn't enough to make her feel the luckiest in the world, Emily was made a business partner alongside Sarah to help expand the tearooms and their new wedding company. Today's wedding was one of many booked in at Trengrouse's farm this year, kick-starting the wedding season.

Emily and Karen finally reached the alter where Tom and Mark stood side by side, both smiling proudly. Mark took a step forward and embraced Emily with a kiss on the cheek and a hug.

"You look beautiful, Miller. Way to brush up," Mark smiled.

"You always were excellent at giving compliments," Emily scoffed, unable to stop herself from smiling back.

"I know. You ready to become Mrs. Trengrouse?"

Emily nodded, her heart racing as Mark led her up onto the platform and placed her hand into Tom's.

"She's all yours, bro," Mark gave Tom a squeeze on the shoulder, then retreated to his position behind Tom as Best Man.

Tom was smiling ear to ear as he brought Emily's hand to his lips and kissed it gently.

"My Emily. You ready?"

"Yes. Absolutely."

It was a day that Emily had dreamt of all her life. Marrying the man of her dreams, being welcomed into a family of her own, a family that loved her and accepted her. She had a job that she loved, working alongside her best friend, and now sister-in-law, whilst living in beautiful Cornwall, a place that had captured her heart. Mark visited often, no longer a stranger to his family.

When Emily had first come to Cornwall, she'd considered herself a broken girl and had been brought into the lives of a broken family. Now here they were, all together - the pieces being glued together with the hope of a bright future and many things to look forward to. Emily had found her happiness, and she intended to hold onto it, indefinitely.

The End

Acknowledgements

So that just happened - I wrote a book and you just read it and I feel a sense of euphoria or something equally as wonderful! Thanks so much to you firstly, for taking the time to believe in me and read my debut novel, which has been sitting so close to my heart now for many years. I am so happy that Emily's story is finally out there for you all to enjoy and be a part of. Please do pop on to my Facebook page to tell me all about your reading experience - I would love to hear all about it. If you enjoyed it, I would be forever grateful if you could also leave a review on Amazon as well. I am right at the start of a very exciting writing journey and I hope you will come along with me where we will meet new characters along the way.

To Martin Ireland, my wonderful husband who has literally showered me in encouragement, love, and support. He has actually read the book - twice - even though reading and romance really is not his thing. How amazing is he? Martin has spent many mealtimes pouring over scenarios of what Emily would do and how Mark would react. With him, the characters and the story came to life. I must also mention my beautiful little boy Henry, who has accompanied me on many long plot walks and continues to inspire me.

To my wonderfully talented editor and fellow writer, Wendy Maynard. Thank you for loving the Trengrouse family and Emily just as much as me. Thank you for helping me polish it up to the very best that it could be and for all the advice along the way.

Writing is pretty solo, but I have been lucky enough to be a member of two amazing writing groups along the way. The first one (Penstraze Writers) I co-founded with the brilliant Toni (TC Harvey - writer of The Farthing and The Devil). James, Janet, and Kerry joined us along the way, and we are still in contact now. Thank you for letting me pester you with random hypothetical questions at various random times over our group chat. The second group, founded by my wonderful editor Wendy, (Clays Writers Group) has given me lots of dedicated writing time with like-minded people. Paul and Gabi have also been on the receiving end of random hypothetical questions, as well as been treated like walking thesauruses. "Give me another word for..."

Thank you to my brilliant friend Chrissi Berry, for giving me that final nudge, after listening to me go on and on about wanting to get my writing out there. Thank you for reading the final proofs (literally in one day!) and for making me feel like I already have a number one fan!

To my wonderful family - especially my Mum for believing in me from the very beginning, for loving my story before she had even read it and just for simply being amazing. Thank you to my sister, Kerry - her bravery and resilience through her own battles with the Beast was where little sparks of the story began. She is yet another person who has endured message after message, helping me to tweak and perfect the medical terminology for Emily's (and Kerry's) rare condition.

I could probably turn this into a long, Oscar-Award-style list of thank yous - but don't worry, I won't. Many friends, colleagues and even brief acquaintances have contributed in some way to the nurturing of this novel and I thank you all. You know who you are!

In the meantime, I hope you enjoyed my first novel and I hope you will be with me again soon for my next one. Watch this space!

About the Author

Lamorna Ireland

Amy Lamorna Ireland is first and foremost a loving wife to her husband and mother to her three-year-old son. She writes alongside her main career as a secondary school English teacher where she shares her passion for the written word with the next generation of writers.
Unexpected Beginnings is Amy's debut novel and she is already in the draft stage of her next project.
When she is not teaching or writing, Amy enjoys her time with her husband and son, dreaming up new story ideas on long walks through the glorious Cornish countryside around their home.

Printed in Great Britain
by Amazon